MW01093054

KILLER HOUSE PARTY

ALSO BY LILY ANDERSON

SCOUT'S HONOR

NOT NOW, NOT EVER

THE ONLY THING WORSE
THAN ME IS YOU

UNDEAD GIRL GANG

THE THROWBACK LIST

BIG BAD

RILEY'S RED WAGON
3040 E. First Street
Long Beach, Calif. 90803

KILLER HOUSE PARTY

LILY ANDERSON

HENRY HOLT AND COMPANY

NEW YORK

Henry Holt and Company, *Publishers since 1866*
Henry Holt® is a registered trademark of Macmillan Publishing Group, LLC
120 Broadway, New York, NY 10271 • fiercereads.com

Copyright © 2024 by Lily Anderson. All rights reserved.

Our books may be purchased in bulk for promotional, educational, or business
use. Please contact your local bookseller or the Macmillan Corporate and
Premium Sales Department at (800) 221-7945 ext. 5442 or by email at
MacmillanSpecialMarkets@macmillan.com.

Library of Congress Cataloging-in-Publication Data is available.

First edition, 2024
Book design by Meg Sayre
Printed in the United States of America.

ISBN 978-1-250-90947-3 (hardcover)
1   3   5   7   9   10   8   6   4   2

FOR KIT CARSON—

THE HOUSE, NOT THE GUY.

We are never "at home": we are always outside ourselves. Fear, desire, hope, impel us towards the future; they rob us of feelings and concern for what now is, in order to spend time over what will be— even when we ourselves shall be no more.

—MICHEL DE MONTAIGNE

Bucktown was a place to leave. A liminal space between cities. A place where the roads clogged each morning with people driving to work in the places they couldn't afford to live, leaving behind a featureless, cultureless suburb they never considered their children would grow up in.

Everyone left Bucktown eventually. The strip malls turned over. The restaurants updated to keep up with the TV commercials. Big-box stores became megachurches that became fulfillment centers for big-box stores.

The only constant was the Deinhart Manor.

As much a fixture of the landscape as the hill beneath it, the manor loomed over town. Everyone knew the stories about the Bad Thing that happened there, but no one knew what was true. Whatever had happened to the Deinhart family all those years ago was lost to time, locked away when the house was boarded up from the inside.

The day the boards came down, light illuminated every window for the first time this century. Everyone in Bucktown noticed.

Which was exactly what the manor wanted.

Every town has a haunted house. The Deinhart Manor was ours.

What happened to the Deinhart family was the first scary story I ever heard. My dad told it to me many times, especially on Halloween. He grew up in Bucktown, looking up at the abandoned house on the hill. He loved the mystery and macabre grandeur of it.

This is his version of the story.

Almost exactly one hundred years ago ... (*It's always "almost exactly" no matter the year, but really it was sometime between World War I and World War II.*)

The Deinharts were the richest family in Bucktown. Mr. Deinhart owned the onion plant (*where the bowling alley is now*) and employed most of the men in town. Mrs. Deinhart wore fur coats and long strings of pearls. They had more money than God. More money than sense.

Back then, Founders Hill was a public park. It was covered in wildflowers and a grove of fruit and nut trees. People would picnic there and look out at the beautiful view of the town.

Until the Deinharts bought the park and the hill beneath it. A fence went up with a sign warning trespassers to keep out under threat of violence. The Deinharts built their mansion there, on the most desirable piece of land in the county.

The people in town watched as the hill's trees sagged with a harvest that the Deinharts did not need. The sweet stench of rotting apples and overripe plums blew downwind and into their homes. Hatred for the Deinhart family grew. Festered. Metastasized into a curse. The town wanted the Deinhart family gone.

And then the Deinharts started to die.

There were five children in the Deinhart family, and they died in the same order they were born. The eldest fell down the stairs and crushed his skull. The second ate one of the hill's apples, bit into the seeds, and died of cyanide poisoning. The third took her own life to escape the terror of waiting for the curse. Then there were two. A son and a daughter. Mr. and Mrs. Deinhart grew terrified that they would lose their last children. So terrified that they made a deal with the devil.

("Really? The devil?" I'd ask. We were only Christmas-trees-and-Easter-eggs religious, not a literal horns-and-pitchfork devil religious.

"The devil always shows up where there's enough money," Dad would say.

This led to me screaming in terror when I got a $50 bill from my grandma on my seventh birthday.)

The devil told them, "Your family is cursed. The only way to break it is for one of you to die. Trade your life for your child's."

Mr. and Mrs. Deinhart didn't believe it. Well, they *refused* to believe it, which is different. Refusing to believe is pretending with the truth stuck in your stomach. They sent the devil away and took their own precautions. They refused to eat anything but canned food and powdered milk. They shut the children away in the manor and boarded up all the doors and windows.

Eventually, one of the kids got sick. No one knows how because the only germs in the house were their own. But the Deinhart parents got scared. Not only out of fear for the child but also fear for themselves. The devil's warning didn't seem so ridiculous now. As the child's fever grew, so did their paranoia. The only way to stop the curse was for one of the parents to die. And neither of them was volunteering. They slept with knives under their pillows. Then they stopped sleeping altogether. They circled each other, sure that the other was planning their death. The house had seen so much death, it could feel that another was close.

Was the curse broken? I don't know. The family never left. Not by foot or hearse.

They're still in that house today, long since dead. And together forever.

Sounds like hell, doesn't it?

After a lifetime of being perfect, I was overdue for something extraordinarily stupid. Throwing a house party in a haunted house was next level.

This was life-or-death. My entire future was at stake.

My parents hadn't spoken to each other without their lawyers for six months. Six months of screaming fights, court dates, U-Hauls, and shitty new houses that smelled like cheap paint.

And then, a week before graduation, they sat me down to dinner at the pupuseria where we used to go to celebrate every report card. Stupidly, I thought they wanted to put aside half a year of petty differences and congratulate me. Maybe there'd be a car with a huge bow or a new computer befitting a soon-to-be Windsor College freshman. Maybe they'd even admit that they'd come to their senses and decided to get back together.

There were no gifts or declarations of love. Just pupusas that turned to ash in my mouth when my parents told me that they'd spent my college fund.

On the Deinhart Manor.

It wasn't like I didn't know they'd bought the manor. Everyone knew. The auction for the place had made the local news. Local Realtors Buy Haunted House.

What I hadn't known (what I could never have guessed) was that in order to win that auction, they had emptied their savings down to the penny. Including the money that Windsor was expecting for my freshman year.

"We're going to make it all back," Dad promised me. "But it's taking longer than we thought."

"Because you threatened to sue each other over the place?" I asked. "And neither of you can even change the locks on the manor until you get through arbitration?"

With her dark brown hands clasped loosely next to an untouched Diet Coke, Mom looked irritatingly calm on the other side of the table. She was wearing an amount of makeup she usually reserved for closing a business deal. Whether she was trying to intimidate me or Dad, I wasn't sure.

"This doesn't mean you'll never go to college, Arden," she said. "You'll just need to defer your enrollment for a year. Or two. There's still time for you to enroll at BCC for the fall. And you're more than welcome to come work with me—"

"Or me," Dad interrupted.

Mom gave a threatening lift of her eyebrows. She had taken the real estate business in the divorce. She had chopped Dad's last name off the sign and photoshopped him out of the print ads. Dad was working for a company two towns over so they couldn't compete over listings.

Besides, it was no secret that Mom had always dreamed of me joining the family business. Both of us in matching blue blazers on the sign, back to back, matching white-strip smiles. Like her favorite TV show, *Mommy and Me Realty*, where a mother-daughter team sold mansions to mysteriously wealthy couples. She'd even "jokingly" come up with a name for our reality realty show: *The Fluffy Flippers*. I told her that my ass wasn't full of fluff. It was adipose tissue. She told me I was no fun. Which was probably true.

"You want me to go to community college?" I asked. The walls of the pupuseria started to spin. The sickly yellow paint reminded me of bile. I felt lightheaded. "I'm the valedictorian. I have a 4.3 GPA. I did everything right! I got scholarships, financial aid—"

"You didn't get a full ride," Mom said, somehow managing to make this my fault. "Even with student loans and your scholarship, we're still on the hook for part of your tuition and your room and board. It's not like you can commute from home. You didn't want to go to a local school. You applied to a private, out-of-state university. It's not cheap."

"Because I got guaranteed admission to medical school after undergrad!" I protested. "I have a future! I have plans!"

Dad ran a hand over the shaved part in his glossy black hair. Ever since the divorce, he'd started going to some Instagram barber who loaded him up with pomade and manicured his goatee. He thought it made him look younger. (It really just made him look like a Puerto Rican supervillain.)

"Well, unless you have fifteen thousand dollars, nena, you need a plan B."

He was right. I needed fifteen thousand dollars.

I told my friends the next day during lunch in the school library, where I could openly weep in peace. (Crying during finals week was normal enough that the librarian looked up only if she thought someone was blowing their nose in a book.)

"The key to fundraising is to have something everyone wants," Remi said, stretched across multiple chairs with one foot up on the table. "Cookies, popcorn, candles—"

Maddy May gagged. "Ugh, that bubblegum candle I bought to support the volleyball team gave me such a headache. It smelled like root beer and gasoline."

"Oh yeah, they were total trash," Remi snorted. "But the uniforms we bought with the proceeds made us look so good. Especially when we won the championship."

I laid my head on the table, letting the weak stream of tears reroute over the bridge of my nose. I'd cried so much since dinner the night before that it didn't even feel cathartic anymore. Just a reflex at having to say it aloud again: *My parents spent my college fund.*

"I don't think there are enough dollar-store candles in the world to make me fifteen thousand dollars in less than two months," I said. I heaved a sigh. "I need something people would pay a lot of money for. And then I need people who have a lot of money."

Remi laced her fingers behind her head and scrunched up her face in thought. "Every senior at Bucktown High is going to have money in a couple of days," she said. "Graduation means graduation cards. Half the reason anyone sends out graduation announcements is to get a check from their long-lost great-aunt or whatever. People make bank graduation week. I assume I'll get a Starbucks gift card and twenty bucks to spend at Sober Grad Night."

"Sober Grad Night!" Maddy May shrieked, jumping out of her chair.

Shushes rained down on her from all over the room. Abashed, her shoulders came up to her ears and she bit her lip to contain her excitement as she half stood on the seat of her chair.

She continued in a frenzied whisper. "The last party of high school is a gym lock-in with teacher chaperones and rented bouncy castles from kids' birthday parties. And it's a hundred bucks to get in! What if we could offer them a real party?"

"A party?" I echoed, not convinced. "I've never even been to a party, much less thrown one worth paying to get into. Where would it even be?"

After my parents split, they had sold our family home (as quickly as they could and for fifty thousand dollars under the asking price). Mom moved into a tiny house with one bathroom and put my loft bed in one of the two bedrooms. Dad rented a condo. I couldn't believe that a man who used to brag about selling one hundred houses before he turned forty was renting a one-bedroom condo with no backyard, no pool, and a homeowners association rule against pets. He lost custody of not only me but also

Spaghetti and Meatball, our pugs. But he still had to chip in on the vet bill when Spaghetti ate a bee and swelled up like a tiny Thanksgiving parade balloon. (Spaghetti was fine but developed a minor fear of flowers since they were the turf of his enemies.)

"Arden, your parents have the keys to every empty house in town," Remi said. "Pick any house for sale with a pool and neighbors who won't call the cops and we're golden."

The idea came to me all at once, fully formed like it had been planted years ago, grown a network of roots, and suddenly blossomed. It was perfect. The thing that everyone in town wanted but only I could provide. The thing that had ruined my life could also be the thing that saved it.

I sat up and sloughed the residual tears from my cheeks. "No. Not just any house. *The* house. The Deinhart Manor. How much would you pay to get inside a real haunted house?"

Remi's eyes bugged. "Literally any price."

"And if there's alcohol and a bong?" Maddy May grinned. "Double any price."

Suddenly, we were throwing a party to save my life.

2

Climbing up to the Deinhart Manor was not for the faint of heart. First of all, the hill was so steep that it would have been easier to crawl to the top (even if you weren't a fat girl with short legs, which I was). Secondly, the house was textbook creepy. Not because it was supposedly haunted. I didn't believe in ghosts. I didn't even really believe that the Deinharts had all axe-murdered one another a hundred years ago. The house looked like a Halloween decoration, even in early June with wildflowers blooming all around it. It had a sharp roof, two turrets, and an attic window that looked out over town like a Cyclopean eye. With its weathered bricks covered in green-blue moss, the house gave the impression of a zombie too hungry to care that its flesh had started to rot.

My entire life, I had listened to my parents argue about how they would save the Deinhart Manor. One of many annoying things about having two parents in real estate: They couldn't pass a house without guessing its square footage and looking up its value online. And since we lived in a town with a huge abandoned mansion on a hill, they talked about the manor a lot. How many bedrooms did it have? How many fireplaces?

None of that mattered. Arguing about whether the Deinhart Manor was more Victorian or Jacobean revival was like fighting about whether the boards on the windows were walnut or oak. It wasn't the point of the house. The point was that it was a mystery. All of Bucktown was fascinated by it. Whether it was because they loved the ancient true crime of it all and the family that locked themselves inside and allegedly never came out. Or because it was possibly haunted by the Deinharts' ghosts.

Anyone who grew up in town had a friend of a friend who looked through the boarded-up windows and saw *something*. A bloody knife on a table (but how would they be able to see the blood in the dark?). An axe stuck in the wall (which wasn't exactly proof that the axe was a murder weapon). Remi's older brother (who also went by Remi) said he saw an entire ghost staring out from the single unboarded window in the attic.

But that's exactly what people went to the house looking for. Ghosts. Proof. Murder scenes perfectly preserved for more than a century.

I knew exactly what was inside the Deinhart Manor. Old furniture, moths, antiques ruined by a leaking roof and a mouse infestation. My parents had done the walk-through of the house together six months ago. It had been the beginning of the end.

The manor's key was surprisingly normal. I'd been picturing something heavy and ornate. Maybe with a skull and crossbones carved into the head. Or a key chain warning *Abandon all hope, ye who enter here.* Instead, it was just a small gold key on a thin strip of crumbling leather. I vaguely remembered Mom saying that the key had been found in the safe-deposit box of the very last Deinhart relative who had died, allowing the house to finally be put up for auction. Allowing people to be inside for the first time since the Bucktown Deinharts had barricaded themselves inside.

Sweating and half-full of regret, I made it to the manor's porch. It had been only a few hours since we'd walked the stage at graduation. Maddy May was probably being showered with gifts (jewelry or a purse that cost more than my entire wardrobe). Remi was enduring lunch with her family for long enough to convince one of her older brothers to buy our liquor.

My parents couldn't decide who should get to take me out for a celebratory dinner, so after I got my diploma they had each given me twenty bucks and told me to go have fun with my friends.

"You'll have more fun with them than you would with your old parents anyway," my dad had said, slipping me cash in a handshake like we were making a secret deal.

He wasn't wrong. Obviously my friends were more fun than my parents, especially since my parents had gone completely batshit after deciding they couldn't be married or business partners anymore. But it was the principle of the thing. You're supposed to spend time with your family after graduation. I should have been crammed into a table at Olive Garden with my parents and my grandparents, surrounded by my entire graduating class and their parents and grandparents. My mom should have been loudly saying the word "valedictorian" and making me keep my sash on to see if the waiter would give us a free cheesecake. Dad should have been quoting back parts of my speech and saying that I got my public speaking genes from him.

But they couldn't celebrate my achievements because then they'd have to remember what they'd stolen from me.

My parents' divorce proceedings and legal arbitration had halted the progress on the Deinhart Manor renovation. There was a sun-bleached COMING SOON Lozano Flack Realty sign nailed into the overgrown lawn, even though Lozano Flack Realty didn't exist anymore. One more thing up on Founders Hill that was stuck in time.

The wooden porch was splintery and rotten. Spiderwebs blanketed the beams overhead. With a shiver of anticipation, I slipped the key into the front door's lock and turned it. The hinges shrieked as the door swung inward. Stale air stinking of dust and carpet and something strangely sweet sighed onto the porch.

I stepped inside and turned on my phone flashlight, sweeping it ahead of me as I searched for a light switch. When I found one, it turned on a single chandelier overhead. Its many arms and crystals were caked in greige dust.

I was in a narrow foyer with a wooden floor, an umbrella stand, and a small cloudy mirror. The mirror was old and dark and about as reflective as a pot lid. Still, in my muddied reflection, I could see that the walk up the hill had taken a toll on my hair. My roots were starting to sweat out. I hoped Maddy May would remember to bring her flat iron.

The bottles in my backpack clinked against the floor as I set it down next to the coatrack. Walking deeper into the house, I found myself at the base of a double staircase covered in carpet. It twisted up the sides of the wall to the second-story landing high overhead. Beneath the second-floor landing, a yawning archway led the way to the rest of the house. It was the sort of endless dark that went on unfazed by the pinprick of light that my phone flashlight created.

"Hello!" I called out into the darkness, wondering whether I'd hear an echo or the squeaks of a dozen mice.

"Hello!" a voice called behind me.

Gasping, I clutched my phone to my chest, smothering the flashlight between my fingers. The front door crashed open. The dark mirror on the wall rattled.

Remi and Maddy May clattered out of the foyer. Both were loaded down with a variety of bags, backpacks, and accessories. Remi had her letterman jacket tied around her waist. Maddy May was wearing the same floaty blue dress she'd had on under her graduation gown. She had definitely been treated to a family trip to Olive Garden.

"Aw, Ardy, did you think we were ghosts?" she asked.

No one else had ever in my life tried to shorten my name from Arden to Ardy. Probably because it wasn't actually shorter, just cutesy. From anyone else, I would have hated it. But Maddy May meant it with enough affection to make it okay. She didn't have a patronizing bone in her body. She never even gave me shit for having a Spanish last name but not being fluent in the language, even though she and all of her cousins grew up bilingual. At her family Christmas party, she'd translated her little old abuelita for me but skipped over every time the word "gorda" was used.

"More like I thought that you were my mom coming to see why one of the lights turned on early," I said. "She's got every lamp set up to a timer so that the house lights up at exactly sunset every night."

Right on cue, the whole house clicked on. Buzzing yellow light from the upstairs bedrooms cut through the stair banisters. The house wasn't more welcoming with the lights on. The carpet on the stairs was bloodred. The walls were scarred, especially near the windows where the boards had been nailed in. In the distance, I could see the glint of something metal in the kitchen. Mom and Dad swore that they hadn't found any corpses during their initial walk-through, but I couldn't help but think of all the stories of how the Deinhart family locked themselves in here and never left. Murdered or not, they must have died here, right?

"Wow," Remi said, her giant blue eyes taking in the whole house at once. She dropped a plastic bag, and a single toilet paper roll unraveled a trail toward the stairs. "You really did it. You got us in."

"Of course I did," I said, hurt by the implication that I could have failed. I'd never failed at anything before. I was dependable to a fault. I was a lifelong straight A student who always carried a spare pencil, a spare tampon, and a borrowable ChapStick (separate from my regular ChapStick because, ew, germs). "You didn't believe I could do it?"

"I knew you *could*. I just didn't want to get my hopes up. We're actually inside the murder house," Remi said. In honor of graduation, she had cut her own bangs, which had turned out only a little crooked. Unused to them, she kept batting them out of her eyes. "Have you found the bodies yet?"

"No bodies, no ghosts," I said. I unzipped my backpack and retrieved the handle of vodka. The contents splashed against the glass, thicker than water. "But I did get this."

"Hell yes!" Remi lifted a case of hard seltzer over her head. "Let's drink!"

"A venue and a Costco-size bottle!" Maddy May clapped her hands together in excitement. "Ardy, you're already acing this party!"

The house picked up the sound, bouncing it from wall to wall. An invisible chorus chanting along.

Party. Party. Party.

3

We took the night's inaugural vodka shots out of deep silver candlesticks in the dining room. I would have been fine drinking out of the manor's cups (there was a cabinet full of cut crystal), but Remi and Maddy May refused. Just in case any of the cups had been full of the poison that killed the Deinhart family.

"We don't even know that they were poisoned," I argued.

"If we're going to find out, I don't want it to be because we get the backwash," Remi said. She filled each of our candlesticks to the brim. I tried not to fixate on the blob of wax clinging to the rim of mine. Wax was safe. It was practically honey, excreted from a different part of the bee. The butt part maybe. But I was going to have to let that go.

"One, two, drink!" Remi said.

We threw our shots back. Vodka, warmed over from bouncing around in my backpack, sucker punched my stomach. It tasted as close to poison as anything I'd ever tasted. For my first-ever alcoholic drink, I should have chosen something less extreme. I prayed to keep it down. Barfing would definitely dock my party grade. And even if fundraising was my number one goal, learning to be competent at a party was my number two. It would be important once I got to college.

A spider skittered across the table. I leaped into action and tried to bludgeon it with my empty candlestick. I succeeded only in smashing divots into the old wood.

"Once I find a broom, it's over for these spiders," I said, breathing heavily. "I'll take down every cobweb and burn them if I have to."

"You can't do that!" Remi said. "Ghosts hate when you start moving things around."

"Even bugs?" I asked. I did not share Remi's love of the paranormal. Whether it was a show, a podcast, or a dubiously produced streaming channel, if it was about ghosts, demons, psychics, alternate dimensions, unexplained phenomena, or an unsolved mystery, Remi had committed it to memory. (She had thankfully given up on *Ancient Aliens* after realizing that it was deeply racist. Egyptians built the pyramids without help, okay?)

"Even bugs," Remi said. "Must I remind you of the *Specter Sightings* rules?"

"You really mustn't," I said.

Remi had already started. "Ghost rule number one: Don't piss them off. That means no name-calling, no taunting, no talking back. Ghost rule number two: Don't take their stuff. Leave nothing but footprints, take nothing but pictures. Like in a national park. Ghost rule number three, and this is the most important: If you smell something, say something. Ghosts smell like rotten eggs."

"So do gas leaks," I said.

I had seen at least a hundred episodes of *Specter Sightings* with Remi, usually during sleepovers because the show's constant jump scares and shrill violin soundtrack were fun-scary in the dark. (Maddy May always got too scared and hid in a mountain of pillows.) But that didn't mean I believed any of it. It was so obviously faked. The hosts pretended to pass through cold spots and had ghost-detector devices that beeped once for yes and twice for no, and every single episode someone would hear a ghost whispering and ask, "Did anyone else hear that?"

If ghosts could whisper, then why did the hosts need the yes/no devices?

"Ghosts aside," Maddy May said, gently interrupting before Remi started listing the subtle olfactory differences between ghosts and gas, "we need to preserve the atmosphere. Haunted houses need cobwebs and spiders. Think of them like Halloween decorations."

"Halloween decorations that can crawl around and bite you." Remi waggled her fingers in teasing creepiness.

"Very comforting, thank you," I said, holding back a shudder. Being the daughter of two real estate agents, I had a healthy fear of all insects. Too much of my childhood had been spent listening to horror stories about infestations. Bed bugs in the carpet. Beehives in the walls. Termites eating through load-bearing joists. Spiders . . . Ugh, I couldn't even think about spiders. It made me want to step out of my skin and throw it in the wash.

"Why don't we get changed?" Maddy May said, dancing in place with barely contained excitement. Whether it was for school, a party, or putting on a costume, there were few things that Maddy May liked as much as getting dressed. She was most at home making every tiny detail of her appearance just the way it was in her head. She started piling her many bags onto the dining room table that took up the majority of the room. "Remi, I brought you dress options."

Remi gave the hem of her floral shorts a self-conscious tug. "Thank God. I can't believe my mom got my graduation outfit from Ross Dress for Less. These shorts feel like they're made of burlap and poison oak. I need to change before Hannah gets here. She's going to help me look for the ghosts."

"Ooh," I said. "Your first date with Hannah, at last."

"It's not a date," Remi said, blushing.

Doing her best to maneuver the vodka bottle with one hand, she poured herself a second shot. Liquor splashed onto the floor, washing a clean spot into the dirt. For the first time, I could see the swirling wood grain of the floor planks, the rest obscured by the patchy rug.

"She's into scary movies, so she has some basic understanding of haunted happenings. Wait, did I tell you that she didn't like *The Amityville Horror*? It's a classic!"

"A classic hoax," I said. "They bought a shitty house and made up ghosts to make their money back. It was a bad real estate investment and a ghost story. Maybe that's what my parents should do."

"Oh yeah," Remi said with a hungry gleam in her eyes.

"They could say that the house compelled them to spend your college fund as a way to make you stay in Bucktown. There are a ton of Deinhart stories about the murders being connected to a grudge or someone trying to take control of the family. Fighting over inheritance and being shunned by the community. Boarding up the doors and windows to make sure that no one escaped the murder spree. I prefer the stranger-danger angle, myself. It's very *In Cold Blood*, just a robbery gone wrong and an entire family slaughtered."

It felt weird talking about the Deinhart murders in their house. Wrong. It made me feel like we were voyeurs looking at the most private moment of a family we'd never know. I was relieved when Maddy May said, "Ugh, enough murder talk, please. It's making me queasy. Remi, you should have plenty of time to get ready before Hannah gets here. No one shows up on time to a house party."

I would have, but I didn't say so. This was the first unchaperoned party I had ever attended. Not that there hadn't been other big Bucktown High parties over the last four years. Maddy May's cousin Nayeli had thrown a huge karaoke party before she graduated last year. At a party in someone's garage, both of the teams known as the Bucktown Bucks (one football, one basketball) had challenged each other to a knockdown, drag-out fight for beer pong supremacy and *lost* to the girls' volleyball team, led by Remi.

I'd been invited to those parties and a couple more, but I'd been too focused on schoolwork, on helping out at my parents' office, on not getting into any trouble. All that and it hadn't done me any good at all.

"Let's look around," I said. "We'll find the perfect place to get dressed."

I thought the house looked big from down the hill, but, moving through the rooms, it was overwhelming. Had we invited enough people to fill it? Maddy May was in charge of our guest list. She was the only one of us who walked between social worlds at Bucktown High. I was firmly planted with the honors-track nerds. Remi (volleyball team, part-time Target employee) knew the athletes and the stoners. Maddy May (drama kid and future University of Nevada, Reno musical theater major) knew everyone and had gone to enough parties to know who could come to a secret party without running their mouths about it or posting a live video that could get us shut down. Plus, in order to not raise suspicions of parents or teachers, some people actually had to go to Sober Grad Night.

Every room in the manor was full of furniture hidden away under drop cloths. I could imagine my dad going to remove the covers and Mom stopping him until they were ready to do a full inventory. She wanted most of this stuff sold off to antique stores. Dad wanted it all kept with the house, a monument to the Deinhart legacy, ready to be turned into a museum or evidence for a podcast. I could almost hear the argument that would have ensued between them. Their voices getting louder and louder until the sound of their fight filled every room up to the extra-high ceilings and rattled against the drafty single-pane windows.

A mushroom cloud of dust bloomed as I pulled off the closest drop cloth. Underneath was a pool table with a red felt top and carved mahogany legs.

"A real live billiards room," Remi said. "Holy shit, no wonder your parents are suing each other for this place. They could make bank selling it."

"They're not suing each other. They're in arbitration," I said. There wasn't much of a difference to me, but Mom always emphasized that arbitration was more private than a lawsuit. Suing each other would have made our family business public record. It was much better for all of us to suffer in silence, pretending that it was perfectly normal to destroy each other over one bad business decision.

Remi traced the art nouveau carvings on the sides of the table. "If we don't find the pool cues, this would be perfect for beer pong."

"You probably don't want to play beer pong on felt," Maddy May said. "Someone always spills, and it'll ruin the table. Won't that upset the ghosts?"

"It would upset my parents," I said. "This place is still supposed to pay for the rest of my college education." I shook the drop cloth back into place over the table. "Let's try not to ruin the antiques. I can't keep throwing fundraisers every summer from now through med school."

"You could," Remi said. "There's a whole town full of people dying to get a glimpse of this place. You could make a mint running tours through here. Especially on Halloween. You could charge way more than a hundred bucks a head."

"Hopefully, by Halloween, I'll be far away from here, deep into my first semester," I said.

Remi rolled her eyes, but I pretended not to see.

Going room to room, I couldn't believe how much money Mom and Dad had spent on this place. And for what? To my eyes, the Deinhart Manor wasn't a priceless portrait of town history like Dad said it was. Or a multimillion-dollar future bed-and-breakfast like Mom thought. It was rooms full of oversize furniture and bad wallpaper. A scary story passed down through generations of Bucktown kids. Surfaces encased in dust and spiderwebs and mouse droppings. It was kind of a dump.

We made our way upstairs. Remi charged into a room at random, phone camera at the ready. I heard her disappointed sigh before I even crossed the threshold.

The room was octagonal, giving one the unnerving feeling of standing in the center of a frozen revolving door. An enormous mirror in an ornate frame took up one entire wall. There was also a wood-framed fainting couch and matching vanity and a skinny door you couldn't pay me to try to walk through.

"No bodies in here, either," Remi said. She slumped against the skinny door, fitting neatly inside the frame.

"You don't really want to find corpses, do you?" I asked. "Actual corpses? One-hundred-year-old skeletons with hair and teeth and bugs?"

"I want to find answers," Remi said, gesturing huge with

both arms. "Bodies, ghosts, whatever. I want to know what happened here. And if I don't find corpses, then I've got a ghost detector app on my phone."

"I'm sure that's scientifically accurate," I said.

I looked over at Maddy May, expecting her to jump in to help me tease Remi, but instead she was staring up at the eight-sided ceiling like she was seeing the northern lights.

"This room is so beautiful," she said, breathless. When she swished around to drop her bags on the fainting couch, the skirt of her dress and the paint of the walls blurred together, the exact same shade of sky blue.

Remi yanked open the skinny door and gestured inside. "This room is a bathroom."

"A powder room, technically," I said. I peered into the open doorway, where a toilet and a sink sat in the dark. "There's no bathtub."

Remi rolled her eyes back until all I could see were irritated whites. "Okay, Zillow Lozano Flack. Are you sure you have to move all the way to Windsor for premed? You could get your real estate license at Bucktown Community College with just one test."

For a second, I couldn't breathe. It wasn't Remi's fault. I hadn't told her and Maddy May about Mom and Dad's offer to have me choose between them and start selling houses. Partially because I was worried that my friends might think that I should give up on med school and surrender to my fate. No money for college? No problem, take a test and have a career. I was great at tests. But that didn't mean that I wanted to give up on my dreams.

Even though it wasn't her fault, it felt like Remi had torn off my emotional scab and gleefully shoved her thumb in the wound. Her smile was too mocking, her eagerness verging on malicious.

"Shut up, Madison," I bit off without thinking about it first, without even meaning to. I barely even thought about Remi as another Madison. I just knew she didn't like it. She hated having to be Maddy R., and Madison Remington wasn't as catchy as Maddy May, so Remi had all but discarded her first name back in middle school.

The sound of her first name snapped her chin back like she'd been socked in the nose. Pale eyes flashing, nostrils flaring, she held her hands up in limp surrender.

"Sorry," she said, not sounding very sorry. A real apology wasn't three sung syllables. "Fuck me, I guess. You have your fancy GPA and a hundred acceptance letters, so you're too good for the 2.0 normies at BCC. I get it."

She didn't get it. Remi had never cared about school, much less college. When she, Maddy May, and I would get together after school to do homework, Remi would get bored and end up watching her paranormal reality shows on her phone, taking out her earbuds to share the goriest details or shadowy figures that were supposedly proof of life after death. While Maddy May and I had spent the beginning of senior year panicking about college applications and test scores, Remi hadn't even taken the SATs.

All I had ever cared about was college. Working as hard as I could to not end up at the same community college my parents had gone to.

But I wasn't going to explain it to her. I didn't want to talk about it. I wanted to have fun. Throw a party. Get drunk for the first time. Show the normies, as Remi called them, that I was more than just the valedictorian with acceptance letters to multiple schools I couldn't afford to attend.

"This is it," Maddy May said, setting her makeup case on the vanity with a *thunk*. "We'll get ready here."

"In the bathroom?" Remi asked. "It's the smallest room we've seen so far."

"It's cozy, like when we used to do our makeup in the bathroom at school," Maddy May said. "We'll all be spread out during the party. And after that…" She trailed off, her face falling.

My stomach twisted. "Why would we spread out during the party? It's *our* party."

"I need to collect money at the door and pass out cups," Maddy May said. "And Remi has to profess her undying love to Hannah. And you have to make sure that no one burns down the house your family owns. This is the last night that things will be exactly the same before everything changes." She bit her lip and looked down at her feet for a moment. When she lifted her head again, her face shone with her million-watt smile. "So let's make it the best night of our lives!"

4

Remi peeled a tight pink dress over her scratchy shorts. "I've been working on my 'I like you' speech. For Hannah."

"Like there was any doubt," I said.

Remi had been sweating what to say to Hannah for the last year. Every interaction was planned, plotted, and then relayed to us in excruciating detail while Remi obsessed over every single second. In every other aspect of her life, Remi generally gave no fucks. She once told a teacher that she hadn't studied for a test because her period was "fibrous and furious." She got one of her teeth knocked out in a volleyball game and took her yearbook photo the next day, smiling wide enough to see the hole in her mouth (which was later filled with a fake tooth she popped out to scare new players on the team). While Maddy May was always polished and picture-perfect, I'd seen Remi literally comb her hair with a cafeteria spork.

But something about Hannah Treu made Remi a

stuttering, self-conscious mess. It was cute enough to justify having to listen to how many times Hannah had blinked at her.

"Do you think a planned speech is the most romantic approach?" Maddy May asked. She was sitting delicately at the vanity in a chair that would have disintegrated in a light breeze.

"She deserves something planned, not whatever idiot word salad would fall out of my mouth if I tried to improvise," Remi said with a huff. She wrestled with the straps of the dress like a fish caught in a net. "I'm going to tell her that she was an inspiring team captain and that I really liked spending time with her during and after volleyball season."

"That speech ends in a handshake, not fingering," I said.

Remi guffawed.

Maddy May gasped and clutched her neck. "Ardy!"

I sprawled out on the fainting couch, ready to jump up at the first creak of the old springs. "Remi, you have been obsessed with this girl for over a year. You don't want to just hold hands and stare into her colorful armpits. You want to tell her that you like her so that she can tell you that she likes you back. Right?"

Remi's shoulders crept up toward her eyebrows. "Obviously."

"And maybe at the end of all the speeches, you end up fooling around while a ghost watches," I said, laughing.

Remi whipped a spare dress at me.

"You should be direct," Maddy May said. All of her hair

products and makeup lined the vanity next to the preheating flat iron. She started arranging them in order of use. "I've always found that a simple 'Hey, I like you' works."

"That's because you're a hot girl with hot-girl privilege," I told her. "No offense, Rem."

"None taken," Remi said. She turned around, revealing the strappy hot pink dress she had changed into. "Maddy May could wear *this* without looking like she was doing the world's worst Barbie cosplay. Where would you even wear this, Mads? It looks like lingerie."

"I wore it to Easter brunch at my abuelita's," Maddy May said. "It's from Nordstrom! I'm just not as tall as you, so it shows less booty cheeks on me."

"Oh my God, get me out of this thing," Remi groaned.

"Does Hannah know you're gay?" I asked.

Remi scoffed. "Of course she does. I'm a Bucktown High queer icon. She asked to borrow my copy of *Fun Home*."

"I own a copy of *Fun Home*, too," Maddy May said.

"That was different," Remi said. "You have it because they turned it into a musical. You own a copy of *American Psycho* for the same reason."

"The musical is better," Maddy May muttered. "The book is sorely lacking in choreography."

Remi shifted her weight from foot to foot as she tried on each of the dresses Maddy May had brought for her. The Remi in the huge wall mirror was even taller and lankier than the real one, the warped glass giving her the proportions of an alien with a tiny head and stretched-out limbs.

"This dress is really short," she said. Her reflection

turned around, its impossibly long neck craned to see the back of the lacy miniskirt. (Presumably to check for visible booty cheeks.)

"That's why it's perfect," Maddy May said, running the flat iron through her hair so that it went from nearly perfect to perfectly perfect. It fell like black ribbons around her face. I envied Maddy May's hair to the point of covetousness. Even when I straightened my natural curls, my hair was never as shiny and well-behaved as hers.

"Arden, are you going to change?" Remi asked.

The question startled me. I looked down at my jeans and T-shirt. Both had a fine layer of the mansion's dust. "Uh, I somehow doubt that Maddy May has anything in a size twenty in her bag of many dresses."

Maddy May's eyes went large with regret. "Oh, Ardy, I'm so sorry, I—"

I held up a hand to stop her. I didn't really want Maddy May to feel guilty for not tracking down clothes my size. I meant it as a throwaway joke. A gentle reminder that not everyone in the room was exactly the same size despite variations in height. Nothing I could ever do would make me the same size as Maddy May and Remi. I wasn't built that way. The last time I wore their size was fourth grade. And by fourth-grade standards I was freakish. I had to wear a beige old-lady bra while everyone else still had cartoons on their underpants.

It would have been nice to have a new outfit for graduation, but neither parent could afford to get me one. Mom had offered to let me borrow something out of her closet, but none of her skirt-suits screamed "cool girl hosting a party."

"It's fine," I told Maddy May. "Really. I'll press my hair and do my makeup. I'll still be ten times fancier than I was for our graduation ceremony."

Once her hair was even more perfect, Maddy May offered me the flat iron. I cautiously took her seat at the vanity and started taming my frizzy roots. Maddy May retrieved a necklace from inside her backpack. A sapphire the size of a nickel hung from a thin silver chain. It glittered in the light as she fastened it to her neck.

"Holy shit, look at that rock," Remi said.

"Do you like it? It was my graduation present," Maddy May said, adjusting the pendant on her throat. It was so big, I was surprised it didn't weigh down her neck. She turned back with a self-deprecating shrug. "My mom's love language is gifts."

"So's mine," Remi said with a laugh. "But that means she buys my favorite kind of Hot Pocket, not gemstones."

"Pretty sure if my mom has a love language it's getting mad at how much laundry I have and then doing it herself," I said.

"That's an act of service," Maddy May said.

"I think it's an act of passive aggression," I said.

If I'd been consulted, I probably would have preferred living with Dad than Mom. Not because Dad and I got along better. Until last year, I never had to consider which parent I got along with more. They used to be a unit. Actually, we had all been a unit. That's the thing about being an only child: You have no choice but to be on a team with your parents. My friends could never understand that. They had siblings. When there's other kids in the family, it's kids versus the adults. Like at school, it's students versus teachers. All of them versus all of us. But when you're the only kid in a world of adults, there's no one else to talk to. My parents were who I played board games with, who I argued over the last piece of pizza with. When it was time for us to pick a vacation, I had an equal say. I went with them to the office when there was no babysitter. I was raised to be a little junior Realtor with opinions on curb appeal and countertops.

I thought that I was on their team. That we were all on the same team. But when there's no team left to be a part of, it's everyone for themself.

"At least this necklace is my style. Plus it's UNR colors. Go Wolf Pack," Maddy May said. She uncapped a lipstick and stepped in front of the mirror. "It's way better than the purity ring I got for my quinceañera."

"Didn't you have to trade that to Keaton after you guys went into the Jacuzzi at the *Romeo and Juliet* cast party?" I asked with a suggestive eyebrow waggle.

"Ha ha," Maddy May said. "She jests at scars that never felt a wound."

Remi laughed, fighting her way out of her bra while trying to stay completely covered by her borrowed dress. "What a classy way to say 'Shut up, virgin.'"

"Virginity is a construct," I said. "It implies that your first sexual experience is a prize to be won."

"Okay, well, we all know that Maddy May's prize went to Keaton, and I lost mine at volleyball camp to that girl from Quincy High," Remi said. "But Arden—"

"Is waiting to find the right person," I finished for her.

Remi rolled her eyes grandly. "I bet you a hundred bucks that the right person is going to be the first premed dude you find in the dorms at Windsor. Bucktown doesn't have enough hot nerds for you. I mean, other than Nathaniel. And you already crushed his soul. Not that he didn't deserve it. Pretentious prick."

I had not crushed Nathaniel Graham's soul. He was uncrushable. We'd met in AP Calc and been paired up for peer grading. He was cute, smart, and insufferable. But I'd overlooked that last part at the beginning of senior year because he was willing to count study dates as real dates and had a car we could make out in. Three months ago, when my parents' marriage had fully imploded and strangers were moving into my childhood home, I suddenly wasn't in the mood to compare extra-credit assignments and do over-the-clothes stuff in the school parking lot.

"Poor Nate," Maddy May said with a sigh.

"Don't pity him," I said with a groan. "He wore that NASA sweatshirt every day for *years*, begging someone to make the mistake of asking if he wants to be an astronaut just so he could correct them and say he's going to be a rocket scientist. Now he can wear an MIT sweatshirt and do the same thing. All of his wildest dreams have come true. He's fine."

I broke things off with Nathaniel to save us both from

having to pretend that either of us wanted to talk about anything other than school. We weren't friends. We weren't even really in a relationship. We were like coworkers who liked kissing each other. Breaking up was no great loss. Except for in the kissing category. I hadn't kissed anyone in three months. A problem that I really wanted to fix at the party.

"Did you invite Keaton to the party?" I asked Maddy May.

"Of course," she said, pointedly not looking at me.

"But... you don't like him anymore?" Remi said, phrasing it as a question even though she and I were pretty sure that Maddy May had totally gotten over her boyfriend the second their production of *Romeo and Juliet* had ended. We'd both observed the change. Maddy May stopped swooning over text messages or disappearing to snuggle in the drama room. I wasn't even sure if she and Keaton had taken a picture together at graduation, which seemed nonoptional for couples pretending like their relationships would survive the end of high school.

"I never said that," Maddy May said. She busied herself swiping lipstick out of her cupid's bow with her pinkie. "It's just different now."

Beside me, the various bottles of foundation and hair spray on the vanity rattled, making me jump in my seat. My pulse slammed as I imagined ghosts blowing through the room, furious at us for getting too comfortable in their powder room. Did throwing dresses all over the floor count as breaking *Specter Sightings* rule number two?

Maddy May's mascara wand held still in the air as if she were detecting a change in the wind. "Do you guys hear that?" she asked.

Distantly, I could hear thumping. Insistent thumping. Too loud to be mice.

Remi tried to contain her excitement by curling her fists into her chest. "It's the front door!"

"Go without me," I said, quickly flat ironing another piece of hair. "If it's the cops, Maddy May, pretend to be me and tell them your parents own the place! And don't let Remi talk to them!"

Remi pretended to look offended, but Maddy May looped elbows with her and pulled her out of the room. Times like this, it was too easy to remember that they had been a pair long before I'd ever met them. Their friendship went back to elementary school. I had met them in freshman year, when Maddy May had caught me eating alone at lunch. There were still plenty of people who thought of them as the Maddys. I was an afterthought, a very late addition.

Alone in the powder room, I finished my hair and sifted through Maddy May's makeup. Her skin was lighter than mine, so her foundation and blush was useless to me. But she had a gold eyeliner that livened up my brown eyes. Preparing to finish the look with a sweep of mascara, I leaned in close to the vanity mirror. Something moved in my periphery.

I spun around. Nothing. It must have been my own reflection caught in the wall mirror. I stood and moved toward it, looking past my face. A haze crept in from the corners, slowly clouding my view of the room behind me. It looked like a breath fogging the glass. But it wasn't my breath. I was too scared to breathe.

I checked over my shoulder again. The room was empty. I could hear the sounds of people talking out in the foyer, footsteps progressing into the dining room. Nothing was in the room with me.

The closer I got to the mirror, the harder it was to make out the fog that had drawn my attention. In the warped glass, my reflection was slightly wider than it was in reality, with straightened hair less sleek than Maddy May's and a frown that looked like my mom's. When my nose was close enough to touch the glass, I couldn't see the fog anymore at all.

I stepped back and took a breath. There was nothing here but backpacks, discarded dresses, and me. Worried about setting the powder room on fire, I tore the flat iron's cord out of the wall.

When I looked back, the wall mirror clouded over in a rush. The fog descended upon my reflection, blurring me entirely. And deep in the mist, something pressed against the glass. A hand.

And then it was gone. No fog, no hand. Only my reflection staring back at me with eyes so frozen in fear that I stopped myself from blinking.

I ran out of the powder room and straight into my own graduation party.

WHAT HAPPENED TO THE DEINHART FAMILY

AS TOLD BY MADISON "REMI" REMINGTON (AS TOLD TO HER BY JACKSON "REMI" REMINGTON)

The Deinhart family was being stalked by a fucking creep. Someone was looking in the windows at night and checking to see if the doors were locked. Clicking doorknobs woke the children up at night. The windows fogged from the outside with hot, panting breaths. Every morning, dead animals were left on the porch. Birds, squirrels, raccoons. Each one methodically cut apart, their intestines unspooled to spell the words "let me in."

Mr. and Mrs. Deinhart barred the windows. They boarded them up and shut out the remaining light with heavy drapes so that no one could see inside. But, at night, they could still hear someone's dirty fingernails scratching at the glass. The rattle of doorknobs turned into hours of pounding against the doors. More animals were left on the porch. Skunks, stray cats, the family dog. Their broken bodies and pools of blood spelled out "let me in."

The Deinharts boarded up the doors. They didn't need

to leave the manor. It had huge stores of food and plenty of entertainment. They'd stay inside forever if they needed to.

The first night, they heard someone at the windows and pounding on the doors. They heard the screams of the animals dying on the front porch. But the boards on the doors and windows held firm.

The second night, they heard someone at the windows and doors, raging and screaming **LET ME IN**. The voice wasn't one they recognized. It didn't even sound human. It was like a demon had been unleashed on them. The family pushed the furniture against the doors and huddled together in one room. No one slept all night as they listened to the howling outside. But the sun rose, and the stalker left.

The third night, a tree branch broke, crashing down on the side of the house. But there were no sounds at the window, no pounding at the doors. The family slept in peace.

For days after, no one bothered the Deinharts, locked away in their manor. The family started to believe that the nightmare had ended. They started to laugh at themselves for thinking they needed to board up the house. They decided that the next day, they would open the doors and go back to their regular lives.

Everyone went to sleep. They didn't hear the attic door open. The manor's heavy rugs and thick carpet muffled the sounds of the stranger stalking down the hall.

The parents died first. Hacked apart with an axe. Then the stranger moved soundlessly from room to room, chopping down the Deinhart kids.

Two of them got away, ran downstairs, and made it all the way to the front door. If it hadn't been boarded shut, they could have survived the slaughter. They could have run down the hill and found help. They could have identified the stranger.

But they were trapped. Their blood splattered against the boards their parents had put up to keep them safe.

The stranger stayed behind, living inside the impenetrable walls of the Deinhart Manor, never to be found.

5

Maddy May blocked the way into the house with a dusty ceramic vase in one hand and a sleeve of red Solo cups in the other. She had volunteered to collect money at the door without being prompted. Probably because she knew that Remi would wander away at the first sign of ghosts or booze, and I would scare people away by telling them not to make a mess.

Tanner Grant (popular, with no known extracurricular activities) was looming over Maddy May. Either unaware of or unconcerned about the line forming behind him, his broad shoulders took up the majority of the space in the foyer. A sweating bottle of beer was clutched in his fist.

Tanner reminded me of the dogs at the dog park who played too hard and scared my pugs. Like a mastiff–German shepherd mix. Part big dumb doofus, part future cop. He was always smiling but in a way that wasn't actually friendly, just a future alibi if anyone ever pointed out he was being a dick.

"Come on," he was saying to Maddy May. His voice was pouty, but his unfeeling smile didn't budge. "You said anyone who brought booze would get a discount."

Maddy May waggled a finger up at him, her nose scrunched in good-natured disapproval. "A forty is a one-person serving of alcohol. Especially for you. You only get the discount if you bring enough to share with the class."

"I could share. I love to share," he said. He lowered his face closer to Maddy May's. "Where's your Romeo anyway?"

Maddy May's eyes darted away, the same way they always did these days when someone mentioned her boyfriend.

"Maybe he's behind you," I said. I stood next to Maddy May and crossed my arms. "You're holding up the line, Tanner. Pay your money or go back to Sober Grad Night."

Tanner stood up to his full height again. His brow furrowed, as though he were confused that a girl he wasn't attracted to had attempted to speak to him. It was a reaction I was used to, especially when it came to dudes who wanted to hit on Maddy May. My fatness made me not invisible, exactly, but hard to categorize for guys like Tanner. I wasn't there to be objectified, but I also wasn't there to fawn over them and make them feel better about themselves. So, instead, they treated me sort of the way they treated a substitute teacher: vaguely human but only a passing obstacle.

Around Tanner's shoulder, a girl I didn't recognize leaned in, cautiously interrupting. She was small and blond and looked even more breakable than the money vase.

"We could go," she said tremulously. One hand landed on

Tanner's biceps. Not possessively, more like she was trying to remind him that she existed. Poor thing.

Tanner swatted the idea away as if he were trying to stop a mosquito from getting in his ear. "Go? No way. We're barely in the door," he said.

"You're *blocking* the door," I reminded him.

Maddy May frowned at me. She hated when I wasn't welcoming. She told me that I wanted to "close ranks" too much, which made us look cliquey and elitist. I didn't want to be elitist. I just liked the friends I already had and didn't have much use for more. Especially not people like Tanner.

Grudgingly, Tanner pulled a wad of cash out of his pocket and peeled off several bills. He barely noticed the Andrew Jacksons falling into the vase as he winked at Maddy May. "Just testing you, M and M."

He swung an arm around his date's narrow shoulders and dragged her into the party, already guzzling from his single-serving beer. Maddy May watched them go.

"Entitled prick," I said under my breath as they disappeared into the party.

"He was kidding," Maddy May said.

"He was flirting," I said. "And so were you."

"It's a party, Ardy." She giggled, charmed by her own rhyme. "People are going to flirt. You should be one of them. Go! Make friends. Kiss strangers."

"There aren't any strangers," I said, motioning at the people crowding into the foyer. I recognized two soccer players and the president of the FFA. "These are our classmates."

"Then kiss a classmate." She grinned. Turning away from

me, she held the vase out to the next person in line. "Welcome, welcome! One hundred dollars to enter, seventy-five if you were kind enough to bring drinks!"

I snagged a Solo cup and went in search of fun.

"Murder house!" Cans, bottles, and red cups lifted in the air in a mass toasting.

The holler went up over the sound of music being pumped into the ballroom from someone's Bluetooth speaker. The speaker was sitting on the turntable of an ancient Victrola, beneath its huge horn. Making it look like the gramophone was playing hip-hop. The furniture had all been pushed to the sides of the room. Some chairs had been uncovered so that people could wear the drop cloths, pretending to be twerking ghosts. Dancers pressed together, much closer together than any school chaperone would have allowed. People were making out in the corners. Two guys were shoving each other near the door, threatening to fight.

So, I thought, *this is a party.*

For the first time since we'd come up with this plan, I worried about getting caught. Getting in trouble. Every bump and shout made me think of cops banging down the door. Or Mom storming in and taking down the names of partygoers so she could individually call their parents.

Everything would be fine. We had graduated, so there was no principal or permanent record to worry about. Almost everyone was over eighteen. We were basically adults, free to do what we wanted.

I wished I was the kind of person who could throw herself directly into the throng and dance like nobody was watching. But I couldn't help but feel like everybody was watching. Maybe that was the only reason people went to parties. To be seen.

A canopy of smoke hung over the room. Someone was smoking weed nearby but not in sight.

Fighting my way through velvet drapes turned greasy with dust and a set of brittle lace curtains, I tried to jimmy open one of the windows that surrounded the room. No matter how hard I pushed, it wouldn't budge. The glass squeaked and squealed under my fingers.

"You want some help?"

I stopped rattling the window lock and looked over my shoulder. "No, it's probably swollen shut. I don't want to break it."

Hannah (girls' volleyball captain, activist against factory farming, object of Remi's obsession) deposited a case of water bottles onto the floor. A smart choice, if not the most fun (which is what I would call a biography of Hannah Treu).

"Good looking out," I told her.

The drapes swung back into place, and I had to lurch out of the way to keep from being absorbed.

"It must have been hard to get that up the hill."

Hannah twisted her shoulder in a shrug. "Can't have these lightweights forget to hydrate. The plastic is unforgivable, environmentally speaking, but a bunch of people drinking for the first time is alcohol poisoning waiting to happen," she said. She paused to adjust the straps of her pink overalls, an outfit that might have looked babyish if she were wearing a shirt underneath instead of a white lace bralette. With her distinctive lavender bob and matching colorful armpit hair, she was head-to-toe pastel and yet somehow managed to seem unapproachable.

"Have you seen Remi?" Hannah asked. "Hosting a graduation party in a haunted house is too perfect. It's like the party is asking the question: What's the real haunted house? The Deinhart Manor or high school?"

I wasn't sure that parties could ask a question. Unless the question was how many wasted teenagers could fit into one mansion. Or whether the plumbing in an abandoned house could withstand having all nine toilets flush at the same time.

"I mean, Remi's one of the hosts. Maddy May and I..." I cut myself off. It didn't matter. It was more important that Hannah thought that Remi was cool. "She's around here somewhere. In a dress so short that she's probably hiding behind something."

"Nice," Hannah said.

I knew that in order to dutifully report back to Remi, I should try to decode what that *nice* meant. Was Hannah excited that Remi was in a hot-girl dress? Or that Remi was present and accounted for? I couldn't tell from her expression. She looked like she always did: curious and detached. Hannah seemed like an adult masquerading as one of us, sent to study the behavior of the average American teen. Remi said that it was because her parents were both social science professors at BCC.

"So," Hannah said as she tore open the plastic wrap and snagged the first bottle of water for herself. "You're going to be a doctor, right?"

"Oh, yeah, I guess." Flustered, I kicked over a black cherry hard seltzer from a tower of unopened cans. What were the rules on touching drinks? Was it like chess where you had to play a piece once you touched it? In a panic, I picked up the seltzer and cracked the tab. The taste was less outright poisonous than my earlier shot of vodka, but it was unpleasant enough that I had to swallow a gag. "You know, Remi was looking for you, too. She really wanted to talk to you about something. I'll go find her for you."

I didn't wait for permission from Hannah. Pushing through the dance floor, I staggered out of the ballroom. I could hear some girls daring each other to go look in the basement. They wanted to find the Deinhart corpses so they could "bring home souvenirs." Where was Remi to warn them about *Specter Sightings* rule number two?

I choked down more seltzer. It wasn't good. It tasted like cough syrup without any of the sugar to help the medicine go down. But it was cold and distracting. The more I drank it, the lighter my head felt. How many cans would it take before I stopped repeating Hannah's question to myself?

You're going to be a doctor, right?

I used to be able to say definitively yes. There was nothing I was more sure about in my life. Until this week, when everything fell apart.

Even though I worked hard and played never. After years of gifted programs and honors classes, I might never get to live up to my potential. I might never get to protect other fat people from the medical system. Not kids whose parents took them to Weight Watchers and made them get weighed in front of a room full of adult strangers. Not adults who were sold on pills and injections and surgeries to "correct" their bodies even though all the fixes were more likely to kill them than keep their bodies the way they were. But at least they'd die skinny, right? (Wrong. Eighty percent gain the weight back, too.)

Fat people shouldn't have to die in pursuit of thinness. It's not like there's a disease that only fat people get. Not diabetes or high cholesterol or heart attacks. Fat people deserve to live just as much as skinny people.

I had always been fat. I was the fat kid in tae kwon do and the fat ballerina and a fat Girl Scout. And for so long I'd thought it was my fault. Even though Mom was fat and her mom was fat and my cousins on the other side of the country were fat. I'd tried diets and "lifestyle changes" and eating only healthy food (an eating disorder in its own right: orthorexia).

But trying to figure out what counted as healthy led me to learning more about nutrition and genetics and how much money the diet industry makes even though the results are terrible. The more I learned about the human body, the more free I felt. Free to look like myself and stop waiting for the day that my weight dropped in half. Because what had my body ever done to deserve being shrunk down to an unnatural size? Of course I had a fat ass and wide hips and a

49

heavy stomach. It all had to carry around my brain and my feelings and my hopes and my dreams. Hopes and dreams heavier than any body could ever be.

Since preschool, I had known I was going to be a doctor. The first person in my family to go to a real four-year university and then on to med school. I wouldn't just have a job, the way my parents had fallen into real estate because they'd needed a job to support their family without a college degree. I would have a career. A title. *Dr. Arden Lozano Flack. Arden Lozano Flack, MD.*

But now, it was a maybe. If I raised enough money. If my parents sold the Deinhart Manor. If. If. If.

Planning the party (in Maddy May's bedroom and outside the Starbucks near Bucktown High, never in text, nothing in writing so we wouldn't get caught), we had been specific about only inviting seniors. But now I couldn't be sure that these were other graduates. Or even if they went to Bucktown High. Every room on the ground floor was crammed full of people. I barely recognized anyone. Sure, there were some BHS letterman jackets. And even a couple of Sober Grad Night shirts (they must have crawled through a window to get out of the locked-down gym). But there was no one for me to stop and talk to. No one seemed to know that this was *my* party.

What I'd told Maddy May hadn't been exactly true. These people weren't strangers to me, but I didn't know any of them. And none of them knew me.

It was even lonelier than walking the halls at school. There, I expected to be anonymous. I didn't have a huge circle of friends. I never belonged to any clubs. Unless you counted taking all the Red Cross first aid and CPR classes as a club.

The prospect of trying to make friends *now*, at the party, was mortifying. *Hey, we've never spoken, but earlier you and everyone else here listened to me give a speech about how the future is ours and we're going to change the world. That was total bullshit. Want to hang out sometime? I don't have any hobbies because I literally only ever needed to be good at school.*

If I couldn't make friends, I could at least get drunk. That seemed to be what everyone else was doing. I could even find a stranger to kiss.

It was a party. I should try to have fun.

Maybe something would surprise me.

6

The dining room was packed tight with people. The long table was quickly filling up. The case of hard seltzer that Remi had brought was now one of many. There were beers, mostly tall cans that were easy to steal from the liquor store inside a sweatshirt pocket. Bottles that were already half-empty. Bags of Funyuns, Doritos, Takis, Cheetos. A sheet cake that read *Happy Graduation, Shaun.* I didn't know a Shaun, but it was nice of him to share his cake. Although, I wasn't going to be the first to dive into it.

Skinny people could get publicly excited about food and nobody ever thought twice about it. But if someone who looked like me said, "Oh, cool, a cake!" then everyone would assume that I was some out-of-control binge eater who couldn't help herself around sweets. Even though everyone likes sweets. Sugar gives us a huge boost of serotonin (aka happy chemical). It wasn't fair that I had to even think about other people's wrong opinions, but I'd gotten enough shitty comments about my weight in my life to not want to hear more. I didn't eat lunch for all of middle school because nothing I ate was ever good enough to make people shut up. Bring a sandwich? *Have you ever tried cutting out carbs?* Eat chips? *Ew, the empty calories.* Eat nothing but cucumbers and hot sauce? *Are you trying to be anorexic?*

I wanted to be a doctor so I could stop people from putting kids on crash diets and instead explain that fatphobia was rooted in a racist fear of looking like me (and Mom and our Black ancestors) rather than white waifs like Remi. And that even if everyone ate the exact same food and exercised every day, we'd all still look different. Because body diversity is real and you can't starve it away.

Also: Your brain needs carbs to function, okay? Look it up.

As far as I could tell, no one was eating any cake. Maybe I should find forks. There probably wasn't poison on the cutlery, right? And, if no one stole any of the silverware, we probably wouldn't be violating Remi's precious *Specter Sightings* rules. No ghosts had gotten mad at us for taking shots out of the candlesticks.

It felt good to have a mission. I elbowed my way into the room, scoping out the china cabinet that I'd spotted earlier. Standing in front of it was a small group of people taking turns trying to yank the cork out of a wine bottle that definitely hadn't come from anyone's parents. The label was sepia-toned, and the bottle itself was covered in a fine layer of dust. It must have come from somewhere in the house.

"You'll go blind if you drink that," Nathaniel Graham (debate team champion, future astrophysicist, my former make-out partner) was saying. For once, he wasn't wearing any NASA paraphernalia. He was in a short-sleeve button-down with new sneakers and a fresh skin fade. His dark brown skin was cocoa-buttered to a high gloss. He looked good. Which was annoying. Personally, I would have preferred if he had fallen off the face of the earth after we stopped hooking up. Or at least suddenly become less cute. Even less hygienic would have been fine. Plenty of other guys had BO or refused to floss or walked around with food on their faces. But not Nathaniel. He remained hot. With only his personality to distract from it.

I pretended not to notice him. I squeezed between the would-be wine drinkers and pulled open the china cabinet.

"Arden," Nathaniel said.

There went that plan. I gripped my seltzer can until the aluminum started to crinkle and glanced over my shoulder.

"Nate. Hi."

"What are you doing here? You hate parties," he said. He was holding a red cup, but I couldn't tell what was inside. I wouldn't have been surprised if it was plain soda posing as alcohol. Nathaniel would have loved to stay sober while everyone else got wild. His superiority complex would have made him an excellent dictator.

"First of all, I don't hate parties. I just don't usually go to them." I yanked open the china cabinet's single drawer and found a pile of silverware. Actual silver. It was heavy and cold and seemed clean enough. I scooped up a fistful of forks and spoons and turned back to Nate with a smile. "Second, this is my party. Didn't you see the sign out front with my name on it?"

"Your last name," he said, pathologically unable to resist a correction. "Wow, so, you went from no parties at all to throwing one?"

There was a *pop!* The group of people trying to bust open the wine bottle cheered. Nathaniel and I watched as purple-red wine was poured into crystal glasses.

"Seems like it's going fine so far," I said. I held out a hand to warn the wine drinkers. "Hey! Careful! Don't stain the rug."

The plates in the china cabinet were all decorated with delicate flowers and swirls. I could only guess how much money they were worth. I bet Mom had a plan to sell them to a collector. It would feel so good to smash one. Maybe I'd let a single plate slip out of my grasp. Remi wasn't around to tell me not to.

"Is the house sturdy enough for this many people to be in it?" Nathaniel asked, interrupting my fantasies of revenge and destruction.

"It's been standing for a hundred years. I'm sure it's fine."

"It's been standing *empty*," Nathaniel pointed out. He had to hold his red cup over his head to keep from spilling as people shoved by, on their way to get some of the old-ass wine being served. "Now it has at least a hundred people inside."

"The guest list was closer to two hundred," I said. Enough people to cover my tuition but less than half of our graduating class.

Done with this conversation and armed with cutlery, I started to walk away. Nathaniel fell into step beside me. It was this kind of persistence and lack of hint-getting that had made him a no-go as a potential boyfriend. I couldn't believe that I'd ever let him take off my bra.

Drowning out *that* particular memory, I took a gulp of hard seltzer and winced. I craned my neck to see what was left on the table. "Ugh, foul. Is there juice to mix this with?"

"Juice?" Nathaniel asked with a sardonic smile that brought out one of his dimples. "You think someone brought a handle of juice to a party?"

"Or maybe Coke. I'd even take off-brand, that's how foul this tastes."

He made a derisive sound, the closest thing he had to a catchphrase. "It's malt liquor. It's not supposed to taste good."

"What do you know?" I asked without looking back at him. "You're as big a nerd as I am. Excuse me!"

I raised my voice as a warning to the people standing between me and the table, loitering around the booze and snacks. Using my wide hips to my advantage, I shoved my way forward. The forks and spoons fell next to the cake with a clatter.

Nathaniel made his way to my side, posting up against a stately wooden chair and helping himself to a handle of spiced rum. He poured a glug into his cup. "I'm not so much of a nerd that I don't know you don't mix White Claw and juice. Just chug it."

"Why? So I can look cool?" I asked with dripping sarcasm. I hugged an armload of plates to my chest. "Who gives a shit? Everyone's here to get drunk and trespass. Mission half-accomplished." I slammed the plates down next to the cake and barked, "Eat up, everybody!"

Nathaniel's eyebrows went up. "You good, Doc?"

Anger detonated inside me, drowning out all the loneliness and disappointment and lingering anxiety that had been trailing me through the party.

I whipped around. Nathaniel was standing close enough that I didn't even have to stretch to jab my index finger hard into his sternum.

"Don't call me that! I'm not one of the seven dwarfs! I'm just a girl hosting a party and trying to get drunk! So leave me alone!"

Murmuring at my outburst, the people who were crowded into the dining room's doorway parted to let me out. My face flushed hot with embarrassment, but I did my best to ignore it. Another swig of hard seltzer and all I could think about was the medicinal, metallic taste and the way it seemed to curdle everything in my stomach.

I thought about slipping out the front door. Leaving the party behind and accepting my failing grade as a hostess and fun person. Who was I kidding, anyway? I didn't even like the taste of alcohol. I should go down the hill and ask for a late admission to Sober Grad Night. That's where I belonged. With the chaperones and the losers and the teetotalers jumping in bounce houses till sunrise.

Maddy May had abandoned the front door. I shouldn't have been surprised. For all her good intentions, Maddy May couldn't stay away from a party forever. Unlike me, she was fun. Smiling, joking, bursting into song. I'd seen her convince entire movie theaters to do the wave during previews and charm the cafeteria workers into giving her free french fries and chocolate chip cookies. She'd probably started a conga line or an epic game of Sardines, where the point was actually to make out in closets all over the manor. Maybe Keaton had shown up and she was somewhere pretending she still liked being his girlfriend. Or maybe she had sneaked off to meet up with Tanner.

The money vase was gone, too. So hopefully wherever she was, she was keeping my future tuition safe.

"Arden!"

With one hand holding down the back of her flapping miniskirt, Remi charged toward me.

I let out a sigh of relief. I did have friends at this party. I just had to stick close to them so that we didn't get separated by the enormity of the house. "Remi, thank God—"

"What the hell did you say to Hannah?" she spat.

This was not the energy I was expecting. I staggered back a step.

Had I said something wrong to Hannah? Had she witnessed my outburst in the dining room? No, I would have spotted her hair in the crowd. Or her overalls. Or her socks with sandals. Hannah Treu didn't blend in.

"Nothing!" I told Remi. "We talked about water bottles. I didn't even call her Hannah Armpits to her face, I swear."

"She said that you said that I had something to tell her!" Remi said.

I let out a relieved laugh. Thank God I wasn't losing my mind. "You do. It's all you talk about. You want to talk to her. Tonight. It's your last chance, blah blah blah."

Remi was practically foaming at the mouth. Her hands clenched into fists, and her face turned beet red. Was she going to hit me? I had never been in a physical fight before. Remi had a volleyball spike that could knock an opposing team on their ass. She could knock me down no problem.

"I can't believe you! I wanted to do it my way!" she shouted in my face.

My eyes were drawn to the slope of her bangs. It made it hard to take her seriously when she looked like a kid with a safety-scissor haircut.

"I had a plan, and you screwed it up!"

"Oh my God, who cares?" I asked. I couldn't believe how worked up she was over this. It was like she was trying to gaslight me into believing that I'd broken some huge promise. I hadn't even broken the *Specter Sightings* rules. "I didn't tell her you liked her. I didn't tell her that you talk about her all the time! I told her that you wanted to talk to her because *she* was looking for *you!*"

Remi gulped, her anger tempered by the thought that Hannah had asked about her. "She was? What'd she say?"

I couldn't reverse my emotions so quickly. My fight-or-flight had been activated too many times already that night and my body was stuck in full-fledged fight mode. I wanted to scream. I wanted to hurt feelings. I wanted everyone to feel as bad as I had been feeling for months.

"It doesn't matter. Nothing matters," I said. Rage pushed the words out of my mouth, vehement and venomous. "Because *she's* going to go off to college. And you'll still be *here*. In Bucktown. Working a shitty little job just like everyone else who lives here. Living at home because even though this place sucks shit, it's still too expensive to rent an apartment! So, what's the best-case scenario for you, Rem? You confess your big secret crush and hook up tonight? And then what? And then she forgets about you the second she leaves town?"

Remi tucked her chin back, her eyes glassy with hurt. "Why would you say that?"

I pounded the rest of the hard seltzer and tossed the can aside. "Because it's true! Because no one who moves away comes back! That's the whole point of leaving. You go to college to find somewhere better."

She threw her hands up, growling in frustration. "You think Windsor is so much better than here! But you've never been there, Arden. You picked it off a list just because someone else said it was the best school."

"Anywhere is better than here!" I yelled at the wooden beams holding up the ceiling. I wished the ferocity of my hatred for this house and this town and this year could call down a lightning bolt that would wipe it all off the map.

Whatever hateful thing I would have said next stuck in my throat, interrupted by someone pounding on the front door.

And screaming.

7

Remi and I tiptoed into the foyer. The single chandelier was burning bright. Beneath it, a blond girl was throwing her body (over and over again) into the front door. It took me a second to recognize her as the girl who had come in with Tanner. Her face was blotchy red and wet with tears.

"He left me here," the girl cried as we came closer.

"Who left you here?" Remi asked.

"Tanner?" I asked the girl.

"Tanner Grant?" Remi asked. She gagged. "Ugh, of course Maddy May invited him. He's been obsessed with her since—"

"Remi—" I cut her off, motioning toward the girl with warning eyes. This probably wasn't a great time to bring up the fact that Tanner had a crush on someone else.

Remi pressed her lips together, chagrined.

I reached out toward the girl as she continued to launch herself at the door, scrambling for the seams.

"Hey, um—" I cleared my throat. "Sorry, what's your name?"

"C-Claire," the girl hiccuped.

"Take it easy on the door, Claire," Remi said with false cheer.

"It won't open," Claire sobbed.

"It opens inward," I said, doing my best to sound patient instead of annoyed. Not everyone had parents who talked incessantly about OSHA standards. Claire had probably never noticed that doors that open outward had panic bars instead of doorknobs.

"It's stuck," Claire insisted. She slammed her hands against the wood hard enough to make the hinges rattle. But not enough to break the door down. "I told him I didn't want to come here. I told him that the house wouldn't like us here. The house will eat us all."

Well, *that* took a turn.

"Do you want a bottle of water?" I asked her, hoping to distract her from the idea of the house eating us. "Or a slice of cake?"

Remi squeezed past us. Ignoring Claire's continued outburst, she took hold of the doorknob and turned. And turned. And turned.

The doorknob spun in circles, as though it had no latch.

Remi looked back at me, panicked, eyes wide. "She's right. It won't open."

Claire wailed again, attacking the door with new force. Clawing at the wood in long swipes. Scratching until her fingernails started to split and shred.

As smears of blood started to stain the immovable door and drip down her wrists, I grabbed her by the waist and pulled her away from the door.

"Stop it!" I said. "You're hurting yourself!"

"I want to go!" she screamed, insensible even as I dragged her backward. She was light in my arms but wriggled like a feral cat, spitting and screaming. I worried that she might start clawing at me the way she had the door. "Tanner left, and I want to leave! I want out! LET ME OUT!"

"Where is Maddy May?" Remi wondered aloud, and I immediately understood why. Maddy May was the nice one. She was so much better at calming people down than me or Remi. She never would have let us start screaming at each other in the middle of a party. She would have been able to reason with Claire before the girl's fingertips turned into hamburger meat.

"She's supposed to be on door duty," I said, craning to see her over the top of Claire's head. "She probably just went to the bathroom."

"Or she got bored and wandered off to make out with—" Remi caught herself this time and stammered to say, "Her boyfriend, who she's totally in love with and faithful to."

Claire didn't seem to be listening to us at all. She kept screaming. "Tanner's gone! He left me here! In the devil's house!"

"It's not the devil's house," I said. I tried to bounce her like she was a fussy baby. "My mom's company owns it. She sucks, but she doesn't rule hell. The devil wouldn't have a closet full of pug-size sweaters."

Overhead, the chandelier's light flared from gentle to scorching. With a pop, the electricity shut off, leaving us in the pitch black. Sounds of protest and alarm went up all over the house. Letting go of Claire, I held my breath.

Could Mom have spotted the partygoers in the windows and come up to shut off the power?

The lights flickered for a minute straight. In the strobing light, I could see Remi's horrified face. Claire's mouth caught in a soundless sob. The small mirror on the wall reflected something swirling, even as we all stood still.

Then the power came back. Stayed on. Like it had never happened.

In other rooms, a cheer went up. Aluminum cans of bad seltzer and cheap beer crunched in tight fists. People were egged on to chug or to score during a round of beer pong. The party resumed.

But in the foyer, there was a soft burbling. Like the sound of too-thick spaghetti sauce boiling on the stove. *Plop. Splut. Blorp.* Remi, Claire, and I stayed frozen. Liquid (syrupy, salty-smelling) oozed out of the seams of the door, covering the brass handle and filling the keyhole. It came up from between the floorboards, gently splashing our ankles and adhering the soles of our shoes to the ground.

A metallic scent wafted around us. Like pennies. Like nosebleeds.

No. That didn't make any sense. It couldn't have been. There must have been a leak somewhere. Maybe a pipe had burst rusty water. But it was unmistakably red.

Blood.

Blood dripped down the door and pooled in the floor's wood grain.

But the floor looked wrong. Wood grain moves in one direction, like ocean waves. Sometimes it's straight lines. Or wavy. Or riddled with knots. Not the floors of the Deinhart Manor. As the blood filled it in, I could see that the floors had circuitous wood grain. Like cursive handwriting. Like someone had carved into it over and over, millions of times. One word, now overflowing with phantom blood to scream at us.

STAY. STAY. STAY.

Remi stiffened beside me, her breathing shallow, as though she were considering whether to start screaming.

Claire knelt down, watching as the blood on the floor continued to collect. She pressed her palm into the ground. It covered a dozen tiny STAYs. When she lifted her hand again, the imprint of the words was gone. Her skin was coated.

Before Remi or I could stop her, her tongue darted out. She licked across the longitude of her palm. Remi and I both cried out and gagged.

Claire peered up at us with bloodshot eyes. An eerie calm settled over her. She didn't even look like the same girl who had torn her fingernails apart trying to get out a moment ago.

"It's too late now." Her tone was flat and emotionless. Her eyes and nose ran freely, covering her face in tears and slime. "The house will never let us leave."

"What the fuck?" I said. To Claire. To the words carved into the floor. To the blood on my shoes.

Sick to my stomach, I staggered away. Thankfully the blood seemed to be concentrated in the foyer. Near the staircase, there was only the faint smell of blood. In all likelihood, it was coming from me.

Remi chased after me. "This is it," she said, breathless and smiling. "It's them!"

"It's who?" I asked. Who would have vandalized the floors *just* in the foyer? What was the point of that, except to make Crying Claire lose her entire mind? "Oh shit, do you think it's Tanner?"

"Who? What? No!" Remi said with a derisive snort. "It's *them*, Arden! The Deinharts. This is classic haunting shit. Power surges, mysterious blood, cryptic messages. Oh my God, Hannah is going to flip out! Do you know how many times she's seen *The Shining*? Like a billion times."

I rolled my eyes. Even in a crisis, Remi could still find a way to bring everything back to Hannah Treu.

"Okay, well, this isn't *The Shining*, and that wasn't an elevator full of blood," I said. "It was a prank. Or, like, a family of raccoons exploded in the basement. It doesn't matter. What matters is that the front door is stuck. So we need to find a way *out*."

"Are you serious?" Remi asked. She gaped at me. "You seriously don't believe this place is haunted? After all that?"

"No!" I said. I couldn't believe it. Things were weird but not inexplicable. Everything seemed worse because we'd been drinking, because of the stories about the house, because it was the last day of high school and we didn't know what came next. I refused to believe that ghosts had anything to do with it. "And even if I did believe it, it wouldn't matter because we have to find a safe way out before anyone other than Claire realizes they're trapped in here. If people panic, then we'll have a full-scale riot in here and people will get hurt. Haven't you ever heard of crowd crush?"

If the doors wouldn't open, then it would be carnage if the whole party freaked out. People would get trampled.

See, this is why OSHA requires panic doors.

"You heard what Claire said," Remi said, flapping a hand back toward Claire, who was still lying in a pool of phantom blood. "The house isn't going to let us leave. The only way we're going to survive is by making a deal with the ghosts. They probably want us to give them a real burial or avenge their deaths or something. That's usually how a *Specter Sightings* episode ends."

I gasped. "Can you hear yourself? Seriously, I know that we just saw something weird and gross, but that doesn't mean that we have to start making deals with ghosts. We need to find an exit and safely get everyone out."

"What? You want to cancel the party?"

"After I saw someone rip their fingernails apart and lick random floor blood? Yeah, I think I'm done partying, Rem."

"Because of one girl? We don't even know her!"

"And yet you're willing to take her word that we're trapped in here."

"I tried the door. It's not going to budge."

I threw up my hands. "Sometimes the doors swell shut. There are other doors. There are windows!" I remembered the window in the ballroom and how it hadn't moved an inch when I tried to open it. I pushed the thought away. "Old houses have weird quirks!"

"No." Her bangs swung as she shook her head. "This is huge. This is what I came here for!"

"You came to watch your classmates tear their fingernails off on a door that won't open?"

Remi shuddered. "At least Claire realizes that something's wrong. You're deluded!"

"I'm being reasonable!" I snapped. All the anger and resentment of our earlier blowup returned in a rush. I remembered the way Remi had blamed me for talking to Hannah and suggested that because I'd never been to Windsor that I didn't actually know that I wanted to go to school there. And that I should just give up and get my real estate license. The particular sting of that one wasn't getting any easier to bear. "If you want to go hunt ghosts, then fine. I'll be the responsible one. That's pretty standard."

I charged down the hall, keeping an eye out, hoping to see Maddy May as I went. There had to be multiple exits in a house this size. There was definitely a back door in the kitchen. And I bet the windows in the ballroom were big enough to fit through. If I could get them to open. I'd smash them if I had to. My parents would need to update all the windows anyway. One broken pane of glass wouldn't hurt.

As long as there were no other power outages or blood storms, we would be fine.

We would all get out alive.

8

No one else knew that anything was wrong.

As I walked down the hall, a couple of people talked about how the house was so old that of course the power had surged after having things plugged into the sockets for the first time in a century. Otherwise, the party had progressed with no signs of phantom blood or stuck doors. A beer pong tournament had started in the billiards room. (I asked them to put down an extra drop cloth to keep the table dry.) The dancers in the ballroom were bouncing up and down, scream-singing along to their music. (I reminded them that there were water bottles, not just alcohol.) Behind a closed door, I found an impromptu séance happening. They had a bunch of lit candles, a Ouija board, and the world's biggest bong. (I told them to blow the candles out before they burned the house down.)

But I didn't find any exits. I wished I had the house blueprints. They had been surrendered to the lawyers for evidence in the arbitration.

The kitchen was at the farthest end of the house. Compared to the rest of the downstairs, it was in pretty bad shape. More than cobwebs and frail furniture, this room was wrecked. Underneath the single window, everything seemed to be actively rotting. Sheets of paint molted from the wall. A squat cast-iron stove was corroded with rust. Underneath layers of grime, the tile counters were disintegrating.

Standing in front of a dirt-covered sink was a small group of people drinking wine from a dusty bottle similar to the one that had been shared in the dining room. From the collection of anachronistic hats and one pair of steampunk goggles, I was able to recognize the wine drinkers as members of the Drama Club.

Keaton (ghostly pale, king of the drama dorks) waved at me. Although he'd been dating one of my best friends for the past few months, I hadn't spent much time with the Romeo to Maddy May's Juliet. I'd seen their play, of course. (It was fine, except that it had been staged as two rival soccer teams, and everyone's cleats were distractingly loud on the floor.) When he and Maddy May hung out, it was usually with the rest of the Drama Club.

I didn't have the stomach for the LARPing that being a drama kid seemed to require, but Keaton and I had endured AP Lit together. Or, rather, I had endured Keaton during AP Lit. We'd gotten into a screaming fight about *The Crucible*. Keaton called Tituba "a complex character for an actor of color." I called her a whipping boy for white feminism. It was one of the only times that Nathaniel ever had my back in class. He had gone to the primary sources to point out that twisting Tituba's voodoo religion into something demonic was part of the racist othering that was integral to the fabric of Puritanical society. It was the only time I had actually kissed him in full view of everyone. (Well, in the hall. Where practically anyone could have seen us.) The next day, both of us had received a handwritten apology from Keaton for not being culturally responsive in the face of his passion for Arthur Miller.

Drama kids. They were equal parts weaponized therapy words and earnestness. And, if you got enough of them together, they were somehow always on the verge of breaking into an orgy. It was as impressive as it was uncomfortable to be around.

Keaton wiped his mouth on his wrist. The deep-ruby wine stain was uncomfortably bloodlike against his skin as he held the bottle out to me.

"Wanna sip?" he asked.

"We think it's a port," added someone wearing a top hat. I couldn't tell if they had brought the hat to the party or if it had been found among the Deinharts' belongings. You could never tell with the Drama Club.

"I'm good, thanks," I said.

"I liked your speech," Keaton told me. "At graduation. Especially the part about how high school was just the soil we were grown in but we'd get to really blossom in adulthood. That spoke to me."

"Maddy May gave me that metaphor," I said. I had torn up my original valedictorian speech in a rage after my parents dropped the bomb about my college fund on me. I couldn't make myself stand up in front of the entire school and talk about how the last four years of hard work had all been worth it. I didn't want to thank my teachers or, worse, my parents. What I'd really wanted to do was blow a raspberry in the mic, flip everyone off, and disappear forever. Remi had supported that plan (and offered me fifty bucks if I actually did it), but Maddy May had given me some nice-sounding platitudes that skirted around any of my prickly feelings.

My eyes scanned the kitchen for the back door that I knew had to be here. There was a door next to the icebox, but it opened into a pantry. Spiderwebs choked the walls, hanging in every direction like ratty curtains. Behind them were the vague outlines of jars and cans, but nothing discernible. Other than the jittery movement of spiders reacting to the light.

I leaped back, colliding with Keaton, who had crept up beside me. It wouldn't have been hard to knock him over. Both of his arms together would have been about the size as one of mine. He was sickly pale verging on greenish, even without a bellyful of century-old booze. I had never considered it until this moment, but he looked a little bit like a ghost. His white-blond hair and buttoned-up tweed vest certainly didn't help. What was it about the theater kids that made them want to wear costumes in real life? Even Maddy May dressed up like she was cosplaying a hot girl rather than just embodying the idea.

Keaton pointed into the spider-filled pantry. "That's

where we found the port," he said. "There's more bottles in there, I think. If you want one of your own."

I inched away from the pantry door, refusing to look again. I couldn't stand to see more bugs. Skittering. Jumping. Silent on their too many legs. Disgusting. Knowing they were there made all the hair on my arms stand at painful attention.

"Hey, Arden," Keaton said, his voice constricted in a poor attempt to sound casual. He really wasn't a very good actor. "Have you seen Maddy May around?"

"She was supposed to be watching the door," I said. "Didn't you pay her to get in?"

"Oh, yeah, but she said she'd be done soon." He swayed in thought. I worried that his knees might give out. They were looking a little rubbery. "If you see her, tell her I'm looking for her. And—and that she 'doth teach the torches to burn bright.' She'll know what it means."

"I'll make sure she gets the message," I said.

Corny quotes and general aura of intensity aside, I couldn't help but pity Keaton. Unless he found someone with a fetish for malnourished Dickensian-orphan types, he might never have a girlfriend as hot as Maddy May again. Even the first time had been a fluke. Maddy May didn't really like Keaton. Keaton didn't own jeans and couldn't grow facial hair and once recited multiple sonnets in the middle of lunch in honor of Shakespeare's birthday. Maddy May liked *Romeo*, who was an invention of the greatest writer of all time. Created to be suave, popular, good with a sword. Unfortunately, for Keaton and Maddy May,

Romeo stopped existing once the play ended. They were both stuck in denial about it.

A glint of brass caught my eye. It was a doorknob, obscured behind the gaggle of wine-drinking drama kids. I lunged for it, too relieved to be polite. The drama kids leaped back, holding on to their many hats. My relief crested and crashed in one motion as the door swung open and revealed...

Bricks.

Where an exit should have been, there was a wall. It was well-made. No empty seams where air could get in or chunks of missing masonry that could have been enlarged into an opening. No signs that it had withstood a hundred years of neglect, bad weather, and nosy kids. It was as though the outer wall of the house had grown over the door. Like blood cells scabbing over a wound.

"Whoa," Keaton said. He reached out to brush the bricks with his fingertips, checking to make sure they were real. "So it was more than just some boards on the windows, huh?"

Top Hat came close, holding the wine bottle by the throat.

"Why would they brick up this door and not the front door?" they asked.

"It'd be easier to brick up a back door in secret," said Newsie Cap. "People need the front door. This could be done while no one was paying attention."

"Whoever killed the Deinharts was thorough," Keaton said. He accepted the bottle from Top Hat and took another swig. He hissed the fumes through his teeth. It smelled like grape jelly and Bactine. "There was never any hope of them getting out."

The hooks of fear stabbed at my guts and pulled. Keaton was right. This house had been meticulously sabotaged a hundred years ago to keep people from getting out. And they hadn't gotten out. Whatever else had happened to the Deinharts, all of the rumors agreed that they had come home one day and then never left again.

If we couldn't open the front door, what hope did we have?

There was a skillet sitting on top of the cast-iron stove, as rotted away as the rest of the kitchen. The rust on the handle crackled like a fistful of dead leaves in my hand as I gripped it. With one swing, I heaved the skillet at the nearest window.

It should have cracked. The window was wood and glass. But instead, the skillet cracked in half, the base falling away like a broken jaw. The Drama Club watched in horror as I threw whatever detritus I could find. The door of an empty cabinet. An old coffee can. A silver serving platter. A hand-crank eggbeater.

Nothing made so much as a dent. The window stood firm. It might as well have been as bricked over as the door.

Like the Deinharts a hundred years ago, we were trapped.

WHAT HAPPENED TO THE DEINHART FAMILY

AS TOLD (AND REENACTED)
BY THE DRAMA CLUB

Mr. Deinhart was a mean drunk. And he was never sober. Crème de menthe was breakfast. It smelled like toothpaste on his breath. He had vodka in a water glass for lunch. Every night, he came home from overseeing work in the plant, stinking like onions and sweat and liquor, and he raged at his family until he passed out.

Mrs. Deinhart couldn't take it anymore. After her husband caved in half her face with his fists, she stopped leaving the house, hiding away her disfigurement like the Phantom of the Opera. She lived in fear that any attempt to stop him could fail and end in her death. Then there'd be no one left to protect the kids. One day he would hurt them beyond what could be fixed with an ice pack and a bandage. But there was no one to turn to for help. Mr. Deinhart was the most powerful man in Bucktown. More powerful than the mayor. Because he was rich and ruthless and stupid.

There was no one to stop him but Mrs. Deinhart.

So she ordered a special bottle of cognac. While she

waited for it to arrive, she started to hype it up to her husband. This cognac was rare and imported. Of the highest quality. For only the most discerning palate. It was a drink of the elite, a favorite of presidents and kings. It was particularly prized for its subtle taste of almonds.

Mr. Deinhart had never heard of this most special cognac, but by the time it arrived, he had been convinced that it was going to be the best drink of his life. After dinner, he accepted a full glass and drank it without pausing to wonder why his wife hadn't poured some for herself. Mrs. Deinhart watched as her husband's eyes bulged out of his skull. His lips curled away from his teeth and turned purple. He choked and gasped! His head slammed down on the dining room table hard enough to knock over his glass. A trickle of blood ran down his chin like baby puke. He died as he lived, drunk and enraged, having underestimated his wife.

Unfortunately, Mrs. Deinhart had talked up the cognac too much and too well. While she served the poisoned cup to her husband, her son snuck into the kitchen and stole a sip for himself. He imagined himself an important man of means, more cultured and refined than his father. More deserving of this life-changing drink.

Like his father, he didn't know that the almond scent came from the addition of cyanide, the rat poison kept under the sink. He, too, died instantly. Slumped on the kitchen floor.

When Mrs. Deinhart found her son dead, she went insane with grief. She tore the hair out of her head and screamed until her vocal cords shredded. The sound of her sorrow echoed for miles, reverberating over Bucktown like the peal of a broken bell.

She boarded up the doors and windows herself, wanting to hide what she'd done from the outside world.

She dressed her husband and son in their Sunday best and sat them down at the dining table. Mr. Deinhart at one end. Their son at the other. Between them, Mrs. Deinhart, bald, bloodied, and mute, lifted a glass and did what everyone had expected of her husband.

She drank herself to death.

9

On the second floor, everything was covered in a plush crimson carpet. *The better to hide mysterious burbling blood*, I thought.

Up here, the sounds of the party below almost entirely disappeared. Holding on to the railing, I looked down at the foyer. The blood was gone. Vanished. Like it had never been there (though the soles of my shoes said otherwise). From above, it was impossible to ignore the wrongness of the wood grain. Even without the blood, I could still make out the looping cursive **STAY**s that covered the downstairs flooring.

Had my parents noticed the writing when they did their walkthrough of the house? Had their contractor? Was it mentioned in the auction notes? Someone had to have carved those by hand. Hours and hours, or even days and weeks, of obsessive scratching. Is that what the Deinharts were doing while they were trapped in here? Slowly (or rapidly) losing their minds and writing messages on the floor?

Is that what would happen to all of us if I couldn't find a way out?

The first room was a study with a desk that took up most of the room. There was a single window that overlooked the west side of Founders Hill. Below, in the darkness, I could barely make out the neon glow of a nearby gas station sign. I unlocked the window latch and pushed. Nothing happened.

The carpet muffled my footsteps as I slowly backed away. I imagined myself breaking through the window, rolling down the roof, and having to explain to the paramedics and my parents that after approximately two alcoholic beverages I had believed that the Deinhart Manor had trapped half the Bucktown High graduating class inside.

But the glass didn't so much as squeak as I threw myself at it and ricocheted off.

I tried again. And again. Until my shoulder started to ache and I realized that I was one broken nail from going full Claire on the front door.

The windows weren't going to open. I would have liked to sit and cry about it, but every second that I wasn't finding a solution to the problem was a second closer to literally anyone else realizing that there was a problem. What I needed was to find my friends and brainstorm together what we could do to free ourselves. The worst-case scenario was having to call my mom, admit what I'd done, and ask her to come free us. Or calling the fire department and asking them to break down the front door. But the fire department would bring the cops. I didn't need everyone to get arrested (or worse) just because the front door was stuck.

There had to be weapons in the house somewhere. One of the most pervasive Deinhart murder rumors was that someone (Dad, Mom, son, daughter, stranger) had hacked the family apart with an axe. That meant that there could be an axe somewhere. The windows might be strong, but they couldn't withstand a hatchet. Could they? No, that was stupid. This whole party (this whole night, this whole *life*) was incredibly stupid.

Leaning against the wall, I dug the heels of my hands into my closed eyes. The small amount I had drunk was making my brain run at half speed while my adrenaline was at full blast. It felt like trying to speed up in slow motion. Discombobulating. And nauseating.

Suddenly, my head began to tip back farther than the rest of my body. Half of me was falling while my feet stayed on the ground. My stomach flipped like I was on a roller coaster launching away from the starting line. It shouldn't have been possible. Up until a second ago, the wall was holding me up. But it was like the back of my head was stretching the wall back. Or I was fusing into it somehow. Like a ghost.

With a gasp, I staggered forward and whirled around. The wall was whole, complete with ugly yellowed wallpaper covered in busy fleurs-de-lis. I pressed my knuckles into the top of the desk. It was cold, real, and solid. I touched my face. Warm cheeks covered solid bone. I was panicking, a little buzzed, and imagining things. But I couldn't make myself touch the wall again. Just in case.

I left the bedroom, closing the door so that I wouldn't have to see the wallpaper that probably hadn't tried to eat me.

The long curving hallway was empty except for Nathaniel. Of course. He leaned against the wall outside the powder room where Maddy May, Remi, and I had gotten ready. One of his sneakers was posted up against the baseboards. A grunt of annoyance slipped out of me before I could even think to stop it. His head snapped up, spotting me.

"I'm not following you," he said with suspicious quickness.

"I didn't say you were," I said.

He hooked a thumb at the door beside him. "I'm waiting for the bathroom."

"I didn't ask," I said. "Have you seen Remi or Maddy May up here?"

"Not unless they're the ones taking forever in the bathroom," he said with a shrug. "I took a break from waiting to look around and came back. All the downstairs bathrooms have superlong lines."

"I hope we brought enough toilet paper," I muttered, momentarily distracted from the bigger problems. I should have stolen some of my mom's decorative soaps for the bathrooms. Hopefully people were sharing the hand sanitizer I'd put out in the dining room.

"I hope whoever is in there is doing their hair or something because otherwise it's going to be grim when I get my turn," he said.

I rolled my eyes. "It's a party, Nate. It's probably two people. Or more. Looking for privacy and flat surfaces."

"I doubt it," he said with a scoff. "We'd hear if it was a hookup."

"You don't know that," I said, laughing at his cockiness.

Like it would be absurd for people to find somewhere private with a lock at a party. "We were quiet enough to hook up in the textbook room at school."

He quirked a smile at me. "Well, you have to be quiet in the library."

I shouldn't have mentioned our history of making out in and around Bucktown High. I wasn't here to flirt. I wasn't even here to party anymore. I was supposed to be in crisis mode. Exits. Weapons. Checking to make sure that Crying Claire didn't tell anyone else that we were trapped.

Shit, where was Claire? I hadn't seen her sitting on the stairs. She could have been walking around, covered in blood, talking about the devil. That would bring such bad vibes to the party.

"I should go find Remi and Maddy May," I said.

"Doc—" Nathaniel wet his lips and corrected himself. "Arden. AHHH!"

With a shriek, Nathaniel belly flopped onto the floor. His arms shot forward. His feet kicked. As he cried out, the wall *reached* for him.

A dozen hands grew out of the wall and wore the wallpaper as gloves. The wall-hands clawed at his feet, his legs, his ankles. One of his feet disappeared into the crush of hands, and he screamed again as he was pulled back.

Into. The. Wall.

I dove for him, keeping my focus on his terrified eyes and scrambling fingers. I did not look at the wall-hands. They were even worse than staring into a nest of spiders. They were horrifying and impossible and trying to draw

Nathaniel into what should have just been insulation and two-by-fours but was somehow porous and spongy.

It was a wall. It was hands. It was a trap. It was hungry.

My fingers wrapped around Nathaniel's wrists and pulled.

"I've got you," I said, long before it was true. I repeated it as my forearms flexed and my shoulders shook. "Nathaniel, I've got you."

I felt the moment the wall-hands gave up. Nathaniel slipped toward me, first an inch and then all at once, birthed into the hallway. The two of us tumbled backward and crashed into the opposite wall. Nathaniel landed on top of my legs.

Breathing hot, gasping breaths, we stared at each other. His eyelashes were wet, and his lips were dry. We hadn't been this close together in months, since the last time we crowded together in the tinted back seat of his car, when I told him that I needed to be done. That he should find someone else to grope during homeroom and lunch. Someone whose life wasn't falling apart.

His nose bumped into mine as he leaned forward, pressing my shoulders against the wall. Between us, hearts slammed and pheromones lit up. Would kissing him now taste as sweet and spiced as his breath? Would it make me as dizzy as inhaling his carbon dioxide? It felt like I would die if we didn't kiss at that exact moment.

But I could literally die, too, if there were hands in this wall that decided to take both of us while we were busy tonguing down.

Remembering the imminent danger we were in broke the

spell. I shoved him back and clamored to my feet. I gulped down air. Fresh air, far from anyone else's mouth.

"Get away from the walls," I commanded. "Just to be safe."

Nathaniel got up and took inventory of his legs, his chest, and his head. His eyes locked on his shoes. They were as bleach-white as ever, but one of his shoelaces was untied. It trailed behind him toward the wall like a fishing lure. He hurried to tuck the stray lace under the sneaker tongue.

"What the fuck just happened? What were those things?" he asked.

"Disembodied hands." I scrubbed my hands over my face. I couldn't believe that I was going to have to tell Remi that she was right. "So . . . ghosts. Probably."

10

"No." Nathaniel gripped his hair and paced back and forth in front of the bathroom door. "No way. There's no way that I was attacked by ghosts."

"Of course not. You voluntarily fell face-first into the floor and then slid backward until one leg went *inside* a solid wall," I said sarcastically.

Remembering made me shiver. My whole body felt cold and tingly, like my circulation was being cut off by fear. Nathaniel had almost been taken inside the frame of the house. Where would he have ended up? How far would he have to go before I couldn't pull him back? How could we keep everyone else at this party from touching the walls?

I bit my thumbnail and chewed in thought. "You saw the same things I saw, Nate. Hands that appeared from nowhere and then...returned to nowhere. A wall that was solid became squishy and then—" I knocked on the wall gingerly, praying not to fall inside of it. "Solid again. Not even hollow. So what else could it be? We're in a known haunted house. The exits have been sealed. And now there's actual literal ghosts."

Nathaniel stopped pacing. "What do you mean 'the exits have been sealed'?"

After facing down the wall-hands, I figured he was entitled to the very sensitive information about our current circumstance. I filled him in on what had happened in the foyer and the bricked-up door in the kitchen.

"And I couldn't break the windows, which might also be because of ghosts," I concluded. "Do you think it's possible for ghosts to create force fields?"

"No! I don't!" His eyes were huge and frantic, darting around as though he could search out a better explanation. I understood the feeling, but having already overcome my own denial, I also felt superior and a little annoyed to have to watch someone else go through it.

Nathaniel sprinted into the nearest room. It was a library. I was bummed to not have found it earlier, in my life pre-ghosts. It would have been a decent place to hide from my own party. The walls were lined with crowded bookcases missing all of their shelves. Instead, the books were stacked in towers. There were leather-bound covers worn soft with use and paperbacks whose glue had long ago failed, leaving piles of pages on the floor like fallen leaves. There was a globe complete with the Russian Empire and Persia but missing four of the US states and the Panama Canal. An armchair that might have once been blue sat facing a fireplace with an elaborate mantel. The upholstery was shot

through with mouse-size holes. The coil of a spring pro-
truded from the seat.

Nathaniel didn't notice any of this. He was transfixed
by the fireplace tools, hanging from a cast-iron stand. He
picked up the poker, gripping it tight with two hands.

"I told you, I tried—" I said.

But he was already charging toward the nearest window.

Swinging from his shoulder like he was trying to hit
a home run, Nathaniel bashed the poker directly into
the center of the glass. The glass didn't budge, but the
reverberation snapped Nathaniel's head back. Undeterred,
he adjusted his grip, lifting the poker over his head. He
brought it down hard, point-first. Iron screeched against
glass, nails-on-a-chalkboard loud, but no mark was left
behind. With a frustrated growl, Nathaniel brought the
poker down again, on the window, on the frame, on the
wall.

The poker tore at the wallpaper, parting two sheets. As
it came down again, the tip slipped effortlessly into the
wall. Then, the entire poker sunk into the wall, like a butter
knife being absorbed into Jell-O. The handle went last, a
glint of metal that got smaller and smaller until it was fully
swallowed by the tear in the wallpaper.

Nathaniel stared at the spot. Lifted a hand. Touched the
flap where the wallpaper was split.

"Nate, don't!" I warned.

His nails scrabbled at the tear in the wallpaper. Shreds
of paper rained down on his feet and the carpet. I came
up beside him, ready to wrench him away or rescue him

from going the way of the poker. But I didn't have to. He stopped, and we both stared at the hole he'd created.

It was nothing. Not wall. Not wood. Not fiberglass or asbestos or even a hidden beehive.

Behind the wallpaper, in a hole about the size of fist, was a stretch of true nothingness. Lightless, limitless nothing. Vantablack. An abyss where a house should be. From where I was standing, it gave off neither heat nor smell. Did it have oxygen? Was it a vacuum? A black hole? Something else entirely?

Nathaniel and I stared into it. If it stared back at us, I couldn't tell. Neither of us even considered touching it. It was like space with no stars. Or the Challenger Deep without water.

"You don't see Cthulhu in there, do you?" I asked, transfixed by the sight.

"Don't," Nathaniel said, voice choked. "Don't joke about that."

"Because it's possible?"

He couldn't bring himself to agree with me. It was against his nature. He balled his fists and turned his back on the nothingness.

"What do we do?" he asked in a whisper.

I turned to look at him. It felt better not looking directly into the abyss. It was there, I knew, but not keeping it in my eyeline made me feel better. More real, somehow.

"Now we look for a way out," I said. "Remi's looking for ghosts. Once I find Maddy May, I'll have her make sure that everyone downstairs stays distracted. And safe."

Nathaniel looked helpless. "How?"

"I don't know," I said, exasperated. "Improv games. Or spin the bottle. Or a dance contest. Who cares? They just can't know how fucked we are."

"Lucky them," he said.

"Do you want to help me look for exits?" I asked. "Or do you want to stay here and have an existential crisis? Both are valid options, by the way. But I've already made my choice."

He shook out his hands like he could fling his fear onto the ground. "I'll help you, but I—I still have to use the bathroom."

"You might as well piss in the fireplace," I said, gesturing to the less-terrifying hole in the wall. "Time is sort of the essence here."

Nathaniel jerked back, appalled. "I'm not staying here alone."

"I'm not staying to listen to you pee," I said.

"Will you—" He squeezed his eyes shut and gritted his teeth. Whatever he was going to ask was obviously deeply painful to him. His jaw worked. "Will you wait outside the door?"

I would have loved to say no and storm off to find Remi and Maddy May. But if the house ate Nathaniel because I was too petty to wait for him, it'd be pretty hard to live with myself. Even if it was only for a little while.

"Fine," I said. "I'll stay within shouting distance."

I closed the door behind me and stood in the middle of the hallway, my hands clasped together as I tried not to touch either wall. It felt like playing Operation, except instead of buzzing the red nose if I failed, I'd get taken by ghosts into nothingness. I distantly considered throwing up out of sheer terror but remembered that the nearest bathroom was occupied. What would happen if I puked into the abyss? Would it cease to exist? Would it fly back and hit me? Would my DNA float off to another planet?

Banging behind me made my heart fall out of rhythm. Muffled by the library's door, Nathaniel was knocking and calling my name.

"Arden! This isn't funny! Arden!"

"I'm not doing anything," I called back.

"Let me out of here!" Nathaniel shouted.

I stared at the doorknob for a long moment, imagining the horrors behind the door, before I reached for it and turned. It opened easily.

Nathaniel spilled out of the room, his face shiny with sweat. He put his hands on his knees and guzzled down air like he'd been drowning.

"The door was locked," he said.

"No, it wasn't," I told him. "It opened on the first try."

"On *your* first try. But I was pulling on that thing until it was ready to break off."

"Sounds like a normal Friday night for you," I said with a saucy eyebrow raise.

He glared at me, chest heaving. He'd never found me very funny. One of many reasons why we hadn't worked as a couple. Or a situationship, as Remi called us. She and Maddy May insisted that you couldn't be a couple if you didn't publicly acknowledge each other. Which was fair, I guess. I'd never wanted Nate to come with me to Remi's volleyball games or sit with us at lunch or, ugh, ask me to some school dance where we would be expected to take pictures and hold hands and make small talk. Those weren't places where we would thrive together. We worked best either quizzing each other with AP flash cards or making out. Quiet activities where he couldn't infuriate me with his debate team strategies for arguing over every last detail.

Nathaniel tried the doorknob for himself, twisting and releasing it a few times to make sure that I was telling the truth.

"What kind of door only opens from the outside?" he asked.

"I'm pretty sure the answer to most of our questions here is going to be 'because it's haunted,'" I said with a heavy sigh. "Let's go."

The staircase I'd come up was much closer than its twin. We'd have to go all the way around the second floor to make it to the other stairs, but I wanted to check the rest of the rooms for Remi and Maddy May. I would feel better if we were all reunited. Plus, I owed Remi a mea culpa about the whole ghost thing.

Nathaniel followed me down the hall, trailing slightly behind me. There were three more doors lining the walls before the hall turned a blind corner. I opened the first door and checked inside.

Furniture hidden under drop cloths huddled together in the center of the room. The floor was bare wood, dull and dusty. A rat with a tail as thick as my index finger scuttled past.

Nathaniel reached past me and slammed the door shut. "I hate rodents."

It seemed like an arbitrary line to draw in our current situation, but I let him have it. I wouldn't have been happy to see a spider, even if it were in the same room as a ghost.

The next room was the primary bedroom. Clothes spilled out of an armoire, wool and silk scattered across the floor. Satin-lined circular boxes had been wrenched open and dumped onto the bed. At least now I had a pretty good idea as to where the Drama Club had found their store of hats.

I closed the door, thought of something, and opened it again. The walls were bare except for a looming silver mirror. I pulled the door shut.

"I just noticed something weird," I said.

"Ghosts are real and life is a simulation?" Nathaniel asked dryly.

"Ugh, I can't live in a world where incel losers are right. Saying we're in a simulation is so boring. Like, all of reality is in a computer? An invention we made millions of years into life on Earth? Every movie and sci-fi book cracked all the mysteries of existence? And what would it even change? We're already in an unknowable existence controlled by who knows what. If it was controlled by a computer, would that be any different from being controlled by physics? Or God? So wouldn't we just be naming the computer God? And isn't *that* just the plot of *The Matrix*?"

"Tell me how you really feel about it, damn," Nathaniel said, lips twitching into a mocking smile.

"I did," I said simply. "I don't understand why anyone wants to name the container that life fits into when we still don't understand all the pieces. Like, we barely understand dreaming. Or yawning. Or *ghosts*, apparently. But we figured out the exact nature of reality?"

"Counterpoint," Nathaniel said. "The Matrix movies rule and if we could wake up from the simulation, then we could fly. Or do kung fu."

"Counter-counterpoint, kung fu is a skill you could learn without downloading it to your brain. But, yeah, okay, flying would be cool."

Nathaniel grinned at me, flashing both of his stupid cute dimples, and I had to force my brain to get back on track. "*Anyway*, there's no art in this house. No paintings. No pictures."

"So?" Nate asked.

"So, it's an old house," I said. "The Deinharts died decades before TV. What did they look at?"

Nathaniel shrugged and motioned at the walls neither of us wanted to touch. "The endless ugly wallpaper? The literal fucking abyss behind it?"

"Maybe," I said. "But there should be something. A landscape, a photograph. It's creepy."

"This just in," Nathaniel said in a cheesy news anchor voice, "valedictorian realizes that the local haunted house is creepy."

I shoved his shoulder with a laugh. "You're right. It's low

on the creepy scale *now*, but if there weren't any ghosts, you'd be like, 'Whoa, that's so fucked up. The people who lived here were serial killers.'"

He cut his eyes at me. "Weren't they?"

I opened my mouth to protest. We didn't actually know what had happened to the Deinharts. But if the house really was haunted, then maybe all the stories were true. The axe murders, the poison, the domestic violence. It could all be real.

The next series of rooms was all bedrooms, connected by inside doors. The beds were tidy with pillows fluffed and the comforters tucked into the brass frames. None of the windows budged no matter how hard Nathaniel and I pushed on them.

The connected rooms came to a dead end in a nursery. It was cozy here, far removed from the feeling of dread and threat of murder that hung over the rest of the house. The wallpaper was covered in painted pink bows. A tall wooden crib had a single moth-eaten stuffed rabbit inside. A dollhouse with a collapsed roof sat in a pile in the corner. A rocking chair sat in front of the fireplace, its seat unraveled.

It reminded me of the rocking chair that had been in my room at our old house. My parents had bought it to rock me to sleep when I was a baby. It was gray wicker with an upholstered white seat and looked more like a patio chair than bedroom furniture. It had never matched anything else in my room, but I'd loved it. There were pictures of me napping on Dad's shoulder there when I was really small and reading aloud to Mom when I was in kindergarten. I'd plastered stickers to the arms and had to spend a Saturday scraping them off, which pulled up patches of paint. I would sit there to read or study or even just scroll through my phone, rocking until the creak of the legs became background noise, a self-propelled ambient noise app.

There wasn't room for the chair in the new house. At least, that's what Mom said when all my other furniture got moved in except the chair. Dad didn't want it, either. He said that having a rocking chair in his living room would make him look like an old man. They'd donated it somewhere. Or thrown it out and said that they donated it. Because, to them, it was only a chair. They had lived without it before and could do without it now. But to me, it had been a fixture my entire life, the first chair I had ever learned to identify with the word. And now it was gone, discarded the second it caused even a moment of inconvenience to my parents. Like our house. Like their marriage. Like my future.

"Hey," I said, nudging the rocking chair into motion. "Did your family take you to Olive Garden?"

Nathaniel was bending down to look inside the crushed windows of the dollhouse. It seemed to be the most likely place to find mice, but I didn't tell him so. He glanced back at me. "Olive Garden?"

"After graduation," I clarified. "Did you go out for a meal?"

He bobbed his head. "Oh. We went to Red Lobster."

"That must have been nice," I said.

My mouth watered at the thought of steaming hot Cheddar

Bay Biscuits. My dad used to love going to Red Lobster so he could call me and Mom "shellfish" for not sharing our crab claws. Classic Dad humor. I used to think it was so annoying. But now I wondered if he'd ever say it again. Would he still make those corny jokes when it was just me and him? Was there even a Red Lobster in his new town?

Nathaniel stood up, brushing the knees of his jeans. "It was pretty good. My mom insisted on using a coupon, so we could only get shrimp."

"And you wanted lobster?" I asked.

"I wanted the option."

I sighed and held the rocking chair still. "I know the feeling."

We gave a perfunctory try of the windows, but neither of us were surprised when they didn't budge. We left the room, closing the door behind us. The hallway curved around ahead of us, leading, undoubtedly, to more rooms full of stuck windows and the sad remains of a disappeared family.

"How many rooms does this place have?" Nathaniel asked.

"Fifteen rooms, nine bathrooms, an attic, and a basement," I said, listing the numbers from my memory of the auction listing.

His lip curled. "This is too much house for one family. It should be a hotel or a bunch of apartments."

"Ugh, you sound like my mom."

"Well, Ms. Lozano Flack must be brilliant and forward-thinking," he said haughtily. "Has she considered becoming a rocket scientist instead of selling haunted houses?"

With a fake gasp, I clutched my chest. "Oh my God, are you going to be a *rocket scientist*? You literally haven't brought it up in twenty minutes, and I was worried that you'd changed your mind."

"Okay, pre-premed, you don't have room to talk shit."

We came around the corner. On the ground, there was a white boy with waxy skin. His pale eyes were unfixed and sunken, staring without seeing. Blood spilled out of jagged wounds all over his body, soaking into the carpet beneath him. He looked like a marionette with the strings cut, left to fall into a heap that wouldn't have been possible with tendons and joints and kneecaps working to keep him together.

"Tanner!" Nathaniel cried.

"Tanner?" I echoed. "Claire's boyfriend Tanner?"

"Who's Claire?"

"Tanner's girlfriend!"

As we argued, ghost hands surged out of the carpet. Each digit was an extension of the textured red pile. In a soundless swoop, they descended, engulfing the body in hands and carpet. Dragging it down into nothingness.

Tanner Grant (popular, with no known extracurricular activities) was dead.

And gone.

11

Nathaniel and I ran. In opposite directions.

I went toward where the body had been, looking for any clues as to where it went. Nathaniel was halfway around the corner by the time he realized that I wasn't with him.

"Doc, come on!" he yelled.

"Where did he go?" I asked, frantic. I dropped to the ground, searching the carpet with my hands. For what? I wasn't sure. It wasn't like he was coming back. His face had been so inhuman in death. Color wrong. Eyes wrong. Lips drawn back. I hadn't even recognized him as the same guy who had flirted with Maddy May at the start of the night.

"We need to go," Nathaniel said. He jogged back, keeping his knees high as he tried not to leave his feet on the floor for too long. "We need to go now!"

"There are ghosts *in* the floor!" I shouted, pounding my fists into the carpet. There wasn't a drop of blood left. "And the walls! It doesn't matter where we go. Nowhere is safe! They can get us anywhere. Anytime they want. They can hurt us. They can kill us, Nate!"

"Come on," he said, gentler this time as he reached for me. His eyes darted around the hallway to the closed doors. He lowered his voice. "We don't know that the ghosts are the ones who stabbed him."

He was right. We didn't know. There were definitely ghosts in the house, sure. But we didn't know that they wielded axes or knives or whatever had chopped Tanner to bits. Someone at the party could have decided that sneaking inside the murder house would be a great time to start killing people. There were even ghosts to take care of the cleanup.

I let Nathaniel help pull me to my feet. My head was swimming even more than it had been from the vodka shot or the hard seltzer. Ghosts were one thing to comprehend. The supernatural, while scary, was also sort of fascinating. The world was bigger and stranger than I had known before the start of the party.

But murder? That was regular, down-in-the-dirt bad. The worst of humanity. Worse than parents who stopped loving each other and betrayed you to prove it. It was sickening. Horrifying. Too plausibly real. The thing we'd all been taught to fear whenever the school called a lockdown drill. It was here in this house with us, trapped between Bucktown High's seniors and the abyss in the walls.

And it was my fault. I had orchestrated this. I had put everyone in the house in this danger. To save my own skin and hold on to my stupid dreams. Unknowingly setting up the perfect confluence of events to make sure that none of us got out alive.

"Tanner Grant," Nathaniel said, swallowing hard. "We went to elementary school together. He sat next to me at graduation today."

"Did you know Claire?"

"No, I don't know anyone named Claire," he said.

"Me either," I said.

Nathaniel looked confused. "Then why are you asking about her?"

"Because." My voice broke. "It's my fault that her boyfriend's dead."

I put my face in my hands. My eyes burned. Someone had died, and it was my fault. All I had ever wanted was to save lives. To go to medical school and make people better.

"Doc—"

"I'm not a doctor, Nathaniel!" I spat. Hot tears streamed down my face and collected under my chin. "And I'm never going to be one."

"Hey," he said softly. He reached for my arm, guiding me forward with a nudge. "We'll make it out of here. We have more processing power in our phones than Apollo 11 had to navigate the moon. We can find our way out of a haunted house."

"It's not the house," I said. A sob burst out of me as the irony slammed into me. "Well, yeah, it is the house. But it's not the ghosts. My parents spent my college money to buy this place."

His mouth formed a little O as understanding dawned on him. "Is that why Maddy May was fleecing everyone for their grad money?"

"It's not fleecing," I protested. Tears leaked into the corners of my mouth, making everything taste like salt and regret. "They would have spent the same amount at Sober Grad Night. It was supposed to be fun. Everyone always makes parties sound fun."

"People make lots of things sound fun that aren't," he said. He rubbed my back as he coaxed me down the hall, one staggered step at a time. "Football games, school dances, Comic-Con. Parties are like that. A huge crowd of people trying to have fun but probably not actually having fun."

"Then why did you come?" I asked.

His eyes, warm brown and penetrating, met mine before bashfully glancing away.

"Maddy May said you'd be here," he mumbled.

I stumbled over my feet. "You wanted to see me? You see me every day."

But, I realized with a drop in my stomach, that wouldn't be true anymore. There was no more school. No more chance meetings in the hallway or getting paired together on assignments. If he had wanted to see me, this would have been his last chance.

I plodded forward with a sigh. "At least if we all die tonight, I won't be the only person whose dreams won't come true."

"That's dark," he said.

"Gallows humor. It's the only way I've survived this far."

Nathaniel opened his mouth and then closed it again. Slowly, he looked over his shoulder. A muscle in his jaw twitched. When he turned back, his eyebrows were drawn together the same way they did when he was rewriting definite integrals to limits of Riemann sum in AP Calc.

"Shouldn't we have made it around the corner by now?" he asked.

"What are you talking about?" I asked. The corner was ten or twelve feet away, past the last room on the left.

"Look," Nathaniel stressed, pointing back at where we'd come from.

The corner we'd come around seemed far away, almost impossibly so. But the next corner wasn't any closer. We were still in the middle of the hallway, even though the spot where Tanner's dead body had disappeared was well behind us.

"Is the hallway getting . . . longer?" I asked.

"No, that's—" His voice faltered. "Impossible."

His shoulders slumped as he recognized that impossible was the name of the game now. For everything we'd seen so far, a stretching hallway was practically charming. An optical illusion in a house of horrors.

"We have to get around to the other side to get down the stairs," I told him. "We'll make a run for it."

He considered this, rubbing his lips together so hard that they looked bloodless. When he seemed convinced that there was no better plan, he held his hand out to me. I took it.

We had held hands before, sitting in his car together, arguing over homework. Then, it was kind of nice. Romantic, even. Our fingers folded together, pulses synchronizing in our palms.

This was definitely not romantic. This was a lifeline, a basic connection to another living thing and a promise not to let go.

"Ready?" he asked.

"Ready or not," I said.

We ran. Until the walls started to blur and the doors whooshed past. Until my lungs burned and my legs cramped and I worried that my bra might not be up to the task.

Something brushed my outside arm. Nathaniel flinched as if he had also been touched. Something banged into my shoulder. A doorframe. Then a doorknob. A small table.

The walls were pushing in on us. The faster we ran, the more the hallway compressed, squeezing until it was barely the size of Nathaniel and me, side by side. Then smaller still, pressing us painfully shoulder to shoulder.

It got harder to run. Harder to breathe. The hallway was getting darker and smaller. The ceiling started to slope, slowly descending toward us. I was terrified it wouldn't let us out. That we'd be crushed in this hallway like a mouse in a snake's throat, swallowed whole and digested slowly.

"Come on," Nathaniel said, tugging me along. "Don't stop now. We're almost there."

We weren't almost there. The narrow point that was the end of the hallway seemed miles away. But believing we were close felt better than not. So I tried to believe it, even as my lungs caught fire and my legs started to feel too heavy to lift.

We came around the corner with a burst of speed, free of the crush. We exploded into a hallway the size of a hallway.

And crashed into Remi, whose nose was deep in her phone, undoubtedly examining her ghost-hunting app.

She squawked as we collided. "Arden! And Nathaniel. Hello, you two."

She blinked in surprise, looking down at our clasped hands and raising a knowing eyebrow. Nathaniel and I immediately let go of each other.

I threw my arms around Remi's neck, so relieved to see her and to see her *alive*.

"Whoa, someone's a happy drunk," she said. She gave me a facetious pat on the back as she tried to extricate herself from the hug.

"Remi, I'm so sorry," I said, reluctantly releasing her. "I shouldn't have doubted you—"

"You definitely shouldn't have," Remi said. "Because I found something totally wild. Bigger than anything on *Specter Sightings*."

Nathaniel blew out an uneasy breath and raked a hand over his tight curls. "Yeah, we've seen some shit, too."

"Not like this," Remi said.

She held up a soda can that I had assumed was her drink. Seeing it closer, I realized that it was filthy and partially crushed.

"Look at this!" she said. She shoved the can so close to my nose it made my eyes cross. "Look at the logo."

"It's old?" I said, unsure as to why she was so excited about garbage.

"Exactly! But it's retro old and not ye olde-timey old," Remi said.

"I don't think a hundred years ago counts as ye olde-timey, either," I said. "I think ye olde predates anything in America."

"Well, actually, there isn't such a thing as 'ye olde,'" Nathaniel said. "When people think of the sign that says 'ye olde' the 'y' is an Old English letter 'thorn,' which is just an antiquated way to make the *t-h* sound. So it's really '*the*' olde."

I rolled my eyes. "Ignore him. He's incapable of ignoring a chance to 'well, actually.' It's a rare case of Black nerd disease."

"Excuse you, little miss half-Black valedictorian," Nathaniel said. "If I'm a nerd, you're a nerd."

"I am not half Black, Nathaniel Graham," I said. "I'm a whole entire Afro-Latina, not a pie chart. Don't count my ass in fractions."

Remi shook the can in the air. "You're both missing the point! This can mean something! The manor has been boarded up for a hundred years, right? So why is there a thirty-year-old soda can in here? The expiration date is from the *nineties*."

I shrugged, unable to make myself care. "I don't know, Rem. We kind of have a bigger problem."

"Bigger than maybe we're not the first people to be in this house?" she asked, staring in disbelief like Nathaniel and I were both sleeping on the discovery of the century. "What if someone moved the bodies? What if someone was living here after the Deinharts died?"

"What if there are people getting murdered here right

now, tonight?" Nathaniel asked. "And all the exits are sealed shut and we're trapped in here? Oh, wait. That's exactly what's going on."

"What? Are you serious?" Remi asked. She looked at me for clarification.

I nodded.

"All of that," I said. "Plus, the house is sort of, um, fluctuating around us. Walls moving, ceilings lowering."

"Ghost hands dragging people to hell," Nathaniel added.

"We haven't seen anything that confirms or denies the existence of hell," I assured Remi.

"Who's trying to 'well, actually' now?" Nathaniel asked with a scoff. "The endless abyss in the walls is straight-up hell."

"But it's not like fire-and-brimstone hell. It's existential-dread hell," I said.

"Wait," Remi said, looking dazed. "You guys have actually seen ghosts? Did they talk to you? Rearrange the furniture? Did they stink?"

"None of the above," Nathaniel said. "They tried to pull me into a wall."

"There was a dead body on the floor. Tanner Grant," I said. "But the ghosts sort of poofed him away."

"They dragged him. To hell," Nathaniel said.

"Holy shit!" Remi exclaimed. "I'm so jealous! I've been up here for like an hour, and all I've found is trash in a fireplace!"

"Not the fireplace in the library, I hope," I said. "That's full of Nate piss."

Nathaniel glared at me.

Remi tossed her soda can aside and started to march past us, toward the never-ending hallway. "Okay, well, show me a ghost!"

Nathaniel put out an arm to stop her. "No way," he said.

"We need to get back downstairs," I told Remi. "We need to make sure that no one else is hurt or captured or killed. And we have to find a way out. One person has already died here. We can't let that happen to anyone else."

But we were already too late.

Downstairs, people had started screaming. Like they were being murdered.

WHAT HAPPENED TO THE DEINHART FAMILY

AS TOLD BY NATHANIEL GRAHAM
(IN ACCORDANCE WITH NATIONAL
SPEECH & DEBATE ASSOCIATION
EXTEMPORANEOUS SPEECH RULES)

In the 1920s, more than one hundred Bucktown residents died in a freak blizzard. That was 10 percent of the population dead in the span of seventy-two hours. Men, women, and children all over town died from hypothermia, building collapse, and exposure.

The blizzard came out of nowhere. The sun just never rose. Instead, the sky erupted, dumping snow on Bucktown. A record thirty inches blocked every roadway, doorway, and window in town. It was the Storm of the Century and the planet had barely begun to warm up yet. But there were no headlines about it in the *Bucktown Gazette* because the entire staff of the newspaper died when the roof of their building caved in under the weight of the snow.

These blizzard-related deaths were senseless, tragic, and preventable. Who had the means to save these people? The Deinhart family.

The Deinharts had money when no one else did. They

had generational wealth, meaning they had more money than they needed to survive. They were the top employer in town, which means that their own workers were dying in the blizzard. And they had a mansion with ample heat and space, not to mention radios, phonographs, and a full library to provide entertainment. But the Deinharts didn't associate with the people of town on the sunniest day, much less in the middle of a blizzard.

So, what happened to the Deinhart family? They barricaded themselves inside their home and left people to die.

At the time of their disappearance, the Deinhart family was worth $300,000, roughly $4.5 million in today's dollars. They could have easily purchased a snow plow for the community. They could have provided what other people lacked. But they didn't.

Mr. Deinhart was the owner of the Zweibel plant, which sold dehydrated onions to the military to use in army rations. (Had he survived to see the second World War, Mr. Deinhart may not have been as successful with his German-branded company and their onion-headed, lederhosen-wearing mascot.) The plant did not stop production during the blizzard. Mr. Deinhart insisted that the heated air of the dehydrator would be enough to keep the employees warm.

It wasn't.

The high water content of the onions made them prone to freezing, and multiple employees reported frostbitten fingers from having to sort through the icy alliums. Eventually, it became so cold inside the plant that the machinery stopped working, presumably frozen in place. Unfortunately, by then the roads were impassable and the workers could not easily leave. They could either remain on-site and live on raw onions or they could brave the storm in an attempt to find warmth and shelter. Many died regardless of their decision.

Due to the prominence of the Deinhart Manor and its position on Founders Hill, many townspeople viewed it as a beacon of hope in the storm. A sanctuary held high above the rising snowdrifts. Inside, there would be heat. Inside, there would be food. Inside, they would be saved. They knocked at the front door, begging for asylum. If not for themselves, then for their children. If not for all their children, then for the babies. But no answer came. People froze to death on the porch, hands still reaching out. Desperate for salvation that never came.

Rather than look at the townspeople asking for shelter, the Deinhart family boarded up the doors and windows. They put cotton in their ears to drown out the screams. They turned their backs on the town, even as Founders Hill filled with corpses. They let their extra food rot and their spare fireplaces stay cold.

But they could never come out again. How could they face the survivors? With every passing day, they became more afraid that the townspeople would kill them. For their complacency. For their greed. For their cowardice.

What happened to the Deinhart family?

They got what they deserved.

12

The screaming stopped as quickly as it started.

Everything was normal. Eerily normal. It was like I'd walked through a portal with a haunted house on one side and real life on the other. Remi and Nathaniel felt it, too.

There was no sign of anyone in distress downstairs. The game of beer pong in the billiards room had expanded to people making bets as to who would win (Nash, the MVP of the football team versus Octavio, an extremely shy kid who placed second in the state science fair). The dining room had a circle of people listening to Kenzie Sullivan (student council vice president, marching band flutist), who was standing on a chair and double-fisting hard seltzers as she recounted the story of the homecoming parade when a bird flew into a tuba.

"And we were all like, 'Oh my God, Eben, did you forget how to play?' It was like he was trying to play a turkey as a bagpipe. The worst sound you've ever heard! It was so bad. And then: *fplfplfplf*—" She slurred a sort of flapping sound and waved her arms as best as she could without spilling her drinks. "This bird shoots out of the bell, and Eben totally nails the rest of the song!"

The three of us flinched as Kenzie's story ended in cheers while she tried to chug out of both of her drinks at the same time. We continued through the house, peering into rooms, looking for any signs of the horrors that had been upstairs.

"Maybe we just need to keep people from going upstairs," Nathaniel said as we passed by a roomful of people playing flip cup on top of an enormous wood desk. "It seems pretty safe down here."

"Or that's what the ghosts want you to think," Remi said in a loud whisper. "They're lulling us into a false sense of security so they can scare the shit out of all of us at the same time."

I was more inclined to believe Nathaniel. Maybe the house just didn't like us traipsing around in the bedrooms. What I didn't understand was *why*. Was it because of how easy it was to peel back the wallpaper and see the abyss? Was it something about keeping us drunk and pacified? Did they want to kill us all at once? Or pick off the strays like they had with Tanner?

The music coming out of the ballroom pulled my attention. Bouncy and bass-less, it sounded like the soundtrack to some ancient cartoon, like the score to Mickey Mouse walking and whistling. The only word to describe it was "jaunty."

"Do you guys hear that?" I asked Nathaniel and Remi.

"The music?" Nate asked. "Of course. You think you're hallucinating jazz?"

"You think that's less weird than someone deciding to put on *jazz* at a house party?" Remi asked with a scoff.

I followed the sound. It was hypnotically out of place at the party and yet perfect for the house. It was music that matched the wallpaper and the china pattern. Music the Deinhart family would have listened to.

I stopped in the doorway of the ballroom. Looking in from the outside was like looking into the past and the parties the manor would have hosted in its heyday, full of rich people in tuxedos and flapper dresses and fur coats. But now it was packed with my classmates, even more of them than the last time I'd come through here. Every single person was dancing to the music, which wasn't coming out of the Bluetooth speaker anymore. The old gramophone was spinning, spewing out squeaky horn and piano jazz. The music was absolutely blaring, so loud that it was a palpable force. A tsunamic sound wave.

Even weirder, everyone was dancing to it like it was the greatest thing they'd ever heard. They all knew the choreography. Kicking feet and waving arms and shimmying hips. Some people were dancing in pairs, rocking forward and back with perfectly synchronized kicks and toe taps. It was like I'd stepped directly into a *Great Gatsby* party. For a moment, it was magical.

Until I saw their faces. While everyone was dancing energetically in time with the music, their faces were contorted into panic, terror, pain. One girl, whose kicks were particularly high, was racked with silent sobs.

Something was making them dance against their will. All of them.

When the song ended, everyone collapsed on the dance floor. Some people held each other. Others wailed in wordless agony. The same screams that we'd heard from upstairs.

The gramophone needle lifted, moved to the edge of the record, and touched down. In a second, the music restarted (a tootling trumpet and plinky piano) and everyone on the dance floor was back on their feet, swinging their limbs in time to the beat.

"What the hell is happening to them?" Nathaniel asked, appearing behind me with Remi.

I couldn't look away from the way everyone's faces clashed with their enthusiastic dancing. "They're possessed."

There was no other explanation. They were being puppeted. What else could have made them all dance with so much force? There hadn't been this many people dancing at junior prom (which I had attended as a volunteer for community service hours to put on my college applications).

Hannah Treu's distinctive lavender hair was in the middle of the dance floor. One minute she was up and dancing as lively as anyone else, the next she was on the ground, holding on to her ankle and crying out. Nobody around her stopped dancing. Feet stamped down on her legs, her toes, her hand. She was moments away from being trampled to death by the Charleston.

"Hannah!" Remi burst into the room. The moment she crossed the threshold, the music took hold of her. Even as she continued to call Hannah's name, her knees bowed like a scarecrow's and her hands traveled fluidly from leg to leg.

She looked back at me and Nathaniel, her face burning red as she started to slap her heels with the tips of her fingers. "Help me! Do something!"

I scanned the room without stepping inside, looking for anything that could stop everyone from dancing. But it wasn't like there was a bag of marbles to throw on the dance floor to trip everyone up. The gramophone was spinning of its own volition, not plugged into an electrical outlet. The crank in the side of it wasn't even moving. How do you stop a haunted stereo?

I had to try something. People were in pain. In danger. Without control of themselves, they could end up dancing themselves to death. Maybe that was the ghosts' plan.

"If I start dancing, tackle me," I told Nathaniel.

"I'm not going in there," Nathaniel said, taking a step back, deeper into the hall. "I refuse to die to music this goofy. I don't care if Black men created jazz. Without drugs, it sucks."

"You are so not helpful," I growled.

I put my fingers in my ears and darted into the room. I could feel the chugging horn of the music in my chest. It made me want to shuffle my feet and flap my hands in the air, but I dug my fingernails deeper into my ears and hummed atonally to drown out the sound. (It wasn't hard. Maddy May had very gently brought to my attention that I'm tone-deaf.)

The music in the air was oppressive. The gramophone speaker was the same shape as a trumpet flower, emitting blasts of music equal to a thousand air horns. It felt like swimming upstream to get closer to it. The sound waves vibrated the bones in my skull, making my teeth buzz and my eyes bounce. The gramophone itself was about the size of the desktop computer in my mom's office.

Steeling myself, I picked it up and lifted it over my head. It was surprisingly heavy and hard to keep hold of as the record kept spinning. With the music pouring freely into my ears, I felt my feet starting to lift from the floor. My knees bounced. My hips twitched.

I threw the gramophone down as hard as I could. Splinters shot off in every direction as the box burst. A crack split the record down the middle. The speaker rolled onto the dance floor, silenced.

A cold wind sliced through the room as everyone fell to the dance floor. A shiver ran down my spine. But my urge to dance was dead. Possibly permanently.

Everyone on the dance floor looked dazed and unsure, waiting for a new song to start to rip them back to their feet again. Questioning mutters passed through the room. No one seemed quite brave enough to name what had happened. I could see people removing their shoes with groans of relief and massaging charley horses out of their calves. More than one person was bleeding from burst blisters and broken toenails.

With the room suddenly still, I looked out into the crowd, hoping to find Maddy May. This would be the perfect time for her to show up, ready to reroute everyone's attention with her infectious smile and an offhand joke (and the vase full of my tuition would be nice, too). I didn't feel like I could comfort or distract anyone. Unless they wanted to forget about how weird being compelled to dance was in exchange for being terrified at the news that someone had already been murdered, we were all trapped, and there was absolutely no plan for how to get anybody out.

I made my way over to Remi and Hannah, whose leg was stretched out in front of her, stiff as a board. A leather sandal dangled from the toe of her thick blue socks.

"My ankle!" Hannah gasped, rocking back and forth. Sweat beaded across her forehead, and her cheeks were the same livid pink as her overalls. "I heard it pop! It might be broken."

Remi set her hands on Hannah's shoulders encouragingly. "You'll be okay. It's probably nothing."

"You were dancing hard in Birkenstocks," Nathaniel said, appearing at my side only after it was clear that the danger had passed. "You're lucky you didn't die."

"Shut up, Nate," I said with a sigh. I knelt beside Hannah's outstretched leg. "Can I take a look?"

"Go ahead," Hannah said, staring up at the ceiling. "I don't think I can stomach it. It feels like being stabbed with a hundred hot and cold knives."

Gingerly, I rolled the pink pant leg up Hannah's shin. Her socks were a chunky knit, obviously handmade. As I rolled one down, I held back a grimace. Her ankle was already swollen to the size of a fist and fiery hot to the touch.

Remi looked from the ankle to me, eyes wild with panic. It didn't take six first aid classes to know that ankles aren't supposed to look like that. The bone was intact, but at least one of the ligaments was torn. A grade 3 sprain, if I had to guess.

"You didn't get into college on an athletic scholarship, did you?" I asked Hannah.

Her eyes bulged. "Yeah, why?"

I pulled the sock back up, took a breath, and turned to Nathaniel. "We're going to need bandages and disinfectant. Not just for Hannah. There's lots of injured people here."

Nathaniel's lips flattened into a sardonic line. "Do you think the haunted house has a first aid kit?"

"We'll make do," I said between gritted teeth. I wished he'd help for the sake of helping. Altruism wasn't in his vocabulary. "You can help me tear up the curtains or you can go get a bottle of liquor to help clean up anyone who's bleeding."

"You forgot to say 'stat,'" he said, chuckling at his own joke. When nobody joined in, he turned on his heel. "I'll go get the disinfectant."

"He's scared that the ghosts are going to come back," Remi muttered.

"Ghosts?" Hannah asked, perking up as much as she could while in excruciating pain.

"Without a doubt," Remi said. "We were all totally possessed. Making people dance is a classic ghost practical joke. Haven't you ever seen *Beetlejuice?*"

"Oh my fuck, of course!" Hannah said. She reached out and grabbed Remi's hands in genuine excitement. "It felt so natural. I always imagined a possession being more like *The Exorcist*, you know? The full Pazuzu: a demon voice and projectile vomiting. But I really had no control over whether I wanted to dance. I just *had to*."

Leaving Remi and Hannah to bond over the supernatural, I got up and made my way to one of the ballroom's massive floor-to-ceiling windows. It seemed impossible that the Deinharts could have found enough wood to cover them up, but they must have. The walls were pockmarked where the nails had been removed. Mom's contractor took down all the window coverings during the walk-through. I wish I'd thought to ask what they were made of. Store-bought planks would mean sealing themselves inside was premeditated. Broken bits of furniture would have been done in a rush. The more I saw of the manor, the less the stories made sense.

Bracing one foot on an immovable pane of glass, I pulled until the curtain rod cracked and released the velvet drape into my arms. A cloud of dust blew into my face, filling my nose and eyelashes. I tried not to think about how much dead skin and dirt I was breathing in. Thankfully, the extremely old fabric put up no fight as I tore it into long strips.

I brought the pile of makeshift bandages back to Remi and Hannah. Remi was nervously smoothing her own skirt in long strokes. This seemed to me like it would have been a pretty good time to profess her undying love. Or maybe not. What did I know? I'd never professed anything before. The first time I made out with Nathaniel was because we got 104 percent on a history presentation and we'd just sort of . . . overcongratulated each other about it. It had never been grand gestures or mushy words with us. I didn't really think about him when we weren't together. Or if I did it was a better version of him, one who didn't annoy me so much.

I wrapped Hannah's ankle as best as I could. I knew that what she really needed was a cast and a prescription for some heavily addictive opioids. But since that would have required being able to actually *leave*, I didn't tell her so.

Nathaniel came back with some of Hannah's flat of water bottles and a bottle of Everclear, which stung my eyes when I opened it.

"Are you sure this isn't rubbing alcohol?" I asked, pulling away from the smell.

"It might as well be," Remi said, taking the bottle from Nathaniel. "That's overproof grain alcohol. One shot could disinfect a port-a-potty."

"Then I'm glad we're not drinking it," I said.

I'd spoken too soon. Remi took a swig directly from the bottle and let out a hoot of distaste.

"Do you think that's a good idea?" I asked her. Personally, I wanted all of my wits about me while I faced down a paranormal threat. Taking shots and getting drunk was for people who didn't know about ghosts.

"It's a great idea. It really takes the edge off being possessed," she said, offering the bottle to Hannah. Hannah took a much smaller sip and shuddered at the taste.

"I think I'd take being possessed again over more of that," Hannah said, gasping. She passed the bottle back to me. "It'll work better as a disinfectant than a beverage."

"Good to know," I said, getting to my feet. "Come on, Nate. You can carry the water bottles."

Ministering to the wounded turned out to be pretty easy with a dare of a drink on hand. The injured could either choose to take a shot of Everclear while I bandaged their trodden toes and sprained ankles or they could rehydrate in peace with a bottle of water. Having the choice meant that everyone was momentarily distracted from the fact that they had all been compelled to dance by a haunted record player. In fact, no one was talking about hauntings or ghosts or possession other than Remi and Hannah. It was almost like nobody wanted to be the one to point out the obvious.

It reminded me of what my dad always said about the difference between not believing and not *wanting* to believe. Probably everyone in the ballroom knew that what had happened to them had been supernatural. But if they refused to believe it, then the night could keep going. Life could keep going. Everything they thought they'd known up until now wouldn't have to be rewritten to include something that could make you do things you didn't want to do, even past the point of injury. Who was I to dissuade them of that? I would have loved to have the choice not to believe in what was happening.

It wasn't long before everyone in the ballroom had been treated (or at least hydrated). With almost half the room full of Everclear and everyone drunk on denial, the party vibe crept back in. No one was rushing to put the music back on (just in case), but Hadley Shao (a girl I knew solely because she had cried in PE every single time she was on a losing team) spun the Everclear bottle on the ground and announced, "Kiss or shots!" A game born in that moment as a way to dive deeper into forgetting what had happened before.

And it worked. Everyone in the room limped or crawled to sit in a huge circle as though they were back in kindergarten and the "make a circle, make it round" song was playing.

I was bummed not to get to participate. I considered staying behind and forgetting about my responsibilities for a little while. At least until I got a chance to kiss someone other than Nathaniel before the manor's ghosts found a way to kill us all. But there was no way I'd be able to take a shot of Everclear without absolutely throwing up my organs. And literally damning everyone to die so I could maybe get one kiss seemed, you know, a tiny bit selfish.

Remi and Hannah recused themselves from the game and stood near the door. Crouched over to be the right height, Remi was helping to hold Hannah upright, acting as a human crutch. With her free hand, she was hugging Hannah's Birkenstocks to her side as though they were the most precious cargo.

"We talked about it," Remi said, lowering her voice so that she wouldn't be heard over the sounds of people cheering on the spinning of the Everclear bottle. "And Hannah and I think that we should try to talk to the ghosts. They're obviously mad at us for trespassing. We need to follow the rules and make peace with them. And make sure they don't hurt anyone else."

Nathaniel folded his arms imperiously. "You want to go shout into the abyss and see if they'll take a meeting with you?" he asked.

"Do you have a better idea?" Hannah asked. It was as much a challenge as it was a question. If there was one thing I knew about Hannah Treu, it was that she was used to being in charge. She led protests and the volleyball team without help. But she had less firsthand experience with ghosts than Nathaniel and me. Lucky girl.

"I have an idea," I said. "We need to crash a séance."

13

I knocked on the door of the grand salon. Not out of courtesy, but because the door had been barricaded since the last time I'd barged in.

"Who goes there?" asked a voice on the other side of the door.

"It's Arden," I said.

"Who?" asked the voice.

Nathaniel snorted a laugh into his fist, then tried to cover it with a weak cough.

"It's my party," I said. "And my house. Kind of."

Furniture scraped against the floor. A lot of furniture, from the sounds of it. The door opened, revealing a group of people. Everyone was sitting on the ground on top of a series of blankets. A Ouija board was set out, as was a small mirror, a bowl of salt, and a stack of tarot cards. Various crystals and what looked like Scrabble tiles carved with runes were scattered around.

The room had a piano and couches shoved into the corners.

Every available surface was covered in candles. Dripping tapers, glass jars full of clashing Bath & Body Works scents, citronella tins, even incredibly melted birthday candles stuck into an otherwise untouched slice of the *Happy Graduation, Shaun* cake. The flickering yellow candlelight was caught in a low-flying fog of weed smoke, giving the room the appearance of the world's most romantic stoner picnic.

In the middle of it all were Yara Molina (small-scale cult leader, self-described witch) and her loyal followers who believed she was capable of real magic (she sold good-luck charms and love spells to gullible freshmen). Yara ran a pretty well-known (even outside of Bucktown) social media account where she wrote horoscopes that were not-so-secretly just her saying mean shit to people under the guise of astrological readings. Like when she wrote that Pisces were "unreliable leaders" after she lost the student council vote to Kenzie Sullivan. I respected the dedication to getting what she wanted, but astrology wasn't for me. As a Virgo, there are only so many ways to be told you're a control freak obsessed with being clean and successful before it gets to be old news. Like, the worst thing about me is that I like to stick to a plan? Oh no, my September birthday is *such* a curse.

Yara's hands didn't budge from the Ouija planchette. Her black painted lips drew down into a scowl. "Oh, it's you again. Our valedictorian. Blessed be. Are you here to bore us with more clichés about how the future belongs to us?"

Embarrassment made me fidget. I knew that my speech hadn't been the best thing I'd ever done, but I still didn't think I deserved to get roasted by a girl unironically wearing a witch's hat on a day that was not Halloween.

To distract myself, I squinted into the smog. "Is Maddy May in here?"

"Does this look like a Sephora with glitter eyeshadow on sale?" Yara asked drolly. "Maddy May doesn't have a bruja bone in her body. She's a perfect little Mexican American princess who wouldn't be caught dead in the same room as a tarot deck. Is that all?"

"No," I said flatly. "I'm here—"

Behind me, Remi cleared her throat, and I corrected myself.

"Sorry. *We're* here to hijack your séance. Have you managed to talk to the house ghosts at all?"

Yara drew her shoulders back and lifted her chin, doing her best to look down at me even though she was sitting on the floor. "We've found some success with using the dowsing pendant and asking yes or no questions."

Remi barked a laugh that smelled like Everclear. "A whole room just got possessed, so you must really suck at this. Move over. We have shit to do."

I sat directly across from Yara. Nathaniel plopped down next to me, looking like he'd rather be anywhere else but in a roomful of femmes and a Ouija board. Remi helped Hannah sit on one of the couches on the far wall.

"Is the bong for anyone?" Remi asked.

"Actually," Yara said in a supercilious tone that clipped each syllable down to the quick, "that's a very special strain intended to open your third eye—"

"Is it laced with anything or not?" Hannah interrupted, waving away Yara's spiel. "I sprained my ankle while I was possessed but that doesn't mean I want to smoke ayahuasca at a house party. Mixing psychedelics and ghosts seems like too much of a good thing."

"It's an indica-dominant hybrid with some hash oil. It should be a pretty potent pain reliever," said one of the other witches, a nonbinary kid named Maze who had successfully gotten one of the bathrooms at Bucktown High to be officially degenderized. Their arms were decorated with impressively detailed Sharpie drawings of their bones from the phalanges down to the radius. They passed the bong to Hannah, who accepted it gratefully.

"Good," Hannah said, speaking inwardly between hits. "Because I am in pretty potent pain, and I'd love to be able to focus on the whole 'ghosts are real' thing."

Nathaniel rubbed his nose with the back of his hand. "How are the candles still lit? There's no air in this room."

"Please be less of a narc for two seconds," Remi said, accepting the bong from Hannah. She inhaled so long, I was shocked that smoke didn't start leaking out of her ears.

"I'm not a narc!" Nathaniel protested. "Arden is way more narc-ish than I am. She's never even been to a party before. She's not going to smoke hash oil." He glanced at me, eyebrows drawn together. "Are you?"

I wasn't, but mostly because I needed to keep my head on straight to find a way to get everyone safely out of the house. When I'd imagined this party for the last few days, smoking weed out of a huge bong would have been exactly the kind of experience I would have been seeking out. The sort of thing that most people had already done while I was busy studying and writing extra-credit papers. Unfortunately, the time for new (non-ghost) experiences had passed.

"Everyone please shut up," Yara said, irritation making her voice squeak, ruining whatever gravitas she might have had underneath her Spirit Halloween hat. "What do you mean an entire room was possessed?"

"The house is haunted. There have been happenings all night, but the entire ballroom was forced to dance to the point of injury," I said in a rush. "So things seem to be getting worse. Can we hurry up and contact the spirits or whatever?"

"No," Yara said, huffing disdainfully. "You can't barge in here and snap your fingers and demand magic."

"Someone fucking died upstairs," I said. The vision of Tanner's body, hacked apart and sucked into the floor, burst into my mind, a still image of grotesque horror. I closed my eyes against it. "One of our classmates was murdered tonight. And we don't know if it was done by a ghost or not. But none of the doors or windows will open, which means that we're all trapped in here with some*one* or some*thing* that has killed and could kill again. So just ask the damn ghosts if it was them or if we need to be on the lookout for a fucking psycho with a knife."

Yara's jaw snapped shut.

"Of course we'll help," Maze said, scooting forward to put their fingers on the planchette. "But we've barely gotten a yes or no from the ghosts so far. We were hoping that things would get easier around midnight, when the veil between worlds is supposed to be thinner."

"We can't wait that long," I said. "We need answers now. Before anyone else gets hurt."

"Fine," Yara said. "Everyone put their hands on the planchette. I will go into a trance state and ask to speak to the ghosts. No one interrupt me or make any unnecessary comments." She shot a dirty look at Nathaniel. "Unbelievers shouldn't touch the board."

Nathaniel defiantly set his fingertips on the planchette. "I've seen shit in the last hour that would knock your hat off, Goody Proctor."

I squeezed my fingers on the planchette next to Nathaniel's. Remi sat between Maze and another witch. Hannah stayed on the couch, cradling the bong like a long-necked glass doll.

Yara closed her eyes. The joints in her neck popped as she rolled her head in a circle. Her chest rose and fell in short, sharp breaths. It reminded me of the fainting game that had been a brief fad in middle school. Before the custodians caught us making each other pass out and alerted the vice principal. Back then I hadn't known enough about human biology to realize that everyone was actually intentionally cutting off the oxygen from their brain to make each other faint. It was stupid dangerous, but we all thought it was a funny way to pass the time. (Isn't it wild that we're all entrusted with a human body years before we're smart enough to keep ourselves—or anyone else—alive?)

"I implore the restless spirits in this house," Yara said in a droning tone. She swayed side to side like she was caught up in a song the rest of us couldn't hear. "Speak with us. We are your descendants, the young adults of Bucktown. We even have the current owner of the house here with us."

Her eyes didn't open, but I felt the jab at me nonetheless. I would have liked to watch her hat catch fire. The nylon it was made of must have been flammable as hell. (Did that make me an unbeliever?)

The planchette didn't move an inch. The candles stayed lit. No messages appeared carved into the floor. The ghosts weren't listening. Yara knew it, too.

"We are here as supplicants to your purpose," she said, voice verging on begging. "You have been alone in this house for so long. It must be so lonely. We are here to visit with you. Can you hear us? Give us a sign!"

The planchette moved in an arc across the board. From A to Z.

"I'm not moving it," whispered one of the other witches. "Are you?"

"Shush!" Yara hissed. Then, in her talking-to-ghosts tone, she said, "Thank you, spirits. We hear you, spirits. Can you tell us who we're speaking to?"

"Whom," Nathaniel murmured.

The planchette zoomed under our hands.

To whom, it spelled.

"What did I tell you about being an unbeliever?" Yara snarled at Nathaniel.

"It wasn't me!" he said. "I said my piece! I didn't need to rub it in."

My house, the planchette spelled. *Not yours.*

"I don't really own the house. My parents bought it at auction. My mom wants to convert it into a bed-and-breakfast. Well, she wants to renovate it and then sell it for a lot of money to someone else who wants to run a bed-and-breakfast out of it," I told the Ouija board, feeling a little ridiculous. I was pretty sure that I was really just talking to Yara. This was another version of getting a mean horoscope from her. *Dear Virgo, tonight you will make a fool of yourself trying to look cool. Don't get too big for your britches, otherwise someone's going to point out the elephant in the room.*

The planchette moved again.

"No?" Maze read aloud. "That wasn't really a yes or no question."

No, the planchette said again. *No changing my house. My house. MY—*

"We get it," Nathaniel said. "This is your house. Arden's mom shouldn't mess with it. And we're sorry that we came in here to drink and absolutely choke out this room with smoke. It would help everyone out if the windows would open. Could you maybe remove whatever protective force field is on them? Or unlock the front door?"

Stay, the planchette spelled.

Stay.

My house.

Our house.

Stay.

Anxiety slithered through my intestines and bit into my stomach. "Stay" was what had been written in the floors and spelled out in the blood. It didn't seem like the sort of thing that Yara would make up to get back at me for interrupting her séance. Now, if the board had told me to shut up and leave, then I would have known it was Yara.

"We can't stay here," I told the board. "We need a way out. Please unlock the doors. There are so many people here. It's my fault. I invited everyone here for this party. We need to be able to leave."

"Arden," Remi said under her breath. "Rule number one: Don't talk back."

NO, the planchette said again.

Everyone stays.

You are home now.

"Someone has already died here tonight," I said. "A boy named Tanner. He was stabbed. You took his body away."

"Arden!" Remi chided me again.

Everyone dies, said the planchette.

Cold fear sliced through me. I took my hands off the planchette and sat back. I examined Yara, hoping to see her betray some smirk that this was her doing. But instead she sat back, too, hugging herself and shaking her head.

"Everyone stop touching it," she demanded. "Whoever is doing this. It's not funny anymore." Her flinty eyes glared at me from across the board. "Tanner Grant?"

I nodded. "His girlfriend, Claire, was looking for him. She said he left at the beginning of the party, but we found his body upstairs."

"I don't know anyone named Claire," Yara said. "But Tanner was my first boyfriend. In seventh grade. He gave me the sweetest piece of amethyst." The silver rings stacked on each of her fingers clicked together as she covered her face with her hands. She let out a soft, mewling cry. "Is he really dead?"

"He's extremely dead," Nathaniel said.

I elbowed him in the ribs, silently begging him to find some tact. He held up his hands, perplexed about what he had done wrong.

Yara slammed her hands back on the planchette. "Who killed him?" she demanded of the Ouija board. "Who killed Tanner?"

"That's a bad idea," Remi said. "Have you ever seen *Specter Sightings*? They're very clear about pissing off the ghosts—"

When the board didn't immediately answer, Yara let out a shriek of rage that had the other witches moving away from her.

"Tell me! My name is Yaritza Molina, and I call upon all the powers of the goddess Hecate to demand to know who murdered Tanner Grant! Was it you, ghost?"

Yes. Tanner is here, the board spelled.

Tanner is mine.

You are all mine.

Stay.

"No!" Yara wailed.

She slapped the Ouija board aside. The planchette cracked against the leg of an unused chair and clattered to the ground, just a plain hunk of plastic again, not a conduit to the other side.

"Um, guys," Hannah said. "The candles . . ."

She didn't have to finish the sentence. Every flame was rising. Stretching. Growing toward the ceiling like dozens of plants desperate for sunlight. The heat was instant and unbearable.

"This is why we don't talk back to the ghosts!" Remi shouted.

Nathaniel dove for the door. When it wouldn't open, he pressed himself flat and donkey-kicked it with his heel. Remi stumbled to help Hannah up. A wall of fire sprang up behind her, cutting the two of them off from the rest of the room.

The tip of Yara's witch hat ignited. Instead of burning, it began to melt. Leaking black polymer crept toward her skull. Maze reached over and whipped it off her head. It flew in a circle around the room before landing on top of a citronella candle. Burning plastic and mosquito-deterring lemongrass came together in a toxic perfume that made me woozy with each inhale. I couldn't faint, not here in a room filled with fire.

I jumped toward the door, twisting the knob in vain. I couldn't think of any way to force it open. Claire clawing at the front door hadn't done any good, but it had brought the phantom blood. I thought about the door in the kitchen, the way the bricks had grown over the doorway so organically that it looked like the outside wall had simply stretched over the opening. Like the house had tried to heal itself.

Like the house didn't want to be hurt. The Ouija board had warned us not to change anything. Wouldn't breaking things count as change?

I grabbed a taper candle from one of the manor's heavy silver holders and held it against the wood.

"Are you out of your mind?" Nathaniel asked. "How are we supposed to get out of a burning doorway?"

"I have a hypothesis, okay? Let me test it," I said. A puff of pure white smoke started to rise from the wood grain. "The ghosts might want to hurt *us*, but they don't want to hurt the house. Or maybe the house *can't* be hurt. Which means that something should stop me from setting it on fire."

"What if that something kills you?" Nate asked shrilly.

As the door continued to smoke and the other candles started to lick the ceiling, a single red droplet landed on my hand. Yara screamed and ducked her head under her forearms as a storm started to splatter us from above. Beads of salty red blood pelted the room. It plunked discordant notes on the piano. It extinguished all the candles and filled the bong up to the neck. It soaked into our clothes, our hair, and washed away the tarot cards. It covered our feet. An inch, two inches, and rising. The smell of copper was suffocating and cloying, wiping away any lingering perfume of the candles or funk of the weed smoke.

Nathaniel reached for the doorknob again, which opened easily as if in denial that it had ever tried to trap us in the first place. We spilled out of the grand salon, but the blood didn't follow. It splashed against an invisible barrier at the threshold. Remi piggybacked Hannah out of the room. The witches stayed behind, trying to gather their belongings from underneath the pond of blood.

As we turned to watch, the rain ceased to fall. Yara was on her hands and knees searching for something. She didn't notice the single stain on the wall left behind from the downpour. It looked like graffiti half washed away. But I could read it: **EVERYONE DIES TONIGHT.**

Out of the floor, a rush of ghost hands surged upward. They came crashing down on top of Yara, pulling her face into the blood pooled on the floor. She sputtered and choked, kicking her feet as though she could swim to safety. Maze and the other witches tried to help her, but the ghost hands were piled on top of Yara in a heap, a heavy blanket of ectoplasm that couldn't be pried away. Yara fought as hard as she could, limbs jerking and splashing. She went suddenly still and floated on top of a pool of blood that wasn't her own. The ghost hands pulled her down into the blood until she disappeared.

As though she'd never been there.

With one earth-shattering crash, the door between us slammed shut in unison with every other door in the house.

And then, silence.

WHAT HAPPENED TO THE DEINHART FAMILY

AS TOLD BY YARA MOLINA (BEFORE THE START OF HER RUDELY INTERRUPTED SÉANCE AND UNTIMELY DEATH)

The Deinharts knew something was wrong with their son the day he was born. But it was too late. They had made him, and what they'd made was evil.

He was evil in the classic textbook definition. He pricked strangers with safety pins. Killed small animals (squirrels, mice, cats, even someone's pet turtle) and never even thought twice about it. Whenever other children were around him, they were victims of ghoulish accidents. One kid suffered three broken ribs when the wheel of his bike came unbolted. Another lost an eye when she fell out of a tree on the Deinhart hill. Multiple schoolchildren came home with bruises they refused to explain and cuts in the shape of tiny fingernails, little crescent moons that would get infected and poison their blood.

It wasn't long before a body was found on the Deinhart property. The postman (or the census taker or the milkman) had been stabbed so many times that his whole body was an open wound. He was just meat, left behind to rot.

Mr. and Mrs. Deinhart covered up the death, buried the man in the backyard underneath an apple tree that, after that day, never bore fruit. For the safety of the town, they decided to board their son inside. No one would ever leave the Deinhart Manor again. Not him, not them.

No one knows how long they lasted there. Or who died first. The son or the parents. But at some point, the Deinhart Manor stopped being a home and became a prison.

And then a cemetery, full of unmarked graves.

14

Yara was dead. Drowned by ghosts in a roomful of blood and dragged into the floor. Just like Tanner.

I staggered back and sat down on the bottom of the stairs. My head was spinning. I tried to take a deep breath, but the stink of blood in my hair and wafting up from my clothes made me dry heave.

"Hey, hey, it's okay," Remi said, sitting down next to me. "Breathe, Arden. You're okay. At least now we know that the ghosts are doing the murders. It's not one of us."

"That is the coldest of cold comforts," I said. I was breathing too fast, my lungs and my stomach fighting to see whether hyperventilating or barfing was the priority. "She's dead, Rem. And her friends are still stuck in there!"

"At least her body isn't in there," Hannah said, resting her weight against the post at the bottom of the stairs. Her armpit hair was the only bit of pastel left on her. Like the rest of us, she was soaked in blood from head to toe.

Nathaniel threw himself into the grand salon door a few

times for good measure, but it stayed shut. The voices on the other side rose, begging for help. Those trapped inside slammed their hands against the wood.

"Don't worry," Nathaniel promised, shouting into the sealed crack of the door. "I'm gonna get you out!"

"You and what army?" I asked as he came over to us and sat down heavily on the bottom stair. "We don't have a battering ram!"

"The fire department does!" Hannah said, fumbling with her phone. Her thumb swiped through the blood on the screen like a tiny windshield wiper. "And I know the cops have riot gear from when they came to monitor the protest I held in the park over factory pollution in the duck pond."

"Wait, does everyone have their phones with them?" Nathaniel asked, head whipping around at each of us. "Maddy May told me that it was a strict no-phones party. So nobody would take pictures and get us all busted."

"Maybe Maddy May doesn't trust you specifically," Remi said, pulling her phone out of her bra.

Nathaniel held an affronted hand to his chest. "Why? I'm trustworthy as hell."

Remi cocked her head at him. "Didn't your parents ruin the egg drop? They complained and got the prizes changed."

"It was a science competition!" he cried, throwing up his hands. "It made more sense for the grand prize to be a trip to space camp. What did tickets to a theme park have to do with anything?"

"The only reason anyone entered was for Great America tickets!" Remi said. "Who wants to go to space camp?"

"Um, everyone?" Nathaniel scoffed. "Space is cool as hell."

"Hold on, Hannah," I said, setting my hand on top of her screen as she dialed 911. "Do we really want to align ourselves with the cops? I mean, they brought riot gear to a duck protest. Do you really think they're going to let us all go peacefully after getting drunk and sort of trespassing?"

Nathaniel blew a raspberry. "If they find out that two people died in here, we'll be lucky to get out of here alive. Especially since one of them was a white boy."

I knew the "we" he meant there was me and him. Remi and Hannah had nothing to worry about. With their porcelain skin and Remi's borrowed rich-girl clothes, both of them could walk out of here, no sweat. They could even chug Everclear all the way down the hill and the cops would offer them a ride home.

Nathaniel and I, openly melanated, would have way more trouble.

Hannah poked her tongue into her cheek and let out a long sigh through her nose. "I'm open to suggestions," she said. "But we can't sit here and wait to be murdered by ghosts."

Put like that, I knew there was really only one option left that wouldn't result in immediate danger. Just a very unpleasant rest of my life. (If I was lucky enough to live past tonight.)

"God, she's going to make me take the real estate exam as a punishment," I grumbled. "I'm gonna be selling houses for the rest of my life to pay for this."

I called my mom. Even as her contact photo came up (a picture of her in a bonnet that she thought I'd deleted), my phone didn't even pretend to make the call. A *no signal* warning flashed on-screen.

With a wave of anxious nausea, I opened up a text.

Mom, I wrote. *I'm trapped inside the D. Manor with some friends. We need help. Can you call one of your contractors to take the front door off the hinges for us? Or the fire department? But not if they bring cops. Sorry. Thx.*

I considered adding in something about ghosts or a picture of the scary messages carved into the floor in the foyer or even asking her to wait to be mad at me until we were sure that I made it out of here alive, but time was of the essence, so I hit SEND. After pondering my request for a minute, an exclamation mark came up. *Message unable to send.*

"Fuck," I said.

"Try turning airplane mode off and on," Nathaniel said, peering over the edge of my screen.

"It's not working," I snapped at him.

I tried sending the text again. Again it failed. Panicked sweat started to swamp up my armpits and the small of my back. Behind the closed doors, our classmates continued to scream for help.

"I have zero bars!" Remi growled. She lifted her phone to the ceiling, searching the empty air for a signal. Flakes of dried blood fell from the screen. "I swear to God, my mom's cheap-ass phone plan is going to literally be the death of me. Of all of us."

"No service," Hannah concurred, checking her own phone. "No way to get help from the outside world. So, what? We're all doomed to die?"

"Unless you have a plan for befriending all the ghosts," Nathaniel said. "Yara's method of screaming and cursing them definitely didn't work."

"Befriending people is Maddy May's job," Remi said, exasperated. She gripped her hair in both hands. "And who knows what room she's stuck in! I haven't seen her all night!"

"We need to figure out how to open the doors," Nathaniel said. "We have to let everybody out."

I scrubbed my hands over my face. "Do we? Maybe they're safer in there than out here."

Nathaniel stared at me in disbelief. "You're not serious. We can't leave them there."

"Why can't we?" I asked. Being completely out of options was making me feel loopier than any of the drinks I'd consumed. My heart was drumming inside my chest, a million beats per minute. I got to my feet. All my pent-up energy had to go somewhere, so I started to pace, trying to think of a plan that didn't end with everyone in the house getting murdered by ghosts. The blood in my shoes squelched unpleasantly with every step. "The ghosts want us to stay here. That's what's carved into the floor. That's what the Ouija board said. They want us here. So maybe we're only in danger if we try to leave."

"But we are going to try to leave," Hannah said, watching me uneasily. "Aren't we?"

"This place has a lot of rooms, but not quite enough for

half the graduating class," Remi said with a forced chuckle. "Plus, the only food in the house is Doritos and cake."

"Setting the séance on fire got us out of the last room," Nathaniel said. "What would happen if we tried to light the whole house on fire? Could that open all the doors?"

"It could," I said. I rubbed the heel of my hand across my forehead where blood-rain was drying in a sticky patch. "But if it didn't work, we'd all just die in a huge fire."

"Fire, ghosts, cops," Nathaniel said. He clasped his knees and rocked back and forth. "Pick your poison at this point, right? I don't know if there's a way out of here that doesn't end in all of us dying."

"There has to be!" I exclaimed. "Use your big rocket-scientist brain, Nate. We're not stuck on Mars. We're stuck in a house within spitting distance of a gas station. We could try to send out an SOS or something? Does anyone know Morse code?"

"Why is everyone looking at me?" Nathaniel asked.

Hannah gave him an appraising once-over. "You have a real Eagle Scout vibe," she said.

"Oh my God, exactly," Remi said, slamming her hand on her forehead. "That's totally your vibe, Nathaniel. Like someone who knows a lot about different kinds of knots. But not in, like, a sexy, kinky way. Or even a rich sailing way. Like you studied knots for a test."

"What the hell?" Nathaniel asked. His jaw dropped in offended shock. "Arden, back me up here. I don't have a dork aesthetic. Look at these sneakers! These aren't the sneakers of an Eagle Scout!"

He stuck out his feet so I could examine his Jordans. They had been clean before buckets of blood sank into the white leather. Despite having been attacked by ghost hands, there were no visible creases. But they were so obviously unused that, I had to admit, they were kind of dorky.

I gave him an apologetic grimace. "They're basketball shoes, and you don't play."

"What? Come on! You don't have to play basketball to wear Jays!" he protested. "You don't have to play tennis to wear tennis shoes. This is racial profiling! Just because I'm Black, I should be able to play ball."

"No one said you should be able to play," I corrected him. "It's not like you're NBA tall."

"I'm the same height as Isaiah Thomas!" he cried. "He's an all-star!"

"Who is old *and* short," Remi said. She let out a braying laugh that was so infectious that it set off Hannah and me, too.

Nathaniel folded his arms and sulked. Taking pity on him, I set my hands on his forearm and gave him an encouraging squeeze.

"Aww, it's okay," I said. "You'll have your college glow-up and prove us all wrong. You'll be hot and successful, doing calculations for launching shit into space, and the rest of us will still be here in Bucktown, standing in line to get food poisoning from Chipotle on a Friday night."

"If I live to see college," he said darkly.

Oh, right, I thought, the laughter dying in my throat. *We're all going to die here.*

"So...," Remi said with a grimace. "That's a no on the Morse code?"

"No," Nathaniel said flatly. "Morse code is antiquated as fuck. I don't even think they use it on ships anymore."

I stood up straight again. The diversion had been nice, but our situation was getting worse by the minute. Everyone but us was locked inside a room, most likely being tormented (and possibly killed) by ghosts. I had to do something. Or die trying.

"Where are you going?" Nathaniel asked, eyeing me warily. "Are you going to sacrifice yourself to the ghosts because you made out with a geek?"

"You two made out?" Hannah asked. She curled her index finger under her nose, intrigued. "I can see that. You have a similar energy."

I held up a finger, prepared to count all the ways in which Nathaniel (and Hannah Armpits) had it wrong. "One, it was a million years ago—"

"Within this calendar year, for sure," Remi told Hannah. "It ended right before spring break."

"She told you?" Nathaniel asked. His eyebrows flew up. "What'd she say?"

"And two," I said, raising my voice over both of theirs, "there are two places in this house I haven't seen yet. The basement and the attic."

"I couldn't find the stairs to the attic," Remi said. "I looked upstairs, but it was all rooms."

"Fine," I said. I didn't really want to go upstairs and get stuck in the shrinking hallway again anyway. "Then I'll start with the basement. There could be tools down there. Or a secret exit. Or a huge fucking monster that swallows me whole, making this whole thing your problem. Won't know until I try."

Hannah gripped the banister and, with some difficulty, pulled herself to standing. "Wait, we're coming with you," she said.

"We are?" Nathaniel asked.

Hannah nodded, resolute. "Haven't you ever seen a scary movie? You don't split up when people start dying. That's hella stupid. We'll all go."

"Yeah," Remi said, getting to her feet and flashing a gummy smile. "If one of us gets eaten by a basement monster, we all do! All for one and one for all!"

15

No one was left in the downstairs corridor. Where there had been throngs of people milling around, now there was only a long line of closed doors, each one almost (but not quite) trapping the sounds of people calling out from inside. It was surprisingly easy to find the door to the basement. It was the only one that wasn't locked.

"That's not foreboding at all," Nathaniel said, shying back as the door swung open. He stood in the doorframe, clinging to the light of the hallway as though considering turning tail and running. Remi pushed him forward. Hannah was hugging her around the neck, getting another piggyback ride down the stairs into darkness.

I held my phone flashlight up and led the way. The stairs were rickety, splintered wood that didn't creak as much as they loudly objected underfoot. With every step, I prayed that they'd hold my weight. Falling to my death would be so embarrassing. Way less dignified than being attacked by vengeful spirits.

"Anyone else feel like they're following the Judas steer?" Nathaniel asked.

"Call me a steer again, Nathaniel, and see what happens to you," I said, bristling at the comparison. It's one thing to worry about my own weight but another to get compared to a literal cow. "I'm sorry if you got your feelings hurt over your lack of apparent athleticism, but if you start making fat jokes, I will throw you over this railing."

"Obviously you aren't a literal steer," Nathaniel said dismissively. "Steers are male. I mean—"

"I get what you mean," I growled. "Now stop explaining yourself before you choke on your foot. Or before I choke you with it."

"What's a Judas steer?" Remi asked. "Let me guess. It's something from an AP Lit Russian classic that's too hard for a normal person to read."

"It's a farming term," Hannah said. "It's the cow that leads the others to slaughter. Sometimes it's a Judas goat. Poor things. They don't know that they're leading their friends to die. They're just doing a job."

"Or maybe they do know," Nathaniel said. "And it's some Stanford prison experiment shit where they go mad with power."

"I don't think that animals would align themselves with the slaughterhouse," Hannah said.

"Why not?" Nathaniel asked. "People work against their best interest all the time. Anything to stay alive."

"For example, going into the basement of a haunted house," I said.

I reached up and pulled on the chain of the room's single light bulb.

The basement was clammy, cold, and largely empty. Load-bearing wooden beams stood guard at intervals, making the room feel claustrophobic despite its expanse. Crumbling bricks made up the walls. How many semesters of college would it cost for Mom to hire a stonemason to fix these gaps? Or to fix the water pipes that crisscrossed the ceiling, leaking (what I hoped was) rusty water?

This place wasn't just haunted. It was a money pit. No wonder Mom and Dad had to divorce after buying it. It needed a new foundation, a new roof, windows and doors that weren't haunted to stay shut. It would be next to impossible to turn a profit on the sale, even without it being the site of multiple ghost murders.

There was no furniture down here. Just heaps of debris. Stacks of narrow wooden boards lined one wall, like a makeshift horizontal fence. I reached out and grazed my hand against one. It was smooth. The wood had been cared for. Waxed.

"Floorboards," I said. I tried to count them but lost track after the first fifty. There were dozens of loose floorboards in these stacks, all of them the same oak as the floors upstairs. Some still had crusty old nails jutting out, but only on the ends.

"Weird," Nathaniel said. "Wouldn't you throw away the old boards when you got a new floor?"

"You would," I said. "But I don't think they got a new floor."

I lifted one of the boards and held it up. The stray nail at the end of the board scraped against the brick. No words had been carved into this floor. There were barely any scuffs to show that it had ever been walked on. But there were frayed edges where I could imagine a hammer or a crowbar cracking the wood away from the wall.

"This is how they did it," I said. "This is how they boarded up the house. They sacrificed the floor."

Why hadn't Mom and Dad mentioned this to me? They'd said their contractor had spent hours taking down all the boards, but they'd never said that they were floorboards.

"But which floor?" Remi asked. "We've seen most of the house. I don't remember seeing any huge holes in the floor, do you?"

"Maybe the house healed itself," I said. "The way it scabbed over the back door."

"What's that?" Hannah asked. She slid off Remi's back and hopped toward a pile at the back of the room.

This pile was in much worse condition than the floorboards. The outer layer had been charred to a crisp, leaving behind a precariously teetering triangle.

"It looks like a summoning circle," Hannah said.

"Holy shit," Remi said. "Do you think the Deinharts could have been killed by a demon they summoned?"

Hannah's eyes sparkled with excitement. "Or maybe they tried to summon a demon to kill whatever was threatening to kill them," she said.

"Demons?" Nathaniel asked drolly. "Really?"

"Ghosts are real but demons can't be?" Remi asked him.

He shrugged. "Ghosts are just people. People exist, they die, they don't go anywhere. Ghosts. Demons imply the existence of angels and God."

"It wouldn't be terrible to believe in God right now," Remi said.

I got closer to the stack, nudging a piece with my foot. It clattered to the ground with an almost hollow sound.

Nathaniel gulped and stepped back. "Oh fuck, is it bones? Tell me it's not bones."

"It's not bones," I said. I pulled the intact specimen away from the pyre. It was wood, ornately carved, with a scrap of canvas dangling from one corner. Using it to push the pile apart, I found more of the same, plus some shattered glass.

"It's art," I said, repulsed by the sight. I forced myself to keep prying apart the pile. The fire had obviously been started from the outside. The deeper in I went, the more intact pieces I found. Bits of picture frames. Half a painted face. Yellowed photo paper burned away except for an apple tree. "It's all the art that was in the house before. Paintings. Photographs. Anything that would burn. Someone put it down here and lit it all on fire."

Hannah aimed her phone light upward. A black circle was burned into the ceiling, directly over the pyre.

"We're not the first people to think of burning the place down," she said. "But obviously it didn't work. It doesn't even look like the fire made it upstairs."

"I bet the house blood-rained the fire out," Remi said. "Its own nasty-ass sprinkler system. Probably made out of all the people the ghosts have murdered."

"Wait a minute," Nathaniel said. He reached a hand into the pyre and pulled out a flattened cardboard box. It was black and yellow with a huge picture of a lemon on the side. It read *Mike's Hard Lemonade*. "They still make this, right? It's a hard seltzer with sweetener in it."

Dread made my limbs feel heavy. There was no way that box was from the Roaring Twenties. Or even the Great Depression. It had once been shiny, even if it was now dusty with ash. It was cheerfully, horribly modern and yet still too old to have been brought here by Mom and Dad or their contractor.

My parents hadn't been the first people inside the house in a hundred years. And we weren't the first people to drink here.

"Dude, I told you!" Remi said, pointing at me victoriously. "I told you when I found that old can! There have been other people here before us! They probably got rid of the Deinhart bodies, which is why I couldn't find them!"

"Okay, you're right," I said uneasily. I panned my phone flashlight across the walls, looking for any more clues as to what had happened down here in the past. But there were no body-shaped patches or vampire coffins or portals to hell to provide an easy explanation. "So, what happened to those people? Why is there just a box and a single soda can left behind? Wouldn't they have told someone if they'd found a bunch of corpses in here? Or if they'd been confronted with, you know, the existence of ghosts?"

"Not necessarily," Nathaniel said. "If I get out of here, I'll probably never speak of this ever again. So I can hold on to my shoelaces and keep my feet out of the grippy socks. Or, worse, end up on one of those corny-ass ghost-hunting shows."

"Hey," Remi said, throwing her bangs out of her eyes to better glare at Nate. "You should be so lucky. *Specter Sightings* is the best show on TV. *Ghost Watchers* is pretty good. *Haunted Road Trip* got bad after the original hosts left."

"I like *Specter Sightings*," Hannah said. "I started watching it after you recommended it, Remi. I'm on season six."

"You are?" Remi clutched Hannah's forearms in excitement, her whole face lighting up brighter than the bare bulb swinging from the ceiling. "Have you seen the zombies of Cross Creek episode? Three girls were spotted in a Walmart a week after their deaths and then—"

"That mysterious fire? Oh my God, it should have won an Emmy!" Hannah squealed. "Totally my favorite episode so far. But I have, like, nineteen seasons left."

Leaving Remi and Hannah to their moment, I turned to Nathaniel. There was no chance of us getting distracted from our mission with flirting. We'd never found anything that both of us liked (other than being good at school). He watched only stuff about space (except for speech-and-debate competitions, which he watched so he could critique them). I liked medical dramas or romantic comedies where Black girls were more than the sassy best friend.

"According to the rumors about the house, there were five Deinhart kids and two parents," I said to Nathaniel. "I'd say that we've seen more than seven people's worth of phantom blood."

"How much blood is in a normal body?" he asked.

"One and a half gallons," I said. "On average."

Nathaniel's lip curled in disgust. "You know that? Without looking it up?"

"I helped run the school blood drive in September," I said, refusing to feel weird about being knowledgeable. "You try watching people donate a full pint of blood and not get curious about how much is left in their bodies."

"How much blood do you think it took to drown Yara?" Nathaniel asked.

"More than ten and a half gallons," I said. If I had to guess, the grand salon was filled with more than a kiddie pool of blood. At least fifty gallons. Sure, the house could have been cycling through the blood after it soaked it up after a downpour. Like water being stored in an aquifer. The same blood that had leaked down the front door might also have been used in the grand salon. But that still meant that at least thirty-three people had died and been absorbed by the house. Thirty-three people's blood was soaked into my clothes and matted into my hair. The next time it rained inside, Yara and Tanner would be included in the storm. Three more gallons to protect the manor.

Creeped out, I rubbed my arms for warmth and leaned against one of the wooden beams. I wanted the longest, hottest shower of my life. I wanted to sleep a thousand sleeps. I wanted massive amounts of therapy. But we were no closer to having a way out than we had been all night. Obviously, burning down the house wasn't a viable option. Whoever had partied here last had tried and failed. Remi was right.

The house had a fire sprinkler system that would drown any flame in blood. Any door could lock itself. And who knew how many disgusting spiders were crawling around.

My dad's story was true. The manor was hell. I should have just gone to Sober Grad Night. Instead of dying in a haunted house, I could have played poker for Starbucks gift cards with the rest of the honors track. (At least there I would recognize some people from my classes.)

Remi pointed her phone light at the pyre. Something glinted at the bottom of the stack. She dropped to the ground, scavenging through the pile like a raccoon through a particularly smelly dumpster.

"Careful," I said. "There's glass in there. You could cut yourself—"

I spoke too soon. Remi came up fast, swinging an axe. It audibly cut through the air. Nathaniel, Hannah, and I all ducked, crying out with different levels of horror.

Remi was delighted. Her whole face lit up; she examined the silver sheen of the axe head. Only one side of it had been touched by the fire that took out all the art, a single line of black that ran down the handle. "Do you know what this is?" she asked.

"That's an axe," Nathaniel said, holding his hands up and standing frozen. No part of him looked like he trusted Remi with a weapon. I wasn't sure I did, either. She was more enthusiastic than cautious even without a blade.

"It's gotta be *the* axe! Like in the stories!" Remi said. She stuffed her phone back into her bra so that she could grip the axe with both hands. Its wooden handle was almost as long as a baseball bat. "This could be the hatchet that killed all of the Deinharts. Shit, I wish I had a black light so I could check it for blood splatter."

"Haven't you seen enough blood for one night?" I asked, thinking of Yara drowning in the grand salon. If I never saw another drop of blood, it would be too soon.

"Yeah, sure," Remi said, barely listening as she examined the curve of the axe blade. She looked up suddenly and grinned. "Now we can cut down the front door! And all the other doors! The ghosts can't keep us here now!"

Nathaniel shoved his hands into his jeans, his shoulders hunched up to his ears. "I mean, I couldn't break a window with a fireplace poker, so I don't know if . . ."

I shot him a silencing look. The axe was the only good thing we'd found in the house so far. Everything else was bad news, leaking pipes, and dead classmates.

"You're right, Rem," I said. "Let's chop down some doors."

WHAT HAPPENED TO THE DEINHART FAMILY

AS TOLD BY HANNAH TREU
(HEARD ON THE BUS EN ROUTE
TO A VOLLEYBALL TOURNAMENT)

Nobody knows why he did it. There were guns in the house. (Hunting rifles. A pistol in the nightstand.) And knives. (The cook's meat cleaver. Paring knives and oyster knives.) There must have been a hatchet or a chain saw. (Something had taken down the fruit trees that blocked the view in the ballroom.)

But Mr. Deinhart killed his family with his hands. He crushed their windpipes. Blocked their airways. Smothered the smallest with one beefy palm.

And when he was done, he put them all back into their beds. Tucked the covers up to their chins. Turned down the lights and closed the doors. Then he trapped himself inside (boarded up the doors and windows).

He sat in the silence and thought about what he'd done. He thought about it over and over and over and over and over and over and ...

16

It was harder to cut through a door than *The Shining* made it look. We started with the first door we came to—the one that led to the kitchen. The first few swings that Remi took only managed to slice off splinters. Nathaniel got macho and took the axe. His strike managed to get the blade stuck in the wood but no closer to getting through to the other side.

It was my idea to use the back of the axe to pop the hinge pins out of the doors. (I'd seen my parents do it at a house they'd flipped when Dad lost the key.) All four of us took turns banging the bottom of the hinges. Sweat and old blood-rain stung my eyes by the time we got out all the pins. The door pulled away from the frame easily. It was heavy, though. Both Nathaniel and I had to carry it away. We hadn't even leaned it against the wall before Hannah and Remi screamed.

The Drama Club members I'd talked to earlier were on the kitchen floor. A single newsie hat had fallen off someone's head, discarded in the dust. The sink was running, spilling water down the front of the ruined cabinets. The old bottle of port I'd watched them pass from person to person had shattered. Chunks of black glass littered the floor.

There was no blood, no signs of injury. But their faces...

All of their faces were twisted into total and utter agony. Six tragedy masks. They hadn't gone peacefully. They had known pain and suffering until the very last breath. It was the worst thing I'd ever seen. Worse than Tanner. Worse than Yara. They had been taken away by the ghosts. But the Drama Club had been left behind. To rot? As a warning? I didn't know.

Hannah covered her face with her hands and turned away. Remi wrapped her arms around her, watching as I leaned over Keaton. His lips were gray-blue from lack of oxygen. A trickle of wine or blood was leaking out of the side of his mouth. Even as my heart raced and my mind screamed to look away, I bent down close to his dead face and sniffed.

"What are you doing?" Nathaniel asked. He stepped forward like he was considering pulling me away, but he didn't want to be that close to the corpses. "You can't just go around smelling dead bodies!"

"He smells like almonds," I said, standing up. I couldn't take my eyes away from Keaton's face yet. Maddy May had affectionately called him "Keats." Did anyone else? Why didn't I know his last name? Was Keaton his last name? He'd been in my classes. He was Maddy May's boyfriend. I had never paid that much attention to him. That theater kid sincerity was hard to look at directly. Like the opposite of an abyss. *An abundance.*

He shouldn't have been here. He belonged at Sober Grad

Night, too. Singing karaoke versions of show tunes no one had ever heard of or asked to hear. Reciting sonnets at sunrise while everyone else tried to sleep. All he'd wanted was to see Maddy May one last time, to steal one more minute when he was a Romeo with a Juliet to adore him.

Swallowing hard, I forced myself to look back at Nathaniel, Remi, and Hannah. "It was poison, probably. Cyanide smells like almonds. It could have been in any of the unmarked bottles they were drinking from. It was definitely the wrong place to play wine snob." I tried to smile, but my mouth wouldn't move beyond a flinch. Any wrong move would end in me crying again.

"There's a story that Mrs. Deinhart killed her husband with a poisoned drink," Remi said, uneasily. "And her kid accidentally drank it, too, so she killed herself."

"There are a lot of stories," Nathaniel said. "That won't bring the Drama Club back to life."

Rasping, choking gasps made all of us jump. Keaton's shoulders seized. Top Hat's eyelashes fluttered. One of the others rolled over and puked black sludge onto the floor.

"Whoa, whoa, whoa!" I stumbled back into Nathaniel, who wrapped a protective arm around my shoulders. Whether he was trying to protect me or himself was unclear. (But I had a guess.)

The reanimated Drama Club got to their feet in jerky, uncertain movements, as though they were all doing an acting exercise where they tried to walk like baby deer.

"They were dead," Remi said in a loud whisper. "You all saw that. They couldn't fake that."

"They're actors," Hannah said. "Maybe they were acting dead."

"You've obviously never sat through one of their shows," Remi said.

Keaton wiped his mouth on the back of his wrist and noticed all of us for the first time.

"Hey, guys," he said. "Is Maddy May with you?"

"We haven't found her," I said. I hazarded a step closer, breaking free of Nathaniel's teddy-bear hold.

Behind me, Nathaniel panic-whispered, "Zombies! Theater geek zombies!"

I ignored him. I could concede the existence of ghosts. But zombies? Absolutely not. Especially not zombies that came back to life to play another round of Zip, Zap, Zop like three of them had started to do immediately, clapping at one another with increasing speed. The guy in steampunk goggles found an unbroken bottle of wine on the counter and started fumbling with the cork.

"Are you okay, Keaton?" I asked.

"Hell yeah," he said. His face was taking turns smiling and focusing his eyes, making it look like closing his eyes powered up the corners of his mouth. Watching it made me feel a little seasick. Or maybe that was the smell of nearby wine puke. "I feel great!"

To prove it, he swung his arms out wide and twirled. He let out a burp that smelled undeniably like poison and smiled again.

"Do you remember lying on the floor just now?" I asked. I pointed at the spot on the ground where we'd found them.

Bits of broken black glass had started sailing over the area on trails of water coming down from the sink.

"On the floor?" He let out a wheezing laugh. His teeth and tongue were stained, purple as plums. "What are you talking about? We've been here all night. You saw us earlier. No one was on the floor."

"Then why is your back wet?" Nathaniel asked. He had one hand gripping the doorframe, ready to bolt, but his instinct to "well, actually" got in the way.

Keaton's laugh faded. Confusion came down over his features, knotting his eyebrows and wrinkling his nose. He reached over his shoulder and touched the back of his vest. It was soaking wet, the satin one long dark stain.

A new bottle of wine popped open. Goggles held it overhead and announced, "'I pray, come and crush a cup of wine!'"

"Yes!" Keaton said, pumping his fists wildly. "More wine!"

"It might be port," said Goggles, eyeballing the inside of the bottle.

"Port's wine," said Newsie Hat, who had retrieved her distinctive headwear from the floor and plopped it back on her head.

Goggles moved to put the bottle up to his mouth. His lips parted. His head tipped back. At that moment, he looked too much like everyone had on the floor.

"You can't drink that!" I shouted. I slapped the bottle away. It smashed against the cast-iron stove. Shards of glass tinkled to the ground in a splash of dark liquid.

"Party foul!" giggled one of the Zip, Zap, Zoppers.

"Come on, Arden, not cool," Keaton said. His shoulders sank down to knees, telegraphing how very uncool he found my behavior. Or how heavy he found his spine. "That wine is super old. And probably valuable."

"And probably poisoned!" I said.

"What?" Keaton laughed. "Because of that rumor that Mrs. Deinhart killed her husband with a poisoned drink? That was cognac!"

"Or maybe brandy," said Goggles.

"What's the difference?" Keaton asked.

Goggles shrugged. "I don't have my phone with me."

"See, it's not just me," Nathaniel told Hannah and Remi defensively. "Maddy May told her own friends not to bring their phones!"

"You're as trustworthy as a guy wearing Victorian protective gear as a headband," Hannah said gently. "Maybe take it easy on the *I told you so*s."

"There's something very wrong in this house," I stressed to Keaton and the rest of the Drama Club. "Weird things are happening. To you! To everyone. People are dying. Tanner and Yara—"

"Everything's coming up roses!" Top Hat announced. They were crawling out of the pantry, holding another unmarked wine bottle in their hand. Dense, dirty spiderwebs clung to them like mummy wrappings. As they stood up straight, the kitchen light revealed the spiders. Crawling over all them. Head to toe. Brown spiders. Black spiders. Hairy spiders. Throbbing fat-assed spiders. Tiny newborn spiders with translucent legs. Spiders that jumped on powerful legs. Spiders that leaped into the air and floated like little poisonous flying squirrels.

One of the flying spiders glided toward me. Its legs touched down on my shoulder.

My skin didn't crawl so much as it revolted against being connected to my skeleton and tried to self-immolate. I don't remember how I got out of the kitchen, but I'm sure I must have flailed and possibly cried. I slapped my arms. Clawed at my scalp. Shook out my hair. Stomped my feet. Smacked every inch of my body that I could reach, trying to kill the feeling that the spiders were on me. DEFCON 1 hysterics from a full-grown fat girl.

When I came to my senses, I was standing in the hallway, surrounded by closed doors. I was aware of Remi's voice telling me, "You're okay. Arden, you're okay. There are no spiders on you. You're okay. You're safe."

"No spiders," Nathaniel said. "But you are still trapped in a haunted house."

"Hm," Hannah said, considering Nathaniel like he was a particularly interesting lab rat. "You really do think you're helping when you do that. Have you considered that constantly correcting women makes you come off as paternalistic?"

"W-what?" Nathaniel asked, doing a double take at her. He seemed to be absolutely choking down the instinct to tell her she was wrong.

"Just something to consider," she said. "I know we're in a life-or-death situation, but it's never too late to examine your behavior."

I gave my arms one last rub, quadruple-checking to make sure that there were no fuzzy legs walking on me. My skin was cold and sticky with dried blood-rain.

"Sorry," I said. My lips and throat had gone dry. I must have screamed at some point. Possibly a lot. "I'm sorry. I know spiders aren't even the worst thing we've seen today; I can't stand the feeling of them. Even thinking about it makes me—"

In the kitchen, glass shattered. Then, there was a sound like wet laundry hitting the ground. A pale white hand flopped over the threshold. It laid perfectly, eerily still.

The Drama Club was dead. Again. Or they weren't. They could get up, find another bottle, and start the cycle all over. Or they could stay dead, surrounded by broken bottles and a nightmarish mix of crawling spiders.

A bone-deep weariness settled into me. I imagined resting against one of the walls and letting myself sink into the abyss beyond the wallpaper. No more terror. No more death. No more guilt about throwing the world's worst party. As I thought about it, the wall started to feel more squishy, like it could hear my thoughts. I jerked myself away before the ghost hands could come take me.

"Let's take the hinges off the front door and get out of here," Hannah said. "Before we're next."

"I'm with her," Nathaniel said, clearly delighted to prove he was capable of being agreeable. "Let's go. You tried to save the Drama Club, Arden, and they didn't listen!"

"We can't go now!" Remi said. She picked up the axe from where it was leaning against the wall and held it across her chest. "We don't even know what the ghosts want. We don't even have proof that they exist!"

"You want to stay long enough to take a picture of a ghost?" Nathaniel asked. "Are you willing to die trying?"

"We could go get help," Hannah stressed. She gripped Remi's arm. "And we could get more equipment for communicating with the ghosts. It's not like they're going anywhere."

I stared at the lifeless drama kid's hand on the floor, willing it to move. To come back to life. It didn't so much as twitch. But it also didn't disappear.

Why weren't the ghosts taking the Drama Club bodies away? Why leave them but take Tanner and Yara? Was it because they weren't really dead? Or were they less useful to the spirits? Did the Deinhart ghosts hate incessant Shakespeare quotes? Not that I could blame them, but it was a thin excuse.

Remi was right. We didn't know what the ghosts wanted. Just to kill us? To keep some of us and not others? It didn't make any sense.

But maybe it never would make sense. There was plenty about the world that didn't make sense. Why were the smartest people the least popular? Why were the comfiest clothes the ugliest? How can people wake up one morning and decide to stop being a family?

Ghosts didn't have to make sense. Death was a mystery and ghosts were an extension. We couldn't win against death. Not with an axe. Not with overthinking.

"Remi," I said weakly. "They're right. We should leave. We'll get help and rescue whoever's left."

"No!" Remi said. "What about Maddy May? We can't leave her here. The house can disappear people! Like what happened to Yara. If we leave, we could come back to an empty house again. Then we'll never find her!"

"That could already be true!" I shouted. I balled my fists in the collar of my shirt. "We could stay here and die along with everyone else, or we could leave and then *someone* would have survived this shit show!"

"Wow, cool point of view from a future doctor," Remi said. "Fuck everyone else and save yourself?"

"I'm not going to be a doctor, Remi! Maddy May took off with my tuition money," I burst out. "I might not have anything to live for, but I still don't want to die!"

A whoosh of air passed overhead. All the lights went out.

And all of the doors creaked open.

17

Nathaniel's voice came out of the darkness beside me. "See, this would be a good time for everyone to have their phone."

"Yes, Nate," I said, fumbling in my pockets for my phone. I turned the flashlight on and shone it in his face. "If we could go back and make something different about tonight, you being allowed to bring your phone would be at the top of the list. Not finding a non-haunted venue."

Remi's phone lit up. She was holding it overhead like a streetlamp so that the weak light illuminated all of us. "Next time we should break into a house with a pool," she said.

"So we can watch someone else drown?" Hannah asked. She swept her phone across the nearest wall. All the doors were standing open, pretending like they hadn't been locked seconds ago.

"Good point," Remi said. "Next time we should break into a trampoline park. Or a room full of bouncy castles. No one's ever died in a bouncy castle."

"What you're describing is Sober Grad Night," I said.

"Yes, exactly," Remi said. "We should throw a Sober Grad Night. But where everyone can get as fucked-up as they want."

"Brilliant plan, Rem," I said with a snort of amusement. "If we get out of here, we'll get drunk in a bouncy house together."

"You're being sarcastic, but that sounds like the greatest party of all time," Remi said.

"It sounds like jumping into ten different kinds of vomit," I said before conceding, "but before that it would be fun."

"This is probably a stupid thing to say in a haunted house," Nathaniel said uneasily, "but does the vibe feel off to anyone else?"

"Turning the lights off always changes the vibe," Hannah said. "Being scared of the dark is human nature. Although when the lights went off earlier, it felt more exciting."

"Right?" Nathaniel said. "This feels more like a threat."

"We have proven the existence of ghosts and watched people die since then," I said. "So maybe the vibe has been bad and the dark is just making us confront it?"

"You could be right," Nathaniel said in a tone that didn't quite ring sincere but still got credit for attempting. "But the last time the power went out, everyone screamed. So why is the house dead silent now?"

My heartbeat pounded in my ears, making me more aware of how it had sped up. I waited for the usual sounds of an old house settling (creaks in the foundation, groaning in pipes crammed full of toilet paper for the first time in a century). But none came. It was truly drop-a-pin silent.

"No one is coming out here," Hannah whispered. "If

you'd been locked in a room, wouldn't you leave the second the door opened?"

"Maybe they still can't leave," Remi said. Her front teeth worried at her lower lip, making her look like a very tall, very anxious rabbit. She spun the axe handle in her two hands. "Only one way to find out."

For a second, I couldn't make myself move. Walking around a haunted house had been bad enough with all the lights on. Now only able to see ahead a few inches in the dim light of our phones, I was frozen in fear. Anything could be in the darkness. And what would happen when our phones ran out of batteries? If we could even find a candle not co-opted by Yara's séance, would the house let us carry around a flame without drowning it in phantom blood?

Something brushed my hand, and I recoiled, thrusting my phone light at it (to make sure it wasn't a spider). Instead, I found long brown fingers and an open palm held still in the light. I looked up at Nathaniel's face. He gave me a sheepish smile, the same *If you wanna* look he used to make at me when we'd both get to lunch at the same time and decide to ditch to make out in the tinted back seat of his car. No pressure, just an open-ended offer.

Intensely aware of Remi and Hannah pretending not to watch, I took Nate's hand. I gripped it from the side, not fingers interlaced. (In case I needed to make a quick get-away.) He gave a reassuring squeeze.

"We find Maddy May, then we cut the front door down to get help," I told the group. "Agreed?"

"Agreed," said Nathaniel and Hannah.

"What about the attic?" Remi asked. "You said you wanted to look everywhere, and that's where my brother said he saw someone moving around on Halloween, and *Specter Sightings* always look in the attic for—"

I shook my head. "Only if Maddy May's there," I said. "Okay?"

"Yeah, okay," Remi mumbled, and averted her gaze. "She'll probably know how to talk the Drama Club into not drinking poison wine on a loop. It might take one of their weird cuddle parties where they lie on each other in a parking lot, but at least they'll stop, you know, dying repeatedly."

"They were pretty cuddled up when they were dead," I said.

Choking down the sourness of fear, I took the first step forward. We crept down the hall toward the dining room's open double doors. Framed in the doorway, the party scene was surprisingly normal. Gathered around the table, people were drinking out of red cups or aluminum cans. The electric blue light of a vape battery glowed in the corner, followed by a plume of white citrus-scented smoke. No one seemed to notice that the lights were off, and no one was talking.

Setting down her drink, Kenzie Sullivan took the knife out of the cake. Wheeling around, she stabbed it (frosting and all) into the air in front of the nearest person (a guy almost three times her size). Even though it didn't make contact, the guy's jaw dropped as he looked down and watched the knife twist. Kenzie yanked the knife backward, and chocolate frosting bloomed on the guy's shirt, spreading like blood. He should have been fine (if a little confused as to why Kenzie had mime-murdered him), but he dropped to his knees and fell face-first onto the rug. Kenzie took no notice. She was still wielding the cake knife, slicing and stabbing at everyone near her. The knife never went into anyone, but they all dropped like deadweight.

Kenzie's eyes were blank, empty as the abyss behind the wallpaper. When everyone in the room had fallen, she paused, licked the frosting off the knife, and smiled.

Nathaniel kicked the door closed.

"What are you doing?" I asked. "We have to help them!"

"They are already dead," he said, voice clipped with finality. "You tried to save the Drama Club, and it didn't work. They'll either get up again or they won't. We have to keep moving."

"Maddy May wasn't in there," Hannah said helpfully. "Kenzie is just pretending to kill some dudes. And honestly? Good for her."

Nathaniel gave an insulted *hmph* and might even have thought of something cutting to say in return if the tip of Kenzie's knife hadn't erupted out of the closed door. The blade wiggled, trying to slice at whoever it could.

We skittered down the hall before Kenzie could cut herself free of the dining room.

"She's definitely possessed," Remi said, panting as she trotted down the hall. "If I couldn't chop through the kitchen door with a fucking axe, there's no way that Kenzie Sullivan's little bird bones could get a knife through wood without being hopped up on ghost strength."

The billiards room was next. Peering inside, we saw that the beer pong tournament had been abandoned. Instead, the floor was covered in bodies, each one laid out like a plank.

Octavio had Nash by the neck, pressing him hard into the felt of the pool table. The veins in Octavio's arms were fit to burst, straining against the skin as his thumbs wedged into the larger boy's windpipe. Spit foamed at the corners of Nash's mouth as he thrashed feebly against the attack. The light in my hand shook, taking the scene in and out of view.

"Shh," Octavio whispered in the darkness. There was no malice in it, no anger. Just a horrible, hideous calm. "Shh, go to sleep now."

One of Nash's hands came up to palm Octavio's face. He tried to push, but somehow Octavio (so much smaller, so much weaker) powered through. Nash's hand fell away, and his body slumped to the ground.

Octavio didn't look up. Didn't notice us. He stood, gripping the edge of the pool table, and laughed until his whole body shook and his voice went hoarse.

This time I was the one who shut the door. It barely muffled the sound of Octavio's maniacal laughter, a wheezing clownish sound (all the more terrible because until this moment, I don't think I'd ever heard Octavio say *anything*).

"Oh my God, of course," Remi said. She pointed the blade of the axe at the billiards room and back at the dining room. "I'm so stupid. We're all so, *so* stupid."

"Literally a future rocket scientist and the valedictorian here, but go ahead," Nathaniel corrected under his breath.

"It's the stories!" Remi said. She shook the axe in the air to underscore her point. "Every story you've ever heard about the Deinhart Manor. And what happened to the family. They were stabbed. They were strangled. They were poisoned. And it's all happening again! Tonight! Right now!"

I gasped as the truth of it cracked open like an egg in my brain. Every rumor I'd ever heard, every scary story whispered at a sleepover, every fragment of hypothetical gore. A century of stories, none that could be verified even from inside the house. All of it blared in my head at once, playing beside the horrors of the night. It was like playing *The Wizard of Oz* and *The Dark Side of the Moon* at the same time. An eerie sync-up of the worst things I'd ever heard with the worst things I'd ever seen.

"Wait a minute," Nathaniel said. He pointed an accusing finger at Hannah before she could even think to make a face at him. "This isn't a correction. It's a question. Can I still be quizzical without being a monster?"

"It depends on the question," Hannah said blithely.

Nathaniel steeled himself, turning over the words in his head before speaking them aloud. "If everyone is living through one of the stories, then why aren't we?"

Remi opened her mouth to answer and stopped. She scrunched her nose in contemplation.

I thought about the night thus far. The phantom blood. Nathaniel nearly getting sucked into the wall by the ghost hands. The abyss in the walls. Finding evidence of other parties, lost to time (and probably ghost murder). Yara's drowning. Tanner's stabbing. Kenzie's knife still sawing through the dining room door. Now the loops of our class-mates dying only to come back and get murdered all over again.

Sounds like hell, doesn't it? That's how my dad's version of the Deinhart family myth went. A cycle of torment with no end in sight. No resolution. Not even the relief of death. Just endless suffering.

"We are, I think," I said. I bit the side of my thumbnail, my mind racing. "What's the one thing we know for sure happened to the family? Without a doubt, they died trapped in their own house. And now we're trapped here with a house full of more murder weapons than a Clue board. Maybe this . . . this *is* our version of the story."

"Wow. We really drew the short straw," Hannah said. "At least everyone else got to enjoy some of the party before they got murdered. All I got was possessed and a sprained ankle."

"We have more of a chance to get out than anyone else," Remi said. "We have the axe."

"Until you get possessed and decide to chop us all to bits with it," Nathaniel said.

We stood in an uncomfortable silence. I was sure that everyone else was also thinking about the dead look in Kenzie's and Octavio's eyes. Neither of them were killing people because they wanted to. Free of ghost possession, Remi wasn't likely to kill anyone. But who knew how quickly a ghost could inhabit her body and cut us down? It had happened almost in an instant on the dance floor, and all that took was setting foot in the wrong room.

"What if we had a safe word?" Hannah said. "Then we could check in with you, Remi, and make sure you're still you."

"Actually, yeah. That would make me feel better," Nathaniel said.

Remi bobbed her head. I was sure that if the light on my phone were stronger, I'd be able to see her whole face and neck turn beet red at the idea of her and Hannah having a safe word. "You'll know I'm me as long as I can still say 'Moose Tracks.'"

"Like the ice cream?" Hannah asked.

"There's a carton in my freezer," Remi said. "My mom got it for me in honor of graduation. I had it for breakfast this morning."

"Very loose definition of the word 'breakfast,'" Nathaniel said.

"It's peanut butter cups and milk," Remi said. She tossed her hair. "It's basically the same as a PB and J."

"Except the J is fudge," I said.

"I think it's cute," Hannah said, nudging Remi with her shoulder. "A breakfast sundae as a treat."

There was no world in which I could get away with having ice cream for breakfast and have it be charming. Not only would my mom go absolutely bugnuts if she found out, but the world would riot at the idea of a fat girl eating extra dessert. It's cute and quirky when a skinny girl eats unhealthy food but supposedly tragic when someone who looks like me does the same thing. Fatphobia and double standards are basically in a codependent relationship.

Before I could school the others in the ways in which

junk food is weaponized against fat people, the house's doors creaked open again.

Kenzie stepped into the hallway, the cake knife glinting at her side. Octavio came out, cracking the knuckles on both hands. Out of the ballroom, a pair of girls covered in blood-splattered drop cloths. Then, Top Hat, still covered in spider-webs, holding a bottle of wine. Maze drenched in blood, with a length of piano wire pulled taught. A hulking football player in a letterman jacket holding a single pillow.

They lined the hallway, standing perfectly still. Watching us. Waiting.

"Nate, take my phone," Remi said. She didn't take her eyes off the line of killers as she held it out. Nate took it gratefully.

"You can't fight off all of them alone," Hannah told Remi. "Even with an axe."

"I can try," Remi said.

"They're our classmates," I said. "And they're possessed. We can't murder them."

"We could slow them down," Remi said. "I'll aim low. Just take out their kneecaps or their Achilles tendons."

"See, now, it sounds like you *want* to chop some people up," Nathaniel said. He shone the flashlight in Remi's face, making her pupils contract down to pinpricks inside her blazing blue irises. "Say the safe word."

"Moose Tracks, geez," Remi said, flinching away from the light. "Fine, I won't use the axe. We'll find an empty room and barricade ourselves inside until the murderers take care of one another. Does that sound better?"

It did, actually. I wasn't sure if the possessed could hurt each other or even if they'd want to. But killing them before we had a chance to find a way to get the ghosts out of them definitely felt like a bad option.

Remi hoisted Hannah onto her back again. Nathaniel and I illuminated the way. Every stiff-muscled step brought us closer to one of the lurking killers. Each one stood sentry beside the rooms full of bodies. I held my breath and waited for one of them to leap out at us, to attack, to even make a single noise. None of them did. They didn't even watch us pass. Their empty eyes looked ahead at nothing, as though they could see through the walls. Directly into the abyss.

The farther we got down the hall, the harder it was not to look back. It was like waiting for a jump scare in a movie, except instead of a flourish of violins and a blur of movement, we were waiting for our classmates (people we'd seen every day for the last four years, people who lived in our neighborhoods) to try to kill us.

We passed under the second-floor landing. The front door was to the right. The stairs to the left. Dropping my hand, Nathaniel dove for the foyer, ready to abandon the party and try for the front door.

"Stay," said the killers. They spoke in one voice. A threatening, rasping whisper that seemed out of practice using vocal cords. There was too much glottal noise, too much pressure exerted on the lungs. It didn't get any better as they repeated it. "Stay. Stay. STAY."

They started to trudge. One foot, then the other. Plodding steps taking them inch by inch away from their respective kills. Their movements felt choreographed. Each step fell in unison with the others. There was a slight zombielike sway to their progress. Their faces lowered as though their foreheads had all become too heavy to hold up. The tops of their heads aimed at us like bulls ready to charge. Not bulls. Bucks. The Bucktown High mascot with its expanse of pronged horns. *Don't fuck with the Bucks*, as Remi said on game days.

"Goddamn it, Nate," I cried. I grabbed him by the T-shirt sleeve, twisting the fabric around my fist so that he couldn't wriggle away.

"I'm sorry! I had to check," Nathaniel said. He tried to jerk his sleeve out of my grasp and failed. "There's someone guarding the front door anyway."

The killers charged. I couldn't tell if they were still moving in perfect unison. I had to focus on running up the stairs.

Remi and Hannah lagged as Remi struggled with the extra weight while also holding on to the axe. Hannah's legs were starting to slip down Remi's hips.

I held out my hand. "Give me the axe, Remi."

"I'm good," she said. Sweat plastered her crooked bangs to her forehead. "I got it."

"Moose Tracks, Remi!" I shouted.

"That's not how we're using the safe word," she protested.

"You either need to drop the axe or you're going to drop Hannah!" I said.

"I'm okay," Hannah said. "I have excellent upper-body strength! AHHH!"

She screamed in pain as her bandaged ankle flopped down, colliding with one of the balusters. The wood broke away from the banister and fell over the side.

Remi gave me the axe. Bouncing Hannah higher on her back, she held the other girl's legs around the knees and jogged, double-speed, up the stairs, passing Nathaniel and me. Behind us, the killers had hit the bottom stair, which had created a bit of a traffic jam. Shoulder to shoulder, they couldn't all fit onto one step. Kenzie, Octavio, and Maze pushed to the front, leading the rest. I looked away, but could still hear the trudge of their footsteps approaching.

Remi hit the landing and kicked open a door on the right.

"No, that's the powder room!" I called out.

"It has two doors!" Remi called back. She and Hannah disappeared inside.

Nathaniel and I hurried to catch up. We piled into the octagonal powder room. I slammed the door behind us, turned around, and found Maddy May.

18

"Oh my God, we finally found you!" I said.

I threw my arms around Maddy May's shoulders and hugged her hard enough that her sapphire pendant dug into my chest. She didn't hug me back. She was angled toward the wall-length mirror, mascara wand in one hand, lipstick and eyeliner in the other.

"I'm so glad you're okay!"

"Are you really doing your makeup in the dark?" Remi asked. "You do know there are ghosts and murderers in this house? Are you trying to leave a pretty corpse when Kenzie Sullivan stabs all of us to death?"

"Ha ha," Maddy May said. She twirled the mascara wand over her lashes in a long swoop. "She jests at scars that never felt a wound."

"No, for real," Nathaniel said. He dragged the vanity across the room to barricade the door. The legs screeched and juddered, protesting the move. Bottles of hair spray and caramel-scented lotion clattered to the floor, leaving a trail of Sephora products in Nathaniel's wake. "She's not joking, Maddy May. There are people out there being possessed by ghosts. Possessed to kill people. A lot of people."

Maddy May sighed. "Poor Nate."

"Poor me?" Nathaniel asked, chest heaving with the effort of moving the vanity alone. "Poor all of us! Just be glad you weren't partying in the kitchen with the rest of the Drama Club. It's act five of every Shakespeare play down there."

"Ow!" Hannah hissed in pain as she lowered herself onto the chaise longue. "My séance high has worn off and my ankle is on fire."

"My backpack is in here," I said. I dumped the axe on top of the vanity. "I'll check and see if I have any pain relievers. There's probably a loose Advil or Midol floating around."

I knelt down on the floor and shone my flashlight under the chaise longue until I found one of the straps of my backpack. I dragged it out.

"You don't carry a first aid kit?" Nathaniel asked me. "Shouldn't they take away your Red Cross certification?"

"I have a first aid kid, but it's not like I'm stocked up on morphine and a medical boot," I said. I dug through my bag, shining the light inside so I could see to the bottom. Without my notebooks, binders, and school supplies, it was practically empty. "I have a couple of Band-Aids, tampons, and allergy eye drops."

"Oh, let me get those eye drops," Nathaniel said. He held out his hand. "All the dust in this place is killing me."

"Seriously?" I asked.

"What?" he asked. "It's not an emergency like Hannah's ankle, but it's still a medical issue."

"Of course," Maddy May said, offhandedly with a flick of her wrist.

"Thank you, Maddy May," Nathaniel said. "Finally someone is on my side tonight."

"Where did you put the money?" I asked Maddy May. Looking around the room, there was no sign of the vase that held the promise of my future inside. "You didn't lose my tuition, did you?"

"I never said that," she said defensively. She didn't turn away from the mirror. "It's just different now."

"Are you feeling okay, Mads?" Remi asked. "You didn't see any ghosts or possessed killers in here, right?"

I found a single ibuprofen in a pocket of my backpack and handed it to Hannah. "Sorry, this is all I have. Do you want help to the sink so you can get some water to take it?"

Hannah shook her head with a grimace, plucking the pill out of my hand. "I'll take it dry. I really don't want to stand up again right now."

"Bad time not to know anyone with a Vicodin addiction," Remi said, throwing a worried look at Hannah's obvious distress. "It's a serious issue and all, but there's never a pill-popper around when you need them. If my phone worked, I could call my brother's friend Jacoby. Then again, if my phone worked, then I guess we could call an ambulance and get you the good stuff in the legal way. I mean, it'd be way more expensive than getting it through Jacoby, but you'd also know for sure you weren't getting, like, meth mixed with baby aspirin or whatever."

I knew when Remi started word-vomiting that she was getting anxious. Apparently, she talked nonstop during her driver's license test and almost failed because she accidentally revealed to the person from the DMV that she'd been parallel parking her brother's car (illegally) for years because he'd never been good at it.

"Hey, Rem," I said. "You have a change of clothes here. You could wear something not covered in blood."

"But being drenched in blood is basically the team uniform now," she said. She spotted her shorts in a heap on the floor. "Although it would be nice to wear pants again. I chafed hard coming up those stairs."

"Thanks for sharing," Nathaniel mumbled.

"Do you guys hear that?" Maddy May asked, a mascara wand held up in the air like she was detecting a change in the wind. Something about it struck me as familiar, but I got distracted by Nathaniel grabbing the axe with both hands, ready to swing.

"Is it the killers? Is it a SWAT team?" he asked.

"Is it Remi's brother's friend Jacoby answering my prayers?" Hannah asked with a pained wince.

We all paused to listen, but I couldn't hear anything other than the toilet running behind the powder room's privacy door.

"I don't hear anything, Maddy May," I said. "What are you . . ."

Maddy May turned around, facing away from the mirror

for the first time. Seeing her face directly in the light almost made me drop my phone. Her face was repulsively slathered with makeup. Layer upon layer of bubblegum pink lipstick dripped from her mouth. It stood apart from her skin like a keloid scar. Her eyelashes (fused together into a few spikes) were so heavy with mascara that she couldn't keep her eyelids open. The eyeliner that had been a delicate flick earlier was now a crayon scrawl up the sides of her temples.

Remi gasped. "Mads, what did you do to yourself?"

"This room is beautiful," Maddy May responded, staring up at the strangely shaped ceiling. The many layers of lipstick weighed her mouth down, making her words sluggish. It had bled outside of the lines of her mouth, filling in her cupid's bow and sliding toward her chin. When she smiled, I could see pink lipstick staining her teeth, piled up in her gums. "This is it. We'll get ready here."

"You're done getting ready!" Remi said, voice sharp with irritation and fear. She gripped Maddy May by the shoulders and ducked her head down, trying to catch Maddy's attention.

Maddy May's glazed eyes looked beyond Remi's face. "It's cozy, like when we used to do our makeup in the bathroom at school," she said. She opened her lipstick and moved to set it against her lips. How many times had she already done this? One hundred? Three hundred times? How many layers of lipstick did it take to pile between your teeth like plaque and start to build on the rims of your nostrils?

"Maddy May, stop it!" Remi shouted. She wrestled the

makeup out of Maddy May's hands, prying up our friend's fingers one by one in order to free the worn-down tubes. Maddy May's face didn't register the assault, her expression blank and serene.

"Remi!" I forced my way between them, using the width of my hips to keep them separate. "Listen to her. She's not talking to us. She's just repeating what she said earlier. This is everything she said before the party. From the minute she came into the bathroom until you guys went to let everyone in."

Remi blinked in confusion? "Why? Why would she be possessed to relive the same moment over and over again?"

"Maybe she isn't possessed," Nathaniel said.

"Well, she'd never cover herself in makeup like this of her own free will!" Remi burst out. She thrust her finger toward Maddy May's slathered face. "If nothing else, she'd be worried about wasting such expensive products. That lipstick alone is like fifty bucks!"

Nathaniel took Remi's phone light over to the mirror. Opening his mouth wide, he huffed a hot breath onto the mirror. A circle of fog came up.

"Push her closer to the mirror," he instructed me.

"I'm not going to push her!" I said, horrified at the suggestion, by what I knew Nate was suggesting.

"Gently guide her, then!" he said, exasperated. "Just—just look for her breath, Arden."

I didn't want to. I already knew what I'd find. But Remi was looking mutinous, arms folded across her chest like she was barely repressing the urge to start punching everyone.

I took Maddy May's elbow and carefully moved her closer to the mirror. She didn't notice.

"We'll all be spread out during the party," Maddy May said. "And after that..." She trailed off, her face falling.

Even close enough for her lipstick to smear on the glass, nothing she said registered against the mirror. I put my hand in front of her mouth. Her next words were muffled against my palm, something about Remi's undying love and burning down the house. My heart sank.

"No heat. No air," I whispered. I looked up at Remi. "She's not breathing."

"But she's standing there!" Remi protested. "She's talking!"

"So were the Drama Club kids," Hannah said.

I set two fingers behind Maddy May's earlobe, searching out a pulse. I couldn't find one. Not in her neck. Not in her wrist.

"This is the last night that things will be exactly the same before everything changes," Maddy May said wistfully. She bit her lip, her teeth sinking in deep to the layers of lipstick. When she lifted her head again, she smiled her horrible, stained smile. "So let's make it the best night of our lives!"

I stepped back, my throat tight. My chest ached. I couldn't make myself say it. But I didn't have to. Everyone knew. Maddy May was here, but she was gone.

Remi couldn't accept it. She exploded, whirling around on each of us.

"Then why didn't the house take her body, huh?" she shouted. Her voice ricocheted around the room, pinging off the many walls. "Why didn't the ghost hands take her away?

Like Yara! Or Tanner. If there's something really wrong with her, then they wouldn't leave her here!"

"There *is* something really wrong with her," I said. "She's not breathing, and she has no pulse. She's...she's gone, Rem. Like Keaton. Like the people Kenzie and Octavio killed."

In Maddy May's makeup kit, I found a package of makeup remover wipes.

"Those are terrible for the environment," Hannah said. "It takes a century for them to biodegrade."

"The house will eat them," I said.

I drew out a few damp towelettes and gently scraped the makeup from Maddy May's face. She talked through it, not feeling the coldness on her skin, not noticing the heaviness being cleared away. She quoted Shakespeare and talked about the UNR Wolf Pack and teased Remi for showing booty cheeks in a short dress.

When I was done cleaning her up, she looked like herself. Fresh-faced and smiling that million-dollar smile, as bright and sparkling as the sapphire around her neck. I knew she would paint herself over again, layer after layer, loop after loop. But it felt good to give her a blank canvas to start with. It was the only gift I could give to someone who was already gone, even while she was standing in front of me, a shadow of the friend who had brought me into her little group of two. It had been just her and Remi for years, through elementary and middle school. Then, one day, Maddy May had noticed me sitting alone during a "Drinking and Driving" assembly. She recognized me from one of our classes together and invited me to sit with her and Remi. Then they found me again at lunch. She had adopted me like I was a stray cat, and she wanted to make sure that I had a safe place to return to.

It was awful to think that she was gone. That this could be the last time we had together.

"We need to keep looking for a way out," I said, using the final makeup wipe to scrub the phantom blood off my face. "We can't hide in here forever."

I motioned for Nathaniel to help me move the vanity away from the door. He didn't even complain that he'd just moved it into place. I got the feeling that no one wanted to stay and watch Maddy May's loops. Especially not if they were going to end like everyone else's.

"What about Maddy May?" Remi asked. "We can't leave her here! She's our best friend, Arden!"

"We can't take her," I said, looking away as Maddy May applied a fresh layer of lipstick and admired herself in the dark mirror. "She's not—she's not present. She's not in there. She's a reflection. An echo."

"We can't help her by staying in here," Hannah said. Even in the mostly darkness, I could see the pain on her face as she pushed herself to standing.

Nathaniel pressed his ear to the door. "I don't hear the horde of killers outside. Unless they're standing still, waiting for us to come out so they can murder us."

"A risk we'll have to take," I said.

"This room is beautiful," Maddy May said breathlessly.

I tried to take some comfort knowing that we were leaving

her in a place she loved. And we weren't really leaving her. She was already gone, a soul missing from its body. But it didn't make it any easier to walk away as she continued to chat and laugh in the darkness.

We filed out into the empty hallway. Closing the door behind us was like closing the lid on a coffin.

"What if she comes back?" Remi asked, her voice breaking. She was still clutching the doorknob. "She could wake up. And she'll be alone here."

"We need to know for sure whether it's possible for her to wake up," I said. "Whether or not anyone could. Maddy May. The Drama Club. Everyone."

"And how do you propose we do that?" Hannah asked.

"We need to ask the ghosts," I said.

"Not another séance," Nathaniel said, staring down at his shoes. "The last one went so, so bad."

"No, we need to ask them directly. I think..." I swallowed. "I think I need to go into the abyss."

WHAT HAPPENED TO THE DEINHART FAMILY

AS TOLD TO MADDY MAY BY HER COUSIN NAYELI ENRIQUEZ

The girl in the mirror was Mary Deinhart. She had the same blue eyes, the cleft in her chin, the freckles on her cheeks, same as the Mary who lived outside of the mirror. The Mirror Mary never smiled. No matter what real Mary did (sticking out her tongue or puffing up her cheeks or flipping up her eyelids, a talent her mother abhorred), Mirror Mary looked like the saddest girl in the world. Tears endlessly ran down her face like rivers after a rainstorm, never slowing or stopping. Real Mary ran from room to room, trying to catch Mirror Mary in a sunnier mood. But she never could. In the dining room, in the bathrooms, even in the polished silver spoon stuck into an ice cream sundae, Mirror Mary cried and cried.

Real Mary got tired of the miserable reflection following her around.

"Cheer up," she demanded.

"I can't." Mirror Mary wept. "I'm the saddest girl in the whole world."

"No, you're not," Real Mary said. "You're me. And I'm the happiest girl in the whole world. See?"

She smiled her biggest smile, the one that showed off all her teeth and her apple-size cheeks.

Mirror Mary cried even more.

"Isn't there anything I could do to cheer you up?" Real Mary asked. She even nodded her head, hoping to trick her reflection into mimicking her agreeableness.

But Mirror Mary just shook her head.

"I could give you my toys," Mary offered. "I have a dollhouse with furniture in every room and a real piano that plays the highest notes you've ever heard."

"There are no toys in the mirror," said Mirror Mary.

"Aren't you bored?" asked Real Mary.

"Every minute of every day."

"I could give you sweets!" offered Real Mary. "We have taffy and rock candy and Mallomars. You could eat it all. Before you got a tummy ache, you'd be happy."

"There's no food in the mirror," said Mirror Mary. "No sweets, no savories. Not even water."

"That sounds horrible," said Real Mary. "Aren't you hungry and thirsty?"

"Every minute of every day," said Mirror Mary. Her tears seemed to swell, now the size of marbles as they leaked down her face.

"Do you exist in the mirror when I'm not looking at you?" asked Real Mary.

"I exist as long as you exist," said Mirror Mary. "Just waiting for you to need me."

"You poor thing, no wonder you're so sad," said Real Mary. "It sounds like you need a hug."

"I've never had a hug before," said Mirror Mary. "I'm all alone in here."

"All alone? Every minute of every day?" asked Real Mary. "Aren't you lonesome?"

For the first time, Mirror Mary nodded.

Real Mary suddenly knew exactly what to do. She took off her shoe and slammed it into the mirror. The glass splintered. Mirror Mary's face fragmented, making her look almost like she was smiling. In the moment before the shards fell, Real Mary felt her own arms closing around her shoulders. She felt her own hair against her cheeks. Her own heartbeat against her chest.

"Thank you, Mary," said Other Mary. "Thank you for setting me free."

And then Mary was falling.

She found herself back in her room, alone and staring up from the floor. Mary was woozy and cold. She rubbed her head and wondered if she had been knocked down by the broken glass. Her mouth tasted funny, like she'd filled the inside of her cheeks with nickels and dimes. She was desperately thirsty.

Standing over her was another Mary. She had the same blue eyes, the cleft in her chin, the freckles on her cheeks. And the world's biggest, brightest smile.

"You're finally smiling," said Mary.

"Yes," said Other Mary. "I'm very happy. I finally get to do something I've always wanted. I will send all of you into the mirror. Your mother. Your father. Your brothers and sisters. Everyone who ignored me in the mirror."

"Don't hurt them," Mary begged. "It's not their fault. They thought you were me!"

"Yes." Other Mary smiled. "And now I am."

Mary reached out to grab her, but her hands collided with glass. She was trapped and could do nothing but watch herself move from room to room of the Deinhart Manor. Stabbing her parents. Stabbing her siblings. Smiling at her reflection as it cried and cried, covered in the blood of her family.

The girl in the mirror was Mary Deinhart. And she was alone. Every minute of every day.

19

"Into the abyss? That is a terrible idea," Nathaniel said, following too close as I started walking toward the nearest bedroom. "Like, the worst idea of the night. Worse than throwing the party. You want to walk into nothingness and see if you can talk directly to the ghosts?"

I stood my ground. "Where else would the ghosts be but on another plane of existence?"

I went into one of the bedrooms that wasn't connected to the others. The doors of an armoire were flung wide, with clothes tumbling out. Hatboxes and suit jackets were strewn across the bed. A glint of light winked off a diamond hatpin. I picked it up. It wasn't very big, about the size of a ballpoint pen and as thick as a pencil lead, but it had a needle-sharp end. I picked it up and stabbed it into the wall, using the end to scrape off the wallpaper.

"Do you want to use the axe?" Remi offered.

"The wall could absorb it," I said. "Then you won't have a weapon if the possessed show up."

"What if you can't breathe there? What if you get stuck?" Nathaniel asked.

"Then you guys will have to come up with a better plan without me," I said, chipping away at the wallpaper. "But people are dying here, and I have to try something big to stop it."

Finally, a corner piece of wallpaper came up. I grabbed it and pulled down, revealing a strip of nothing in the wall. It was hard to tell in the light from my phone, but it did seem like I'd punched a hole to the abyss. Knuckle by knuckle, I reached inside, waiting to feel the bite of teeth or the frost-bitten cold of space or even just a recessed two-by-four. But I didn't feel anything. Not even the other side of the wallpaper.

"Whoa," Remi said. She crowded in close to me and stuck her hand inside, wiggling her fingers in the void. "Let me come with you, Arden. Every episode of *Specter Sightings* says not to try anything without a trained professional. And I'm basically an amateur professional."

I set a hand on her shoulder. "You are. That's why you should stay here," I said. I couldn't take the chance that Remi wouldn't survive, either. It was bad enough that Maddy May was a shell of herself stuck in a loop. If Remi came with me, there was a good chance that none of us would survive this absolutely idiotic party. There needed to be someone to lead the way.

"Come on," she stressed. "Two heads are better than one. Even if one head isn't a genius."

"It has nothing to do with being smart," I said. I lowered

my voice to a sharp whisper. "Nate's right. This is probably the stupidest thing anyone's ever done. If I don't come back, you have to make sure that people get out of here alive. You take the axe and protect Hannah and Nathaniel and whoever else is still alive. Promise me."

Remi rolled her eyes, obviously wanting to push the point. Finally, she sighed. "Okay, fine, I promise."

Now there was nothing left to do but step into the abyss.

I set my foot inside. It didn't immediately fall into nothingness. But the ground was spongy and pliant. Like those playgrounds made out of shredded tires (minus the smell).

"Wait!" Hannah said. "I have an idea. Have you ever seen *Poltergeist*?"

I paused, half inside the wall. "No."

"*The Mist*?" she asked.

"Nope."

Nathaniel and Remi shook their heads, too.

"Wow," Hannah said, resting her weight against one of the posts of the bed frame. "Really? None of you watch scary movies? How do you practice emotional regulation?"

"Is that something we're supposed to be practicing?" Nathaniel asked.

"Yes. Otherwise every time you get a jolt of adrenaline, you'll immediately fall into fight, flight, or freeze," Hannah said. She started to laugh, looking to me and Remi to join her, but we both stared back blankly.

"And that's not what's supposed to happen?" I asked. I thought back to Remi and I screaming at each other at the beginning of the party. And when I'd yelled at Nathaniel not to call me Doc. Fight or flight was basically all my body knew how to do. (Although it seemed like it chose to fight every single time.)

"Oh, um," Hannah faltered. "They're acceptable responses. Totally human. There's just other ways to be." She cleared her throat. "Anyway, in both of those movies, when someone goes into the other side—a portal to purgatory or a fog full of monsters—they're tied to a rope to pull them back if they get too far. We could make you a rope out of bedsheets. Like people do when they're trying to crawl out of a window. Except for an abyss."

"It couldn't hurt to try," Remi said.

I wanted to say no. To dive into the abyss and find answers. Or just escape the horrors for a minute. But that was stupid, verging on suicidal. Safety precautions meant there'd be a better chance that I could come back and report what I found on the other side. If I found anything at all other than darkness and weird-textured floors.

I stepped back into the room. "Okay. Let's make a sheet rope."

Nathaniel stripped down the bed, sending a burst of dust into the air. We tore the bedsheets down the middle for extra length and knotted them together. When we ran out of bedding, we added in whatever we could find in the armoire. Jackets and ties and silk handkerchiefs. No one talked, not even Remi. The silence seemed to pour out of the abyss and settle over all of us, leaving only the task at hand.

When we'd run out of things to tie together, I wrapped

the makeshift rope around myself, feeling more than a little self-conscious about how many jacket sleeves and ties it took to loop around my waist. The same amount of rope would have looped around Remi twice. But I was the one who had insisted on going alone.

"If you need to get out fast, pull on the rope three times," Hannah said. She demonstrated, tugging the rope in a simple one-two-three pattern. "And we'll pull you out."

No one expressed any worry about their ability to pull me out, and I wasn't going to be the one to voice concern. It wasn't like they could tap out and have other people help. As far as we knew, it was just us left.

Standing in front of the hole in the wallpaper again, I was more apprehensive. Having the rope reminded me that I might need it. And that it might not work to pull me back. We didn't know where I was going. Or what I would find when I got there.

"Good luck," Nathaniel said. "Don't take too long."

"It's only an endless abyss," I told him. "How much could there be?"

I stepped inside the wall to find out.

There was air to breathe. That was good. I wasn't quite weightless, but I felt like I was floating more than walking, like I was a plane in a jet stream, buoyed along a predestined path.

It wasn't cold. Or hot. The air didn't smell or taste of

anything. I could see, even though there was nothing to see other than my own hands and feet. Everything around me was nothingness. My phone light was no help at all. It couldn't make a dent in the oppressive perma-darkness. But it felt better to have it on, to pretend that I would be able to see something coming for me.

I could feel my heartbeat pulsing in the crooks of my elbows and the palms of my hands, places my pulse always was but I never thought about.

Focus! Stay alert. Remember why you're here.

I walked slowly, feeling the sheet rope trailing behind me. When I looked back, the hole in the bedroom wall was a slightly lighter shade of black, a strip of charcoal against onyx.

Ahead, something glowed. The appearance of real light was so harsh, I might as well have been looking directly at the sun. Eyes watering, I squinted and moved toward it. I couldn't help but think about angler fish, those deepwater predators with the light on top of their head and rows of needle teeth. Was I just a stupid crustacean, falling for an evolutionary trick? I could have been walking directly into the jaws of some monster. (Or fish. Or eldritch horror.)

But the abyss wasn't the deep ocean. Or space. Or even an absence of place.

It was the manor.

I was staring in from the outside, as though my face were pressed against the window. But behind me was darkness, not the scraggly fruit trees or bright lights of town.

The light was coming from the crystal chandelier in the

foyer. I recognized the umbrella stand. There was no sign of the blood-filled words carved into the floor. The chandelier itself was sparkling, clean, and shining down on a white woman with steel-gray hair and a hammer. She was in an old-fashioned dress with a high collar and pointy-toed boots that would have gone perfectly with Yara's witch hat.

Despite the color of her hair, she was probably the same age as my parents. Her skin wasn't wrinkled, even though she was so thin the bones of her skull showed through her face. She had deep-set eyes and a downturned mouth that looked like it had never smiled.

There was no natural light in the house. The windows near the staircases were hidden behind bars of wood, long planks. Pieces of the wooden floor pulled up and nailed to the walls. The house itself had been cut apart to create the cage. Like a skin graft sliced from the thigh and sutured over a wound.

The gray-haired woman held a board over the front door and nailed it into place. It wasn't a floorboard. It was too dark and polished, like a piano bench or a shelf in a bookcase. Now it was part of a house-size jail cell. The front door. The last step.

The woman swung the hammer. This was a ritual she had performed many times. The nails held in her teeth, sticking out at angles. The hammer struck in a rhythmic pattern, a tune that only she could hear. When the board was in place, she retrieved another and another. Until the front door was almost entirely hidden.

When she was done, she unlocked the door and pulled

as hard as she could. She pulled like she was desperate to leave. Like she was the prisoner. When the boards didn't budge, she relaxed, pleased with her handiwork.

She turned back, looked up the stairs. There was a boy there, around my age, with his hair parted down the middle and oiled to his scalp.

"It won't work," he said. "You can't keep us here forever, Mother."

"We'll see," said the woman. Head held high, she flounced past him, up the stairs. I tried to follow her but couldn't. I wasn't in the house. I'd forgotten. I was looking in. I was in the mirror in the front hall.

Turning back to the abyss, I moved around the outside of the house, searching for another square of light. When I found it, I was in one of the upstairs bedrooms, the one with the crib and the dollhouse. It was as empty as it had been when Nathaniel and I had found it.

The steel-haired woman, older now (or just aged) sat alone in the rocking chair. Deep lines in her face marked the well-worn trails of her frown. She rocked back and forth in the chair, staring at the blocked window as though she could see out. The axe was laid across her lap like a pet. She was sharpening the blade with a chunk of stone, so practiced that she didn't even have to look down. The sound of stone on steel was awful and set my teeth on edge. But the woman didn't mind. She kept sharpening and rocking. Seemingly all alone.

I banged on the glass between us. "Hello?" I called. "Hello!"

But she couldn't hear me, and I couldn't stand the grinding of the blade, so I left.

The next window I found showed me a trio of teenagers. They were all boys, in matching overalls with grease stains. They obviously worked for a living. Two of them were puking in the kitchen sink. Above them, the kitchen window (which I had tried to smash with an eggbeater) was open, a single floorboard flapping to the side as though it had been kicked down.

"Come on, don't chicken out now," said the only non-puker. "I told you old man Deinhart musta been dead in here. That's why there's no one to sign the checks at the plant. You wanna work for free forever?"

One of the other boys lifted his head from the sink, eyes bleary. "They looked awful. Something real bad happened here."

"You thought you were gonna find pretty corpses? The rich die just as dead as the rest of us, furs or no," said the non-puker. "Now, no one's gonna pay for some dead bodies. We need to find cash or jewels. Clean yourselves up."

The steel-haired woman charged into the kitchen with her long skirt billowing behind her.

"Vagrants! Trespassers!" she hissed. "My husband gave you work and this is how you repay him! You come into my house? My house! MY HOUSE!"

The boys didn't even look at her. They couldn't hear her, like she hadn't been able to hear me. She was a ghost. And maybe I was, too. I couldn't be sure without pulling on the sheet rope, and I wasn't ready to leave.

The boys disappeared down the hall. I tried to follow them, but leaving my view of the kitchen brought me ahead in time. Now the house had a man sliding down one of the bedroom chimneys. Despite his mode of entrance, he looked nothing like Santa. He was young and shoeless and wearing too-big pants cinched hard with a belt. Ice froze his hair into points. Snow slush squelched out of his shoes as he landed on the hearth.

He went straight to the bed in the room and curled up under the covers. His teeth chattered so hard that it made his entire body tremble.

The old woman appeared suddenly, bending down over the headboard so that her face was inches away from the man's.

"Looks like you need a place to stay," she said. Then, she called out, "Boys?"

Six ghost arms shot up from underneath the bed frame and pulled the man down until his body was inside the mattress. The same way Tanner and Yara had been pulled into the floor.

In the next window, a young girl with tangled hair and a dirty face was alone in the front room. She was on her hands and knees, and the soles of her feet were so filthy it looked like she'd been marching through dirt. Her clothes were loose on her, like she'd either recently lost too much weight or she was wearing someone else's wardrobe. It was hard to tell.

Sawdust was strewn all over the floor around her. Over her shoulder, I could see the knife in her hand. It had a pearl handle and a silver blade that looked razor-sharp.

Concentration made her eyes squint and sweat pour down her temples as she carved deep into the floor.

I knew before she blew the dust away what would be there. One of a million cursive words carved into the floor. Only looking at it from this angle, high above her, did I realize that the handwriting didn't match. There were so many different versions of the word. Some small. Some cursive. But all the same four letters. **STAY.**

I ran past more windows. I watched so many people find ways into the manor. Squeezing through holes in the roof. Crowbarring boards off the windows. Climbing the drainpipe to break into the attic. All of them thought they were the first. Just like we had.

Kids who dared each other on Halloween.

Unhoused people looking for shelter from bad weather.

Teens looking for somewhere to drink or do drugs.

People looking to hook up.

People looking for the truth behind the rumors.

Years passed by and the house accepted them all. Took them all. Killed them all.

The deaths happened in the same places that they had at our party. Poison in the kitchen. Strangulation in the billiards room. Stabbing in the dining room. An axe cutting through all three of the connected bedrooms.

Sometimes it happened fast. People would come in and immediately get taken by the ghosts of the ones who had come before. The old woman stood apart from the other dead, barking orders at them that they seemed compelled to follow.

I didn't see anyone get out.

One group got close. The ones who tried to burn down the house. Their clothes didn't look like stereotypical hippies (the kind you could buy in a bag at Halloween), but there was something about the psychedelic print and acid green and yellow that made me think that this must have been the 1960s or 1970s. One of them looked like my grandma in pictures when my mom was a baby, in a super-short skirt with her hair pressed straight and teased into a bouffant.

My view of them was skewed. I was looking up from the bottom of their pyre, trapped in a mirror while flames licked at my frame. Everyone standing above me was blood-soaked and shell-shocked. In the distance, someone pounded on the door.

"I don't believe it. He killed them," said the girl who looked like my grandma. "He killed them all."

A white girl with long blond hair shook her head, clutching at the collar of her shirt. "It wasn't him. It's the house. It's cursed. Let's just burn it down and get out. We'll go out the way we came in."

She pointed to a window in the basement that definitely hadn't been there when we'd been down there earlier. It was tiny, the size of a doggy door, but it was open. A clear exit. Or maybe it was a trap. A trick the house was playing on them.

"It's the same thing that happened to the family that used to live here," said a guy in pants so high they almost touched his armpits.

"No, it isn't," said the blond girl. "They threw a party the day the stock market crashed and danced themselves to death."

"No way," said the guy. "They were murdered during a blizzard!"

A thin ghostly mist peeled away from the wall. Slipping through the air like a kite, it billowed around the room, creeping close to the people standing around the fire. Nobody noticed. It seemed to be scanning them for something. It had the shape of a person (head, shoulders, arms, and legs) but no distinct features. So it couldn't literally smell them with a nose or look them up and down with eyes, but it appeared to be doing both. Sensing something about each one.

It seemed most interested in the woman who looked like my grandma. It wafted around her, rustled her hair, rubbed against her dark brown cheek. Then it started to pour itself into her ear. Inching inside of her like a Q-tip far beyond the point of safety. Her breathing went shallow and panicked. She wrung her hands. As the very last bit of mist disappeared under the conch of her ear, her face sagged. Her hands fell to her sides. Her eyes went blank. Like Octavio. Like Kenzie.

"It's not the house," she said. All the emotion was gone from her voice. "The house is a home. The house is for all of us. You just have to want to stay. You just have to accept it. We belong here."

The axe was in her hands. I didn't even see her pick it up. It must have been beyond my vantage point in the pyre. But I could see her swing it in an arc overhead and chop into the carotid artery of the girl beside her. Blood sprayed every-where, including onto the glass of my mirror. Another swing and it cut into the abdomen of the guy in high-waisted jeans.

Behind them, the dog-door window shrank down to nothing.

I turned and ran, covering my ears to block out the sounds of their screams. I tried to find my way to the front of the house, where I'd started, where I could easily find the way back to the right side of the manor.

But a familiar voice stopped me dead in my tracks.

"Did you see the leaks in the basement? And that kitchen with one-hundred-year-old water damage. An absolute nightmare. The whole place is one strong wind away from being condemned. We're screwed."

"Kitchens always need to be gutted. Especially in old places like this. What would we do with a pristine woodburning stove?"

I pressed myself to the nearest glass, straining to hear them. My parents. Gloria and Rogelio of Lozano Flack Realty. Doing their walk-through of the manor, back before everything changed. When they were still married and I was still going to college and we were still a family.

Mom's hair was hidden under a scarf. She was prepared to get dirty but not willing to chance having to wash her hair on a weekday. Dad must have come from showing another property. He was in a short-sleeve shirt and tie, with dress shoes so polished that I'm surprised they weren't the mir-ror I was looking through.

The two of them stood in the music room where Yara

drowned. Dad knocked on the top of the piano. It rang out, hollow and slightly discordant.

Did Dad's hands itch to open the top and pull out one of the wires? How many had been cut away to murder people in that room?

"We could always keep things as they are," Dad said, admiring the room's intact crown molding. "Instead of a full flip, we could patch up the holes and keep it as a monument to town history."

Mom raised an eyebrow at him. Her *You've got to be kidding me* face. I'd seen it many, many times. (Most recently when I'd asked whether I could have a car for graduation.)

"You want to run a museum?" she asked flatly. "On top of selling houses?"

"We don't have to run it ourselves," Dad said. "Maybe the Bucktown Museum would buy it."

"Come one, come all, and see the house where some old rich family was murdered!" Mom said with a derisive laugh. "Museums are nonprofit, Ro. And we are decidedly *for* profit. Always on the verge of another market crash, always the threat of people undercutting us with cash offers or selling directly to apps. And now we have to think about Arden's college on top of it all. Four years of undergrad, six years of medical school. We need to be solvent. Beyond solvent. We need to be downright profitable and fast."

"And we will be," Dad said. "Maybe Arden takes a year off and helps us with the renovation. Every kid in Bucktown wants to see inside the Deinhart Manor. I bet she'd love to get a peek inside this place."

You'd bet wrong, I thought. The Deinhart Manor had been many people's dream (Dad's, Remi's, probably the hosts of *Specter Sightings*) but not mine. To me, it had always been just a house. And now, it wasn't even that. It was a mousetrap that had already taken the lives of my classmates and had the rest of us cornered.

"She could take a gap year," Mom mused, tapping her chin as she talked herself into the idea of taking away my future. "You know, it wouldn't take her long at all to get her real estate license through the community college. She could make some good money and save up for college. Med school isn't cheap."

Dread weighed down my limbs as I listened, knowing what came next. Mom and Dad would decide that my tuition was too expensive. That I was asking too much by wanting to go to Windsor, even though they'd always told me to reach for the stars before. Before we could no longer afford for me to be whatever I wanted because the money was already spent on a house full of blood and ghosts.

I almost wished that a ghost would take them over, that their eyes would go blank like so many others before them. At least if they were possessed, then I could say that they hadn't chosen the manor over me on purpose. That they'd had no choice.

But no. They'd had more choice than anyone ever had here. They chose the house.

"This place is special," Dad said, taking in the music room with the same intensity that he looked at heated floors and concrete countertops. "You can feel it, can't you?"

"The draft from the single-paned windows?" Mom asked.

"Ignore that," Dad said. He put his arm around her shoulders, planted a kiss on her temple. My heart ached to see them together again, so casually comfortable. This was the family I remembered. The one I missed with my whole heart. "No, there's a quality here. A sense of calm. It feels like we belong here."

"I feel it," Mom said with a sigh. She leaned into his arms, holding his hands in hers. "We were meant to have this place. To be part of its history. No museum, though. I want to get rid of every inch of carpet in here."

"Get rid of the carpet?" Dad said, tensing up. "You're crazy. It's in excellent condition!"

Mom pulled away from him. "No one is going to set foot on a hundred-year-old carpet! It needs new floors, Italian marble counters, state-of-the-art heating and air. It could be a dream home. A dozen dream homes. A bed-and-breakfast or an apartment building."

Dad waved her off, not listening. "You'll see my vision. You'll get on board. I've got the best feeling."

Wrong again, I thought.

Watching them, it felt like I was really seeing them as though for the first time. I'd never noticed before how hot and cold they were. How Mom was never charmed by him. How Dad was never impressed by her big picture. How they listened mostly as a way to pick apart what they disagreed with.

It reminded me of me and Nathaniel. (Ew.)

They left the room, arguing about flooring options.

Why could they walk out when no one else had? If our conversation with the Ouija board was to be believed, the ghosts didn't want the house renovated and definitely didn't want anyone else to own it. So why were Mom and Dad the first people in a century to get to leave this place? Was it all just a trap to get me to throw the party here? Could the ghosts see the future where I came into the house and brought along a bunch of seniors to possess into murder and be murdered?

I started to follow my sheet rope back toward the entrance to the abyss. Taking one last look into the backside of a mirror, I saw a fat girl with high cheekbones, brown eyes, long hair with frizzy roots. She was alone in a pale-blue powder room with its many walls.

It was me. At the start of the night. My makeup was still intact, the gold eyeliner a little too fancy for the jeans and T-shirt I was wearing. My hair was freshly straightened but could have used a hit of argan oil to make it shiny. But even as the me on the other side of the mirror paused, listening to see what was happening downstairs, unsure of being left alone, I could see that I was visibly excited. Nervously excited, but hopeful that the night would change the course of my life.

I was so right and so wrong all at once.

For a second, I thought she could see me. That *I* could see me. But I remembered how dim the mirror was, how impossible it was to make out even my own face in it. Little did I know that when I was trying to see myself in the glass, I would be able to see it hours later, covered in blood, wrapped in sheets and dead men's clothes, the witness of too, too many deaths.

I slammed my hands on the mirror, begging her (*me*) to get out, to never come back. But instead I just scared her off, sending her running downstairs into the party. There was nothing I could do to stop her. To stop the party from starting. To stop the murders from happening. All I could do was watch.

"She can't hear you," said a familiar voice.

I nearly screamed. The voice wasn't coming from inside the house. It was here in the abyss. With me.

Huddled on the ground, knees drawn up to her chest, eyes red.

It was Maddy May.

She wiggled her fingers in a self-conscious wave. "Hi, Ardy."

20

"Oh my God, are you alive?" I fell to my knees and held my hand in front of Maddy May's mouth. "Are you breathing?"

She started to protest, but when I wouldn't move my hand, she huffed an irritated breath onto my palm. It was hot and clammy. Hope sparked in my chest.

"Are you really you?" I asked. I clambered to take hold of her wrist and pressed my fingers to her pulse. Her heartbeat fluttered, elevated but steady. "Are you possessed? What's your secret opinion about Nayeli's nose job?"

"It's too small and now she always sounds like she has a cold." She wriggled out of my grasp. "Arden! I'm fine."

"You're fine? Can you see where you are?" I motioned around at the abject nothing that surrounded us on three sides and tried not to look at my past self running out of the mirror version of the powder room. The back of her/my hair looked awful. I'd missed a section with the flat iron.

"We're on the other side of the looking glass here, Mads. Inside the walls of the Deinhart Manor."

"Okay, so, other than that, I'm fine," she said. She hugged her knees to her chest. "I'm safe here."

"But you're not here," I argued. I pictured the Maddy May whose face I'd cleaned while she spoke the same words on a loop. "You're not *all* here. You left some of you behind. Your body, I mean. You were out there, in the powder room, putting on more makeup. You didn't have a pulse! I thought... We all thought..."

The words stuck in my throat. It would be ridiculous to cry over Maddy May's death when she wasn't dead, but my eyes stung with tears as I remembered leaving her behind. I held back the urge to check her pulse again.

Her brows knit together. "I'm still there?"

"You were just repeating things you said earlier when we were getting dressed," I said. "Like you were stuck on repeat."

"Oh." She picked at her cuticles, avoiding my eyes. "That makes sense."

"It does?" I goggled at her. Nothing about tonight made any sense to me, but this least of all. How had Maddy May's body and spirit separated? Why was Maddy May's body left behind putting on makeup over and over again? What was the abyss, and how were we inside of it, breathing and talking to each other and not being attacked by ghosts? Were we ghosts here, too?

Maddy May let out a long sigh and waved a hand at the powder room mirror. "Look."

Sitting up on my knees and holding my breath, I peered into the mirror. I don't know what I was expecting. (A jump scare? Kenzie and the cake knife? Ghost hands waiting to pull me out of the abyss?) But what I found was . . . us.

Maddy May, Remi, and I were walking into the powder room. We set down our backpacks. Remi yanked open the skinny door and gestured to the toilet. Maddy May set her flat iron on the vanity to preheat. I knew everything that would happen before it did. The beginning of the night played like a movie on the other side of the mirror.

"We get ready. Remi and I go to answer the door. You finish your hair," Maddy May said, only half turning to see what was happening. "Then you come close to the mirror, get scared, and run away. It starts over."

I glanced back at her, really taking in how puffy her eyes were under her waterproof mascara. Even though she seemed calm right now, she had recently cried. "How many times have you watched this?"

She gave a dejected shrug, eyes downcast. "A lot? I don't have my phone. I don't know what time it is. I think it might always just be the time it is inside the powder room? Anyway, you can't interrupt them. Us. The beginning of the party. You can bang on the glass and scream all you want. They can't hear you. Believe me, I tried everything."

"But I saw a hand in the mirror," I said. "Earlier. Just now. That's what made me leave the room."

"But we don't know whose hand you saw," Maddy May

said. "It could have been yours. Or mine. Or someone else who was back here a hundred years ago. Or a hundred years from now."

The idea made the hair on the back of my neck stand up. Maddy May might think we were safe in the abyss, but the surrounding darkness made me feel exposed. Anything could be watching us in the darkness. Waiting for us. Time could have been racing past in the real world, leaving us stranded in the past.

Careful to keep the sheet rope around my waist secure, I got to my feet. "Let's get out of here. Remi, Hannah, and Nathaniel are waiting for me in the primary bedroom. How did you get in here? Is there a hole in the powder room wall?"

"No," Maddy May said, evasive. She shifted uncomfortably, as though debating whether to tell me something. She'd looked the same way when I'd asked if she thought I could pull off green hair. "Something... someone pulled me into the mirror. It was me, I think. The me that's still there. My reflection. I know how it sounds—"

I cut her off. "It's a haunted house, Mads. Nothing is too weird here."

"Ghosts are real?" she asked.

When I nodded, she gave a watery smile. "Oh. Remi must be so happy."

"She'll be happier when she sees you! She still thinks you're dead." I held out a hand to help her up. "Come on. They'll pull us back to safety if I tug on the rope."

She shrank away from me, scooting closer to the mirror. "I can't go back! I can't face it, Arden. I can't face what I did to *him*."

I thought about the Drama Club heaped like laundry on the wet floor of the kitchen. Had she already seen them in one of the windows into the past?

"Keaton?" I asked.

"Tanner." She put her face in her hands and let out a sob. "I think he's dead, Ardy."

"He is," I said. The image of his dead body flashed behind my eyelids. The blood. The ghost hands. The place on the carpet where he disappeared. My stomach churned. "I found his body hours ago. Well, Nate and I found it, but he was no help, obviously. What happened?"

"It was awful," she said. Her hands slid down to the sides of her mouth, as though waiting to clamp down if she started saying something they didn't like. "I came upstairs to put the door money in a safe space so I could go join the party. Tanner followed me. You were right—I shouldn't have been flirting with him."

"You can flirt with whoever the hell you want," I said, seething at the idea of Tanner Grant stalking my friend across a party, cornering her when she thought she was alone. "You're flirty. It's allowed. It doesn't mean it's your fault when some asshole has no boundaries."

"We were in the hall," Maddy May said in a small voice. "He was drunk. His forty was empty. He asked if I wanted to join him in one of the bedrooms."

"What an absolute pig," I said. I thought about Claire

having a full-blown meltdown when she thought that Tanner had abandoned her at the party. When really he was upstairs, being a drunk creep.

"I told him no because I was with Keaton. Sometimes a guy will leave you alone faster if you have a boyfriend," she said, scrunching her nose as though she weren't proud of having to do whatever she needed to get out of a bad situation. "I told him that Keaton was expecting me to join him downstairs for a drink. But Tanner got in my way. He begged me. It was kind of embarrassing actually. He said that he had a crush on me for all of high school. And I told him too bad because high school was over. Which was too mean, I think. I went too far."

"You did what you had to do to get it through Tanner's thick skull that no actually means no," I said.

"I told him it would never happen between us. That I wasn't going anywhere with him. And then. And then."

Her voice broke. She looked up at me with wet eyes, mouth trembling.

"Maddy," I said, dead serious. I was ready to murder Tanner twice. To dive into every mirror in the abyss until I found a portal back to kill him before the ghosts could. "Did he hurt you?"

"He hurt himself," she whispered. "He smashed his empty beer bottle against a table. God, I was so scared. I didn't know what he was going to do. And then he started..." She mimed stabbing herself in the shoulder, in the stomach, in the neck. Everywhere Tanner's corpse had bled. "Over and over. But he didn't scream. He didn't even flinch. I thought maybe he was pretending. Until blood started *pouring* out of him. So much blood. It was everywhere." She covered her eyes again, as though she could block out the memory. "I ran away. I left him there. I didn't know if he was going to try to hurt me, too. I didn't know what to do. I just . . . I just hid. Here. At the beginning of the party, before anything went wrong."

I wanted to tell her that I understood, but I didn't. Not really. Everyone had their own response to the horror show that was our party. Nathaniel wanted to run away. Remi and Hannah took every shot or bong rip that came their way. I had to keep going no matter what happened. Slowing down too much would mean feeling all of it. The guilt. The shame. The rage. The fear.

Maddy May needed to hide to feel safe. Unfortunately, that feeling was a lie. As long as we were inside the manor, we'd never know safety again.

"You did what you had to do," I told her. "There's nothing pretty about survival, Mads. But you can't stay here forever. You'll become part of the house. We have to find a real way out. I won't lie to you. Things at the party are bad. Like really bad. But the house wants us to stay. And we can't give in. We can't give it what it wants just because it's too scary to say no. Right?"

Maddy May took in a deep breath and nodded, more to herself than to me. Slowly, she pushed herself to standing and smoothed the lines of her skirt.

Together, we looked back into the mirror at the girls in

the powder room, who laughed and teased one another in the warm glow of the blue room's light.

"We were so happy," Maddy May said.

"Idiots," I said. "They should have run when they had the chance."

I offered her my hand. She took it.

I tugged on the sheet rope three times, and we flew backward as Remi, Hannah, and Nathaniel pulled us into reality.

21

I stumbled out of the hole in the wallpaper, falling backward into the bedroom and onto my ass. Maddy May somersaulted into the bed frame.

"Maddy!" Remi screeched. She scooped Maddy May into a vise grip of a hug. "Holy shit, you're back!"

"Why is it so dark in here?" Maddy May asked. She combed her fingers through Remi's matted hair. "God, Remi, you're a mess. Is that blood?"

"It's not mine. The house rained on us," Remi said, offhand.

Nathaniel appeared above me, his concerned face upside down. "Are you okay? What happened?"

I felt dazed. Like I'd woken up from too much sleep, my brain murky and overstimulated. I scrubbed my face with my hands. "How long was I gone?" I asked.

"Gone? You just went in!" Hannah said. She helped me untangle myself from the sheet rope. Her hands were quick where mine were sluggish.

"Tell us everything," Nathaniel said.

I sat down on the floor and rested my head against the elaborately carved foot of the bed frame. Remembering the vision I'd seen of the man being taken by ghosts into *this* mattress, I scooted forward. Remi and Nathaniel sat on either side of me. Hannah sat with her good leg curled under her on a backward chair, her injured ankle stretched out. Maddy May hung back, closest to the hole in the wall, as though thinking about sneaking away again.

I turned my phone light on and set it in the center of us, so we could see one another better.

"Well, most important, I found Maddy May," I said.

Maddy gave an uncomfortable smile. "Sorry if you guys were worried about me."

"Worried does not begin to cover it," Remi said. "You are never allowed to die again, missy!"

"I didn't die," Maddy May said in a small voice. "I just . . . wasn't here. I'm okay."

I'd never seen Maddy May cringe at attention before (I had once seen her tap dance in a Starbucks), but she seemed embarrassed at the fact she'd been hiding while the rest of us ran for our lives. She hugged her arms to her chest, making herself physically smaller.

"Do we think this means the other Maddy May won't be in the powder room anymore?" Hannah asked, drumming her fingers on the back of her chair. "Or should we mark this one so we don't get her confused with her clone?"

"It wouldn't be that hard to tell them apart," Nathaniel said. "One is normal-looking and the other is a zombie with no pulse stuck in the past."

"The other me should be gone, I think," Maddy May said. She rubbed her heavy sapphire pendant between her thumb and forefinger. "That's how the story goes. There's one girl in the mirror and one in the real world. They can't both be in the mirror."

"But you were in the abyss," Remi said.

"The abyss is on the other side of the mirror," I said.

"And it's in the past," Maddy May said.

"This is making my head hurt," Remi said. "Dumb it down. Way down."

I did my best to explain the topography of the abyss. An outside perspective of the house. Peering through windows and mirrors. Rooms stuck in the past on a loop. A hundred years of ghosts and possession and murder.

"So many people have been here before today," I said. "And all of them died. They were either killed by the ghosts of the people who came before them or by the people they came in with. All the murderers were possessed. They had the same look in their eyes. A blankness. Most of them even wanted to leave before a ghost got in them and made them kill their friends. Some people died immediately. Others lasted longer."

Like us. I didn't say it, but I didn't have to. We all knew that we were on borrowed time. That at any moment, someone could reach for the axe and no amount of asking for the safe word would save the rest of us from the slaughter.

"It all looked random from the outside," I said. "People who come into the house die. All of them. Except..." I choked down a laugh, even though the situation wasn't funny at all. "Except my parents."

"Your parents?" Hannah asked. "What makes them special?"

"I don't know," I said.

How could I objectively view my parents? They were the people I loved most who had also let me down more than anyone else ever could. They'd given me everything I had but also shattered my dreams. Every thought I had about them was a contradiction of loving hate. (A phrase I'd heard somewhere before.)

"Nothing? I mean, they weren't the only people of color to come into the house. Or the only couple or the only middle-aged people. They were maybe the only ones to come through the front door because their contractor took the boards down."

"But everyone came through the front door tonight. It didn't stop any of them from getting murdered," Nathaniel said. He drew his knees up to his chest, folding in on himself. "Tanner didn't crawl through a window. The windows don't open!"

Maddy May winced at the mention of Tanner. I didn't want her to have to relive watching him kill himself. It wouldn't get us any closer to an answer.

"Nate," I said. "What exactly happened when the ghosts tried to pull you into the wall? Maddy May went willingly into the mirror. But you fought."

"Damn right I did," he said with a toughness that did not at all align with the shrieks I remembered from when the ghost hands took hold of his legs.

"Do you remember what you were feeling just before the ghosts showed up?" Hannah asked.

Nathaniel cocked his head at her, quizzically. "Do you mean was I suddenly homicidal?"

Hannah rolled her eyes. "Contrary to popular belief, men can have big feelings unrelated to anger."

"Um, I was waiting for the bathroom without my phone, so I was pretty bored," he said. He sucked his teeth in thought. "My bladder was full, so I was uncomfortable. I was wondering why I came to the party when most people I know are at Sober Grad Night. Then I saw Arden come out of a room and she said she was looking for Remi and Maddy May...then, boom. Ghost hands. It felt like they were trying to eat me, but they were just a bunch of hands. So, it was sort of like being attacked by puppets. Except without the puppets, you know? Just the puppeteer's hands."

To illustrate, he clacked his fingers against his thumbs. On the wall behind him, his hands became two gigantic shadow puppets.

A jolt of possibility made me sit up straight. "They were trying to eat you? It looked like they were pulling on you."

"It didn't feel like pulling," Nathaniel said. His brow crinkled. "They were surrounding me. Pushing me down. I was sliding backward, but it felt like they were trying to absorb me, starting with my feet, since that's what was closest. Or because they liked my shoes."

"Absorb?" I echoed. I sat up on my knees and gripped his arm. "Did you say they were trying to *absorb* you?"

He flinched away from my excitement. "Yes?"

Realization felt like the first breath of air after drowning. I shot to my feet and threw out my arms. We had been thinking about it all wrong. The ghosts weren't evil or demons or even necessarily conscious. They were a security system, the same as the phantom blood. The same as the bricks growing over the doors.

The house was trying to stave off an infection. And the infection was *us*.

"They're leukocytes!" I cried.

Nathaniel gasped, but he was the only one. Everyone else looked at me with utter lack of comprehension.

"I love your energy, Ardy, but what are lewd coal…?" Maddy May trailed off with a wince.

"Leukocytes," Nathaniel repeated.

"White blood cells," I clarified.

"In the blood rain?" Hannah asked.

"Yes! But no. Yes, metaphorically," I said. It all started falling into place in my head. A diagram that I had studied, memorized, and applied a million times just overlaid onto a different skeleton. "Think of the house as a body. Anyone who comes in from the outside is a pathogen. Bacteria. Something to be destroyed. So the ghost hands, like white blood cells, are in charge of fighting off the invasion."

"Like an army?" Hannah asked.

I started to pace. I would have given anything for a dry-erase board right now. "Not quite. An army *kills*. White blood cells *absorb* and break down. They digest bacteria. Chew them up and spit out the waste. So we haven't been watching the ghosts pull the dead into the house. When Yara died, it looked like they pulled her into the floor. But they didn't.

She wasn't in the basement. She wasn't in the abyss with me and Maddy May. She was *absorbed*. And so was Tanner. That's why there was no sign of his blood on the carpet. The ghosts absorbed it!"

Nathaniel got up, gripping his forehead. "I can't believe I didn't see it sooner." He suddenly pointed at me. "Shit, Doc, they're even diapedetic!"

"Yes! Oh my God! You're right!" I said.

The two of us jumped up and down, too giddy with understanding to think about drawing attention to ourselves.

Remi's head flopped back. "Guys. Explain. Not everyone is a medical savant."

"You guys didn't take AP Bio?" Nathaniel asked, pausing to look down at everyone's confused faces. "Arden and I both got As."

"But only one of us scored a five on the test," I said smugly.

"Humblebrag later," Remi said flatly. "Dumb it down for the dummy, please."

"Remi, you're not dumb," Hannah said. "Dumb people aren't curious about anything. You're curious about everything!"

Remi covered her cheeks as though any of us could detect her blushing in the mostly darkness of a couple of phone lights. "Oh, thank you. That's really nice." She rubbed a hand over the back of her neck and looked down at the floor before remembering that Nathaniel and I were in the middle of the world's biggest brain wave. She coughed. "Sorry. You guys were excited about a blood thing."

"Diapedesis," I reiterated. "It's when blood cells push through blood vessels and get into tissues."

"So . . . Like the ghost hands coming through the walls and the floor?" Remi asked.

"Exactly!" Nathaniel said, punching the air. "And white blood cells don't last long. They burn up in a few hours. Three days at most. That must be why the house needs so many people. The ghost hands burn up over time. So then the house needs to make more to protect itself."

The longer I thought about it, the more it made sense. The phantom blood fighting off the flames against the music room door and Claire's attack on the front door was an immunity response. The way the house was trapping us together in groups, rounding us up so that the ghosts could possess one person to kill the others. It was the same way that antibodies agglutinate antigens so white blood cells can eat them in one go.

"One of the worst—and weirdest—things I saw in the abyss was a possession," I said. I pictured the woman in a short dress who looked like my grandma. "A single ghost entered a person and made them murder their friends. But she wasn't the first person the ghost encountered. It went person to person, looking for the right one. It passed over two other people first. Which is something that a cytotoxic T cell does. It looks for diseased cells. Then it basically marks them for death by stabbing them with an enzyme. What if that's what the possessions are? A ghost recognizes that a person would be a good host and fills them with a murder enzyme that makes them cuckoo for killing."

"What is it that makes someone possessable?" Maddy May asked.

"I—" I faltered. I had been on such a roll but now came to a crashing stop. I wished I had a quick answer, one that could alleviate the guilt she felt over Tanner's death, but I didn't.

"I don't know. I couldn't tell from the outside. The woman didn't seem different from the others. She was even talking about how she couldn't believe that someone else had murdered a bunch of people. The ghost sensed she was right and went into her ear."

"Her ear?" Nathaniel stuck his tongue out and retched. "Disgusting. I hate knowing that. I don't want anything near my ears."

"What about everyone else?" Hannah asked. "Everyone who's trapped in a loop downstairs. Are they dead? Are they alive?"

"Could they be hiding somewhere, too?" Maddy May asked. "Other mirrors? Or different points in time?"

"Maybe," I said. I bit my lip as I realized that we'd been backed into another corner. We had found the shape of reality but not the cause. Knowing why the manor was killing us didn't get us any closer to how to get out. "I think we have to do what *Specter Sightings* would do."

"Recite the alphabet and see what the ghosts respond to?" Remi asked.

"We need to confront the only ghost who's survived this long," I said. My hands trembled. "The woman who boarded up the house."

22

"We just have to find the stairs to the attic," Remi said, helping Hannah to the bedroom door. "That's where the ghosts are. It has to be. According to rule number three, we should be able to follow our noses."

"I don't know if rule number three is applicable here, Rem," I said. "I haven't smelled anything rotten all night."

"But we haven't found the big bad yet, either," Remi said.

"Didn't you fail to find the stairs earlier?" Nathaniel asked Remi. "Back when the lights were on and no one was chasing us?"

"I also didn't find the abyss behind the wallpaper or the hallway that tried to eat you," Remi said. "Or Maddy May. Obviously, I wasn't looking in the right place."

Maddy May self-consciously tucked her hair behind her ears. "To be fair, I found a very good hiding spot."

"You were always the queen of sardines, Mads," Remi said with a grin.

"Remi's right," I told Nate. "The attic is the last place

to look. That's where her brother said he saw a face in the window. It could have been the old woman."

I wasn't any more excited to be searching out ghosts than Nathaniel. If the old woman was the ghost who I'd briefly chatted with via Ouija board, I wasn't thrilled at the idea of introducing myself as the daughter of the people fighting in court over who got to renovate the manor to their very niche preference.

And the old woman was old even before she died, so she could have been a real old-school capital "R" Racist. The kind who grew up with slaves, minstrel shows, lynching picnics, and *Song of the South* all in one lifetime. The kind whose slurs were so old and obscure that they made the N-word look gentle. She might have a problem with three brown kids and two queer girls traipsing around her house.

She could kill us on sight. Or have the other ghosts do it. Or have our possessed classmates do it.

All we could do was try to reason with her. Or die trying. It's what *Specter Sightings* would do. Minus the cameras.

It would have been nice if the odds were slightly more in favor of us living than us dying, but we'd already made it farther than most. Luck could take us only so far.

I held my breath and pulled open the door. No one was on the other side. The upstairs hallway was dark, empty, and silent. The blind corner at the end of the hall felt like a trap. It was where Nathaniel and I had found Tanner's body. Where the walls and ceiling had closed in on us. It seemed like the most likely spot to find something important. Why else would the house try so hard to keep people out?

None of us were rushing to be the first one there.

"Are you sure the old lady is the one we're looking for?" Nathaniel asked. He was holding the axe but kept moving it from hand to hand like he wasn't entirely comfortable being in charge of it. "It doesn't feel right. How often does someone's grandma murder a bunch of people?"

"Female serial killers are rare but definitely not impossible," Remi said, walking slowly so that Hannah could limp along beside her. "And old-lady killers are totally a thing. The Death Row Granny, Russia's Granny Ripper, and Dorothea Puente, who doesn't have a cool nickname but killed people for their Social Security checks. The thing about female killers is that they're harder to catch. Sneakier. Way more likely to use an undetectable poison to kill their victims."

Maddy May shuddered. "You know I hate when you talk true crime."

"I don't feel like gender would be a big deal in the afterlife. It's a societal concept, not a burn on your soul," Hannah said. Her phone light waggled with every lopsided step, flicking up toward the ceiling, then straight ahead again. "Besides, maybe the old lady doesn't know that the other ghosts are killing people. She could be an innocent bystander."

"Maybe," I said. I thought back to what I'd seen in the abyss: the old woman sharpening the axe over and over again, then the hippie girl possessed into murdering her friends with it. I hadn't mentioned that I'd seen the axe in Nathaniel's hand kill two people. We might need it to get through a locked door, and I wasn't sure how everyone else would feel knowing that we were carrying around a murder weapon. It seemed better to let them live in blissful ignorance.

We made it to the bend in the hallway and came to a gradual stop. My heart sped as I remembered Tanner's hacked-apart corpse sprawled across the carpet.

Peering around the corner, my insides felt hollow. Nathaniel adjusted his grip on the axe. Maddy May screamed.

Kenzie. Octavio. Maze. Top Hat. The drop cloth ghosts. At the other end of the hallway, all the party's possessed murderers stood shoulder to shoulder with their chins to their chests like they were all mid-nod. But their eyes were staring up from under their eyebrows.

Behind them was a slim door.

We froze in place, Nathaniel standing in front. When he realized he was an inch closer to danger than the rest of us, he took a generous step backward. (He wasn't chivalrous, but he was consistent.)

"They wouldn't guard the door if it wasn't important, right?" Hannah asked in a tight whisper.

"It could be a trap," Nathaniel said tremulously.

"The whole house is a trap," I said. I smothered my phone light against my chest. "If they don't want us to go through that door, there's probably a good reason."

We shied backward. Hannah had to hop, which made muted thuds on the carpet. Each one made my breath hitch. It wasn't reasonable to be more scared. The group of killers had already seen us (at least I assumed they had; I wasn't sure if the ghosts puppeting them could see through their eyes), but drawing attention to ourselves seemed like waving a red flag at a bull.

We hung close to the open door of a bedroom. Not near the walls (in case of ghost hands) but close enough that we could dart inside if we heard movement.

Fear sent an ice pick of adrenaline into my spine. Cold sweat stung my eyes and pooled above my upper lip.

"We have to get them away from the door," I said.

"Okay, great," Remi said with a manic, disbelieving laugh. "How? It's five against at least eight. We have one weapon, one injury, and Nathaniel. That's a lot holding us back."

"Hey! I'm the one with the weapon right now," Nathaniel said, as though anyone could overlook the blade resting against his shoulder.

"It's not about the weapon, it's about knowing how to use it," Remi said.

"We need a plan," Hannah said, wavering as she kept all of her weight on one foot. It was hard to tell with only a cell phone light to see her, but she looked pale and pinched, like the pain of her ankle was getting worse but she didn't want to bother anyone by saying so.

"Are we sure I can't just kill them?" Remi asked. "I could take the axe—since I'm the one who found it and: finders keepers—then, chop, chop, chop. We get through the door."

"Remi!" Maddy May spluttered. "You're not seriously suggesting *killing* our classmates?"

"Not killing them," Remi protested. "Stopping them. They're possessed."

"Exactly," I said. "They're possessed. Not zombies. They don't deserve to die!"

"They're not *not* zombies, though," Hannah said diplomatically. "They are a mindless horde of infected people who may or may not be dead, who have a shared objective to kill."

"Now who's correcting people too much?" Nathaniel muttered.

I pinched the bridge of my nose, staving off an irritation headache. I'd been getting them more since my parents had started fighting over the manor.

"I concede that they *might* be zombies," I said. "But Maddy May's right. That doesn't give us the right to kill them."

"Fine. We wouldn't want to stoop to the level of zombies," Remi grumbled. Her phone light winked out of existence, leaving us with one extra patch of darkness. She slapped the side of her phone and swore. "Out of battery."

"I'm at thirteen percent," Hannah said.

I checked my phone and felt my stomach drop as I saw the battery icon no longer green. "Thirty-two," I said.

"I don't have my phone," Nathaniel said with a dark look at Maddy May. "*Someone* told me I wasn't allowed."

Maddy May fixed him with an unimpressed stare. "You live stream too much, and you don't even have a private account! Plus, there was the egg-drop thing."

Time was running out. As unlikely as it seemed for any of us to find a way out of the house, the chances without any light at all seemed even smaller. It was hours until dawn.

"We'll take turns using our flashlights," Hannah said. "We'll use mine until the battery dies, then switch to yours, Arden."

It was a good idea, even though I hated being more in the dark. I switched off my light and held back a wince as Nathaniel disappeared from my view. I could see only the faint glimmer of light shining off the axe.

"We can't fight off the possessed," I said. Talking made the dark less scary. I wasn't alone. There were people to talk to and plans to make. "They already overpowered everyone else. We have to outsmart them."

"What about a trap?" Nathaniel suggested. "We need them all distracted for long enough for us to get through the door."

"They could follow us through the door and then kill us," Remi said.

Nathaniel let out an exasperated growl. "The ghost hands could come out of the carpet and absorb us into nothingness at any moment! We still have to try!"

"They want someone to kill. Or to kill all of us," Hannah said. "We could lure them with bait." She lifted her light and scanned it over each of us to gauge our reaction.

"Not it," Nathaniel said immediately.

"Obviously," Remi said. "You're too much of a coward."

Nate glared at her. "Reverse psychology won't work on me, Remington."

"Oh, it's not reverse psychology," Remi said, matter-of-factly. "Just the honest-to-God truth. I think that if we tried to use you as bait, you'd legit die of fright. Or trip and fall on Kenzie's knife. Not worth the risk, honestly."

"Then you do it," Nathaniel said in a huff. I could almost see his pride visibly dinged by Remi's tactless truth. A common problem of spending too much time with Remi. If you weren't in the mood to have yourself reflected back by her unflinching mirror, you were going to end up burned by honesty. Like when she'd told me that my favorite winter coat made me look like an old couch. It hurt, but I needed to hear it.

"I'm the bait," Remi said. Her posture deflated a bit as she realized what she'd signed on for. "So, what should I do? It's not like we have a big pit we can cover over with leaves."

"Or a ton of time," I said, biting my thumbnail. "We don't want them to follow us up to the attic. It would be best if we could lock them in a room since the house won't do it for us. Then, even if we don't find anything in the attic, we could be less worried about them, you know, murdering us."

"Could we build a barricade?" Maddy May asked. "Like in *Les Miz*. Just stack a bunch of furniture in front of the door so they can't break through."

"It would take too long," Nathaniel said. "The June Rebellion had a hundred thousand people to build barricades and they still failed." He looked around at our stunned expressions. "What? I read *Les Misérables* for AP Euro test prep."

Remi bounced up and down, electrified by an idea. "I know! We can tie two doorknobs together. Lock them in one room, then make it so that they can't open the door because it's tied to the door across the hall. My brothers used to do that to me with a jump rope on the bathroom doorknob tied to the hall closet. It was impossible to break free."

"That would be great if we had a jump rope," Maddy May said.

Hannah's face lit up with a smile. "We have a sheet rope," she said.

I ran back to the bedroom with the hole in the wallpaper and got the sheet rope. Remi tied it to the doorknob and snaked it across the hallway so we could pull the door shut from the opposite bedroom and tie the doors closed.

"You'll have to run really fast," Hannah said, pressing her phone into Remi's hand. It was more important that Remi be able to see while running than we be able to see while waiting and hiding.

"Of course I'll be fast," Remi said. "You were my captain. You know I crush running drills."

Hannah held herself up by gripping the door. "This isn't volleyball, though. It's life-or-death."

"Same difference," Remi said, flashing her cockiest smile. It was almost hard to see the glint of fear in her eyes.

Hannah looked away, her face crumpled in worry. It was the least chill I had ever seen her. She fiddled with one of the straps of her overalls and tried briefly to hold herself up on both feet. With a huge sigh, she turned back, set her hands on Remi's cheeks, and pulled her face down to kiss her full on the mouth.

Remi clutched the back of Hannah's head, her knees bowing drunkenly as she melted into the kiss. It went on long enough that I heard Nathaniel open his mouth to say something. I elbowed him in the ribs to shut him up. Making out with Hannah was Remi's dream come true. It was only right that she should have it, unrushed, before risking her life to save the rest of us.

Hannah broke the kiss first, pulling back with a smirk.

"Now you have to make it back," she said.

Remi blinked, looking utterly disoriented. "Something to live for, cool," she said.

"No dying allowed, Madison Remington," Maddy May told her.

Remi saluted and sauntered into the hallway. The light pointed up at her chin, illuminating her jack-o'-lantern grin.

Watching her go, I knew that it was completely possible that this could be the last time I saw her. That the murderers could swarm her. That one could get lucky and take her down. Or that the ghost hands could decide that she needed to be absorbed.

I wanted to tell her how much I appreciated her friendship. That having her and Maddy May by my side was the only thing that had gotten me through the last few months. That she was the loud, overly confident, beautiful mess that I wished I could be. Never afraid to take up space. Never worried about being too much.

But instead I just told her, "Knock 'em dead."

Which made her laugh.

She stretched her arms overhead, then pulled her feet to her butt to stretch her quadriceps. She didn't look back again before she took off like a shot around the corner, shrieking, "Who wants to see if they can outrun a Bucktown High queer icon?"

From behind the bedroom door, we couldn't see whether

Remi had successfully lured the horde away from the door. But Remi (ever helpful, never subtle) shouted from somewhere near the second staircase, "They're chasing me! Oh fuck, oh fuck, oh fuck!"

I wasn't sure if the panic in her voice was sincere or a show to keep the killers on her trail, but I wouldn't have been surprised either way.

"What if they come in here instead?" Nathaniel asked in a panicked whisper.

"Then you need to use the axe," I told him.

"What about not killing our classmates?" he asked.

"It's a last resort!" I hissed back.

The door rattled on its hinges as Remi and the horde approached. I held my breath, terrified that a killer would come through the door ahead of Remi. Or that all of them would. Or that we'd have to listen as Remi was brutally murdered. I'd seen so much death. I couldn't handle seeing hers. If I had to, I'd take the axe from Nate and kill the possessed myself.

But Remi tripped and fell over the threshold, gasping for air and saying, "Do it now!"

We pulled the sheet rope as hard as we could. Immediately, I could feel it tug back as the horde tried to free themselves from the other room. I looped the sheet rope around my forearm and yanked it taut, while Maddy May tied a triple knot around the doorknob.

"Let's go, let's go, let's go," Nathaniel chanted, eyes darting to the door across the hall. "If any of the knots in the middle give, then we're fucked."

Remi put Hannah on her back and cheered the whole

way back to the attic door. I kept looking over my shoulder, convinced that the possessed horde would burst out of the locked room and stampede toward us, a single-minded mass with only one place to aim its killing energy.

We made it to the attic door without the hallway shrinking or collapsing in on us. Nathaniel reached out, grabbed the knob, and stopped. It clicked in his hand like an empty pistol. It was locked.

"Goddamn, bodyguards and a locked door?" Remi said, panting for air and holding Hannah high on her back. "There'd better be something good behind there because this is overkill. I mean like gold or whatever-was-missing-from-Al-Capone's-vault good."

"We'll cut the hinges off," I said. I looked at Nathaniel, waiting for him to do the honors of breaking us into the attic. He hadn't moved. "Nate?"

Hannah shone her phone light at the doorknob. Nathaniel's hand was still gripping it. So hard that his veins bulged, wormlike, all the way up his arm. The axe head dropped to the carpet with a dull thud.

Nathaniel staggered back a step, gripping his stomach like he was about to throw up. Through his clenched fingers, wetness spread. Blood. Stark red against his palm.

He looked at me, eyes wide. "Doc?"

The tip of a knife was sticking out of the door's keyhole.

I couldn't process what was happening. I watched as the handle turned. Kenzie stepped out. The cake knife, tip dripping with Nathaniel's blood, was in her hand.

In the air.

And then, with a flash, stabbing me.

23

Kenzie Sullivan stabbed me the same way that my mom hit the key fob on her car: once out of habit, two more times to make sure the job was really done. The first one hit my shoulder, the second sliced my arm, the third was in the meat of my thigh.

The axe came out of nowhere. The flat of the metal head connected hard with Kenzie's temple and sent her flying back. Nathaniel roared with pain as he swung, but he'd hit her hard enough to make her slam into the opposite wall.

"Not lethal," he said, head and shoulders drooping as the axe (and the hole in his stomach) weighed him down. "But I should have killed that zombie."

"Where did she come from?" Maddy May asked, frantically looking around for signs of the other possessed. "Why wasn't she with the others?"

"I swear, I thought she was following me when everyone started running," Remi said. "Arden, are you okay? Are either of you okay?"

"Okay?" Nate asked. "We got stabbed!"

I didn't want to consider whether I was okay. I didn't want to register the throbbing pain radiating down my right side. At some point, I had dropped my phone on the floor. Stooping down to pick it up was worse than the actual stabbing. I could feel all of my wounds open wider, three mouths screaming in simultaneous agony. But I scooped the phone up and stuck it in my back pocket.

"Gotta keep moving," I said. If we couldn't get free, we couldn't get to a hospital. Blood was flowing freely down my arm, coating the old phantom blood with my own plasma. I was hot and cold and woozy. I was worried about the arteries in my shoulder and thigh. If the cake knife had nicked either of them, I would bleed out. Nathaniel's stomach wound was even more dangerous. He could have a perforated bowel, a ruptured spleen, or damaged intestines. We could both get tetanus from the old cake knife or some kind of blood infection from getting stabbed with a communal murder weapon.

Basically, we were fucked without an ambulance and a way out of the house.

But the only way out was up. Up the attic stairs to see if there was anyone to reason with. Remi closed the door behind us.

We froze. The staircase looked more like an air duct than a passageway. It was a dark, cramped hole that only one person would fit through at a time.

"It'll be fine," Remi said, tremulously. "We'll climb up like it's a tube slide. No problem."

"So you're going to go first?" Nathaniel asked her. He was doubled over in pain.

Remi gulped. "Sure."

We watched as she wedged herself into the hole, head first. It took a moment of struggling for her long legs to make it inside. Once she was in, there was no sound of her. No creaky floorboards or colorful swearing. Not even a scream. Just silence.

Maddy May, Hannah, and Nathaniel looked at me in mirrored panic.

I knew that the point was to make us give up so that we would turn around and die. And I would be lying if I said I didn't consider it. The hole to the attic was small enough that I worried about getting stuck, legs dangling Pooh Bear style as my hips and stomach trapped me half-in, half-out. But that would be embarrassing. Staying down here would be lethal.

"Make a fist," I told Nathaniel.

When he did, I said, "Now press as hard as you can into your wound."

Bellowing in anguish, he pulled his hand away immediately. "Why would you make me do that?"

"You need to staunch the blood flow," I said. Taking a taste of my own medicine, I shoved my knuckles into my shoulder, which hurt the most of all my wounds. I bit the inside of my cheek to keep from crying out. "You need at least seventy percent of your blood to live."

"I really hate your blood facts," Nathaniel said. But he put his fist back over his stomach with an anguished grunt.

"I'll go next," I said.

It was humiliating to get down on my hands and knees in order to fit into the hole. I tried not to think about how utterly unflattering a view this would be (because God forbid I didn't look hot while crawling for my life). I set a hand inside on the first step. My fingers passed through the unmistakable clinging gauze of spiderwebs.

I yanked my hand back. Nausea rolled over me. My mouth started to sweat. My skin crawled. But if I puked in the hole, I'd be damning myself and everyone else. It wouldn't make anything better. It would make everything worse. If I let my fear show, the others might not come in after me. It was a choice they had to make for themselves.

I started crawling.

Spiderwebs broke all around me. Sticking to my hair. Trailing from my clothes like streamers. I couldn't see anything. Not Remi ahead of me. Not the attic stairs behind me. I didn't know if Maddy May, Hannah, and Nathaniel had followed me in. The constricted ceiling and walls scraped against my arms and legs. I was so focused on the pain that it took me a moment before I noticed the spiders.

They were everywhere. Crawling all over me. Scurrying over my hands. Plunging into the deep cuts on my shoulder and thigh. Biting the thin skin of my eyelids. Burrowing into my ear canal, skinny legs scraping against the membrane of my eardrum.

I stopped moving. Hot tears seeped out of the corners of my tightly shut eyes. Spider fangs pricked everywhere my pulse pounded (under my jaw, the crooks of my elbows, the backs of my knees) like they were trying to flood their venom directly into my veins.

Quick, ragged breaths made my diaphragm jump. Every second was a torment, hell on earth. My impulses bypassed fight, flight, or freeze and went straight to give up, lie down, and die. I wanted to scream until all the ghosts found me and tore the soul out of my swarmed corpse. At least then I'd have peace.

But choosing to die (here, halfway between the known and the unknown) would be damning so many other people. Remi, alone in the attic. Maddy May, Hannah, and Nate, waiting to follow me up the endless stairs. Everyone downstairs caught in a murder loop at a party I'd thrown to save my own ass.

It's discomfort or death, I told myself, clamping my teeth together. If I opened my mouth, there was no telling how many spiders I'd choke down. *You can stand the discomfort if it means surviving. You have to stand the discomfort. That's all there is.*

I made myself crawl up another stair. And another. There were so many. Too many. I lost count after the first thirty. Was the house stretching them out like it had done to the hallway? Making us climb until our legs gave out or we bled to death?

It felt like forever, but (finally) there were no more stairs to climb. Just a landing with another closed door. Remi stood there, waiting.

There was no light source (no lamps, no candles) but I could see clearly for the first time since the abyss. Looking down at myself, I was shocked to see that there wasn't a single cobweb stuck to me. No bites on my arms or spiders in my hair.

"No bugs?" I asked Remi.

She checked me over, parting my hair and dusting off the back of my shirt.

"No bugs," she confirmed.

I let out a long sigh of relief, even as my skin continued to crawl.

Maddy May came up the stairs next. Shivers wracked her body. She squeezed between Remi and me, linking elbows with us like we were about to follow the yellow brick road.

"I'm f-freezing," she said.

"You are?" Remi asked. "I'm still sweating from the climb."

I set the back of my hand against Maddy May's forehead. "You feel normal to me, Mads."

Her teeth clattered indignantly. "Are you kidding? It was, like, negative one million degrees in there!"

Hannah came out with her fists over her eyes. When she peeked up at us, she said, "It was like the top of the house didn't have a roof. The wind was so realistic. It felt like it could sweep me away."

Nathaniel fell up the stairs, out of breath and kicking wildly. He stopped when he saw the rest of us standing there.

"Did you not see all the rats?" he asked with a shudder.

"I didn't feel anything in there," Remi said. "No light, no sound. I couldn't even feel the stairs. I thought I was already dead."

"It was spiders for me," I said. I scratched the back of my neck, trying to get the goose bumps to lie flat.

"Oh." He gulped. "The house is customizing nightmares for us now. Great, just what we needed. I, personally, was tired of seeing all the same horrifying shit as everyone else."

"Did the house make us see it? Or did our brains?" Maddy May asked.

"I don't know if it matters," I said. "The point was to scare us."

"Mission accomplished," Nathaniel said.

"Ready?" Remi asked.

She didn't wait for a response before she opened the door.

It was the shape of an attic. Pointed roof, a round window looking out onto the broken roof of the front porch. But everything else was blackness.

I thought back to the stacks of floorboards in the basement, the ones the contractor had pulled down from every door and window in the house. They had to have come from somewhere. There hadn't been any huge holes in the floor downstairs. Like Remi said, no holes in the floor to cover with leaves.

This was the hole.

Floorboards, clapboards, even the joists and beams had been dismantled to board up the doors and windows. So much of the wood had been taken that the house had only this faint memory of the shape of the attic.

The abyss, shaped into a third story.

The abyss, holding up the roof.

The abyss, with a single round window, like a porthole looking out over Bucktown.

Standing at the window with her back to us: a steel-haired woman in a high-collared black dress.

"Mrs. Deinhart?" I guessed.

She turned around. An unbearable putrid smell stole the air from my lungs. It was cloying sulfuric sewage. Pure putrescence that went far beyond rotten eggs. And underneath all of it, something strangely sweet. Like a single flower blooming out of the wet muck of a fetid corpse.

The woman smiled.

"I expect you want an explanation," she said.

24

The old woman didn't look much like a ghost. Sure, her clothes were PBS-costume-drama old. And her hair was in the same gray Gibson girl bun I'd seen her wear before, the sides fluffy and confectionary soft. But she seemed solid and real. (Although that could have just been in contrast to our immaterial surroundings.) Still, it was impossible to ignore the stench coming off her in waves. *Specter Sightings* rule number three was apparently true. Ghosts smell absolutely awful.

"Deinhart is my married name. I used it when my husband was alive," she said. With an ironic sort of smirk she added, "When *I* was alive. But I always preferred my birth name. I was born a Buck."

"A Buck?" I asked, my eyes watering from the smell. "As in Bucktown?"

"Just the same," Mrs. Deinhart said with a haughty flick of her wrist. "My grandfather founded this town. Built the first house on the land. He even planted the fruit trees on this hill with seeds he carried in his pocket across the ocean. Before him, there was nothing here."

"Pretty sure the local Indigenous tribes would have a less flattering story about how that went down, but okay," Hannah said.

Mrs. Deinhart ignored her. "This hill was a gift from my parents. My husband, Gerd Deinhart, built the house here as my wedding present. The manor was built to house generations of Buck descendants. A place where we could survey the town we established and maintained in honor of our forefathers."

"There are no Buck descendants," Nathaniel said. He crossed his arms tight, his fingers digging into his biceps. His throat audibly clicked as he worked to stop himself from gagging. "Or Deinharts, for that matter. The last distant cousin died, which is how Arden's parents finally bought the place at a bank auction."

I tried to swallow my surprise that Nathaniel remembered all that. Back when we were still hooking up, I'd told him about the bank auction and my parents' dream to renovate the manor. I'd never assumed that he'd actually been listening or committing the details of my life to memory.

Mrs. Deinhart's eyes clicked over to me. The way she looked at me was territorial, almost vulturous. In that second, I knew that she was the voice in the Ouija board.

More than any other time that night (including getting stabbed, being offered poisoned wine, and being trapped in various rooms and hallways), I was horribly, chillingly aware of my proximity to my own death. So many people had died in this house, and I would be just one more, punished for my parents' hubris in buying the Deinhart Manor and my own stupid decision to throw a party in it.

But Mrs. Deinhart lost interest in me, allowing her gaze to be drawn back to the round window. I couldn't see what was pulling her focus, only the soft light of town twinkling like artificial starlight.

"The house was built to accommodate generations of Deinhart children," she went on. "There was room enough for my children and, eventually, my grandchildren to all live on the property. Room to grow in the event that we ever needed more space. Gerd and I had five children, three boys and two girls. I imagined a future where all of us would live in the manor for many years. But that, as you already know, is not what happened."

"You killed them," I said. Blood loss was making me dizzy, reckless.

Mrs. Deinhart's posture stiffened.

"I did what was necessary," she said simply.

The lack of denial made me shiver. Or maybe that was the multiple stab wounds. They had started to pulsate like speakers broadcasting the metronome of my heart.

"How?" Remi asked, breathless with anticipation. "How did you do it? Which of the rumors is true?"

"Rumors are vulgarities told by the covetous to distract from their envy," Mrs. Deinhart said sharply. Her fierceness made her face come into sharp relief, revealing the cruel lines of her skull. "You are all drawn in by the stories. Wanting to be the ones to know. Wanting a taste of someone else's misery. Our deaths are nothing to you but entertainment."

She was right. Telling the story. Hearing the story. That was what brought all of us to the manor. Without the rumors, it was just some old house. No amenities. No treasure. Just a shell full of gruesome possibilities.

"That's what they all come for," Mrs. Deinhart went on, dropping back into a more musing tone. "To be the ones who know the truth. But it's not yours to know. It's not your story. Until you're forced to live it. And thus, over time, each of those stories has come to fruition. You've seen that tonight, haven't you? What does it matter which was true first?

"In death, I intended to reunite with my family. My children, my parents, the brother I lost to scarlet fever, my grandfather the founder."

"But none of them were there," I said, thinking back to what I'd seen in the abyss. Mrs. Deinhart, alone with the axe and the rocking chair. How long had she been alone in the manor? Months? Years? "Here, I mean. You were here and they weren't."

"Not even Gerd," said Mrs. Deinhart. "I was alone in the house in a way I never was in life. Houses are built for families. As are towns, as a matter of fact. This town loses more families with each passing year. As young people, like yourselves, eke out more freedom, more selfish desire to uproot yourselves and start over alone, you leave and never come back. You leave behind the parents who love you, and they, in turn, can choose to either die forgotten or follow you like pathetic little pets. Because you won't stay where you belong. Here. At home."

"Is that why you let my parents leave?" I asked. "Everyone else who comes here dies, but you let them leave. Why?"

"Your parents?" Mrs. Deinhart repeated, casting back through her long, long memory. "Oh, the people who think they can own a piece of history. They sacrificed something that no one else ever has. They sacrificed *you*."

"What?" My breath caught. "No, they didn't. I saw them here, in the abyss. I watched them..." I trailed off, remembering Mom and Dad's conversation in the music room. Standing on the spot where Yara would one day drown in phantom blood. Long before they'd figured out what they wanted to do with the house or how they'd sic their lawyers against each other for the right to pick out the new flooring, they had come to one decision.

That I would help them. That I wouldn't leave for college in the fall. That I would stay here.

"My future," I choked. Bile rose in my throat. "They sacrificed my future. To you."

"To me?" Mrs. Deinhart threw her head back and laughed. The ghost smell intensified with each peal. "Heavens no. To the manor. Without families, a place withers away to nothing, forgotten and empty. The manor refuses to wither. Thus it needs family."

Maddy May made a strained sound that I assumed was pain. I started to reach for her but stopped when I followed her gaze to the other side of the attic.

Out of the darkness came ghosts. Hundreds of them.

Misty, grayscale forms that seemed to be walking toward us from miles away. Featureless, faceless ghosts of everyone who had ever died in the house.

"Our family is not born, but it is still bound by blood," Mrs. Deinhart said. "Each comes, answering *l'appel du vide.* The call of the void. Then, they see the beauty of the manor and become part of it. They transcend who they were and become what is needed. They protect our home. Shore up the gaps. Invite in new guests who would be a good fit for our family. The house accepts the unwanted and the afraid, the dutiful and the pragmatic. Outside, there is loneliness and illness and war and failure. Here, there is comfort and kinship. A home needs a family. Without it, it's only a house. And a town is only land. Together, we make it something truly alive."

The repulsive smell in the room became overwhelming as, again, Mrs. Deinhart's face changed. Her eyes became empty hollows, her mouth a hungry, sucking void. It was as if the guise of her humanity had faltered, removing the filter on top of her ghostliness. Beneath it, she was an embodiment of consuming, fathomless rage. I wondered if she was the abyss itself, projecting an avatar to have a voice. Or if it was the other way around. If the abyss was built out of her memories and the madness of a woman driven to kill her family in order to keep them.

"Welcome home, children," she said.

The ghosts swarmed us.

25

With a sound like a gale-force wind, the ghosts came together in a single fog. The cloud of the dead was less a walking mass of arms and legs than it was bodies walking through bodies, faces fused together, hands sticking out of chests. It was cold. Everywhere they touched us burned like dry ice.

The good news was the heavy, hungry fog dampened the smell of Mrs. Deinhart. The bad news was that we were all utterly doomed.

As my legs disappeared into the cloud of ghosts, I thrashed my arms, wanting to stay afloat, wanting to stay upright as the cloud tried to press me down. The stab wound in my shoulder burned, and I tried to focus on the pain, the reminder that I was still alive, even as my legs became impossible to feel. I screamed until I felt like my vocal cords would snap and bleed.

I'm going to spend the rest of eternity as a ghost forced to protect this house. Stretched out over a window, taking whacks from fireplace tools and kitchen debris as future Bucktown kids try to escape Mrs. Deinhart's trap, I thought. Because that's what the manor was: a trap. A soda bottle with the neck pushed inside, entrancing people with the sweetness of mystery and discovery, only to drown them like flies.

Maddy May kicked and shrieked, fighting as hard as she could to beat back the ghosts encircling her legs.

Nathaniel ran for the door, but the darkness grew, pushing the door farther and farther out of reach until it looked like a dot in the distance. Unreachable.

"Hannah!" Remi cried as she pushed her way toward the other girl, each step as labored as if she were pushing through hip-deep snow.

"Remi!" Hannah said.

I could see only her torso, sticking out from the mist. She was sinking, becoming shorter inch by inch.

"I should have told you earlier!" Remi said, shouting over the whooshing air of the ghost miasma. "Before we got trapped here. Before you got possessed. Before we graduated."

"Told me what?" Hannah shouted back.

Remi grabbed Hannah's hands and laced their fingers together. "I think you're the coolest, smartest, most capable person I've ever known. I love your style. I love your colorful armpits. I love that you led us to the championships! I just—I like you so much, Hannah. I always have. I wish I'd told you before we were going to die, but—"

"I like you, too!" Hannah burst out. She pushed herself closer to Remi, their folded hands pressed between them, palm to palm. "I mean, I thought it was pretty obvious when I kissed you earlier, but I've wanted to kiss you for two years."

"Holy shit! Me too!" Remi said. "Since you called the vice principal a fascist when she tried to dress-code you for wearing your 'Pro-Choice, Pro-Planet, Pro-Science' sweatshirt."

"She is a fascist!" Hannah said with a dopey, starry-eyed smile. "Sometimes, I'd think I was getting a vibe from you, but I was never sure. You're that girl who flirts with everyone whether they're queer or not, and I could never tell if you were flirting with me."

"I was! But I didn't want you to know because then you'd know I liked you."

They kissed, laughing. Remi freed one of her hands and buried it in the blood-soaked lavender of Hannah's hair.

The ghost cloud started to dissipate around them, the ectoplasmic mass swirling away like fog burning off at sunrise. Neither Remi nor Hannah seemed to notice, too distracted by tonguing each other down.

I was happy for Remi and the fairy-tale ending of her planned speech. Although that happiness was abstracted by roaring pain and a terrifying growing numbness as the retreating ghosts glommed on to me and swallowed the stab wound in my thigh.

Nathaniel staggered toward me, the cloud only reaching up to his ankles. Ghost hands clawed at his knees and hips, searching for purchase as he walked through them.

If I could have felt my stomach, I'm sure it would have dropped. I knew what was coming, and I didn't know if I had the energy for it. Facing the choice between an honest conversation and death, I truly considered lying down and letting the ghosts absorb me.

"Arden," he said.

"Hi, Nate," I said. It sounded more like a multisyllable groan as I strained to stay afloat in the swarm of ghosts. "I'm sorry that you came to the worst party to see me. We should have just gone to Sober Grad Night with the other dorks. Or stayed home. That would have been smart."

"It's okay," Nathaniel said. "I'm glad I came. I wanted to see you one last time. You broke my heart when you dumped me, Doc. But I couldn't get over you."

It was the beginning of a declaration, I knew. It had worked for Remi and Hannah. It had worked for every fictional character in every romantic comedy. Why shouldn't it work for us? We were so alike. If you could pick two people out of anyone at Bucktown High (living or recently dead) to create a perfect couple, it would be hard to find a pair who worked better (on paper) than us. Driven verging on obsessive, smart verging on pretentious, attracted to each other. If we were truly lucky, we could even go on to be survivors of Bucktown's greatest tragedy.

Wouldn't it all be worth it if, at the end, we were together? If out of something gruesome came true love? After all, it was the last day to have a high school sweetheart.

He reached for me and I reflexively reached back, curling my hand at the nape of his neck, leaning into his lips. Kissing him fit the same way as a well-worn shirt. Despite the holes and busted seams, it was familiar and comfortable. I momentarily forgot that we were both bleeding to death and that I was being consumed like an antigen by an army of white blood cell ghosts.

Nathaniel's lips were insistent, passing along every ounce of passion he felt. For me. For life. He kissed me like it was an antidote to dying.

And it was.

For him.

The ghosts bled away from his legs. They passed over to me like I was a dropped Popsicle and they were a starving colony of ants.

"Arden, I like you," Nathaniel declared.

"I—" My throat caught as my shoulders disappeared into the cloud and my esophagus was squeezed by phantom hands. "I know."

Nathaniel's face fell. His jaw dropped and a weak cough fell out. Honestly, he seemed more hurt by my words than he had when the knife entered his stomach.

"I'm sorry," I quickly added. I couldn't believe that my last words were going to be crushing Nathaniel Graham. I was a monster. I should have lied to him and taken the truth to my ghostly grave. "I know you want me to say that I like you, too. And I do! Sometimes. When you're not correcting me or insulting me. But it's not enough, I think. To save me."

"Obviously," he said with a grimace. Almost every ghost in the house was surrounding me, doing their best to drown me in their oppressive cold. "You're still being absorbed."

"Looks like it," I gurgled. I strained to keep my face out of the cloud. "I mean, if I don't get to go to college, I guess I might as well die in a haunted house with the rest of the graduating class. I'm not special."

"Oh my God, Arden, shut up," Remi said. She dropped the straps of Hannah's overalls and turned to me. "Of course you're special! You don't have to go to Windsor and be a doctor to be special. I'm so sick of you talking like there's only one choice for you!"

"Are you really going to pick a fight with me while I'm literally being eaten by ghosts?" I asked.

"Yes!" she shouted. "Because we don't all come out of the womb knowing exactly who we're gonna be! Some of us need to try stuff out first. You could try stuff out! Maddy May agrees with me. Don't you, Mads?"

Maddy May froze, arms and legs akimbo with ghosts dripping from her like tinsel. "Oh. Um. Are we doing this now?"

"Now or never," I said.

"Okay, well," Maddy May said, clearing her throat uneasily. "Remi and I have wondered why you're so opposed to trying community college for a year or two."

"Because it comes off classist as fuck," Remi said. "Like you're too good to go to school with poor people."

"What are you talking about?" I gasped. "I'm not rich. Maddy May is rich!"

"Not that rich. I still only applied to state schools," Maddy May said. "Even though I would have loved to go to a real theater school like Juilliard or RADA. You applied to schools so expensive that even with scholarships, you can't afford to go."

"Without bilking the senior class for their grad money," Nathaniel said.

"Shut up, Nate, this isn't about you!" Remi snapped.

"Arden, did you ever consider the fact that every single time you talked about how you couldn't fucking stand to stay in this town, what you were saying is that you couldn't imagine doing what I *have* to do? I can't leave here. I don't get to go off to college and reinvent myself. I'm going to live at home and work at Target and go to community college."

"Wait," I said. I thrust my chin out, pushing the ghost cloud down to my chest so that I could fully see Remi. "You're going to BCC? You never told me that."

"No shit!" she said. "You kept talking about how your worst nightmare would be having to go there. And every time you were saying how awful it would be, I was thinking about how absolutely fucking cool it would be if you were there, too. I could have my best friend with me in college!"

"I thought Maddy May was your best friend," Hannah said.

"We're all best friends!" Maddy May insisted. "All three of us! We're all one team!"

"Best friend is a category, not an elected position. You can have more than one," Remi said. "Arden, you and I could be legit everyday best friends. We could take the same classes at BCC. We could make new friends together! College friends. We could go to parties that don't end in everybody dying!"

"Even if I don't die in the next thirty seconds, do you really think after tonight any of us will ever go to a party again?" I asked. I couldn't imagine a day when the taste of hard seltzer didn't make me think about death. "And I don't even know what I'd do at BCC. What would I study? Real estate?"

"What? Of course not!" Remi said with a snort. "You don't want to work for your parents. That's a punishment worse than death."

"They have a nursing program. One of my cousins went through it," Maddy May said. "There are other ways to be in the medical field. The choice isn't actually doctor or nothing."

"You'd be a killer EMT," Hannah said.

"Or a dietician who doesn't hate fat people," Nathaniel said. "You taught me a lot about carbs when I told you my mom was eating keto."

"You could even just study random shit," Remi said. "History. Philosophy. Welding. There's more to life than getting a job."

"I don't know," I said. My own words became muffled as the ghosts spread over my ears. "I've never wanted anything else."

"But you could try!" Remi said. "Leave yourself open to the possibility that there's something else to live for! Because there is!"

"There's old friends and new friends and music and milkshakes!" Maddy May said. The ghosts swarming her started to dissipate as she kept emphatically listing, "And sex and rainbows and puppies and whiskers on kittens!"

"And roller coasters and staying up all night and parrots and fireworks!" Remi added.

"Yep, that covers basically everything good about being

alive," Nathaniel said. "Except parrots. I don't know what those were doing in there."

"It's a pet that can talk to you," Remi said, as though this were incredibly obvious. "That's the dream!"

"If you need a reason to live," Hannah said to me, "imagine how many people you could personally stop from coming here ever again. You *have* to stop your parents from renovating this place. Everyone who comes here dies."

They come to see the beauty of the manor and become part of it, Mrs. Deinhart had said. I refused to see the beauty of this death trap. Or choosing to be absorbed by the ghosts of those who had been tricked. Because the manor wasn't beautiful. Its beating heart was the deranged ghost of an old-lady serial killer. Mrs. Deinhart had killed her whole family in an attempt to manipulate them into staying with her. And when it hadn't worked, she'd stolen hundreds of souls from Bucktown and subjugated them into becoming a security system for her house.

She was a despot who preyed on the vulnerable and the hopeless.

The *hopeless*. That was it. That was what the dead had in common. And what I had in common with them that Remi, Maddy May, Hannah, and Nathaniel didn't. The ghosts and I were people with nowhere else to go. People who lost hope that there was a way out of the house. People who had heard the rumors, seen the reenactments, and given them-selves over to the house.

Tanner, who had faced rejection for the first time in his life.

Yara, who crumpled in the face of true, evil magic.

They lost hope, and Mrs. Deinhart struck.

College had been my only hope for most of my life. Starting in elementary school, when our teachers made us chant "We are college-bound!" as a way to program us with the idea that higher education was the only way to stay respectable.

I had never hoped for anything outside of school. Perfect grades, aced tests, awards and medals and ribbons, acceptance letters, the promise of an enviable job. Excelling at school was the only thing I knew how to do. The only thing I knew how to want. It's where all of my praise came from.

Without it, I had been floundering. I didn't know who I was unless I was working toward a bigger goal. I had only survived the night thus far because I had believed that there was a way out of the house, a way to solve the puzzle of the unbreakable windows and locked doors. And that when I got out, I could spend the party money on tuition.

But what I hadn't seen in all this time was how much my friends had held me afloat when I felt the most adrift. Even now, when I was literally drowning in ghosts, Maddy May and Remi were here to call me on my bullshit and drag me to safety. I didn't have best friends because I was great at school. There was something in me that was more important.

For the first time, I imagined a life after high school. Not college. Not the classes I would take or the grades I would earn in them. But waking up and being more than just the world's best student. Waking up at nineteen. Twenty.

Thirty. Fifty-five. I could live the rest of my life, the majority of my life, years and decades, experiencing so much more than I had ever hoped for. Love and puppies and sex and milkshakes. Kissing boys I liked more than Nathaniel. Making new friends in non-dire situations. Spending time with the friends I already had and discovering new things to love about them. Discovering new things about myself that I had buried under years of perfectionism.

Wasn't that reason to live?

The ghost cloud drained away from me slower than it had the others, reluctantly uncovering my ears, my shoulders, my hands, my knees. Coming out of the fog, everything hurt ten times more than it had before. Every stab wound was on fire. The skin of my palms was skinned raw. My throat ached from screaming.

But I was alive. Alive and ready to keep fighting.

Remi and Maddy May bounded toward me, grinning from ear to ear as they crushed me in a hug. I whimpered, flailing my arms in an attempt to hug them back and escape as quickly as possible. (It turns out that stab wounds do not like to be hugged. Who knew?)

I must have made an awful sound (or they heard the squelch of my wounds) because they both let go of me.

"I'm sorry," I told my friends. "I've been so focused on sticking to my plan that I couldn't think about anything else. And it's made me a shitty friend. I'm sorry, Rem. I think it's awesome that you're going to go to BCC. You're right. It would be fun to go there together. I never even thought about having friends in college. I guess I assumed that

I would just keep my head down and study for ten years straight."

"Oh, honey, we know," Maddy May said with a sad smile. "That's what you were like when we found you."

"I'm glad you guys found me. And that you didn't give up on me," I said. The corners of my eyes burned. I choked back tears. "I know I'm not a fun person—"

"Hey," Remi cut me off. "You are fun. You're just not good at remembering that you like to have fun. That's not the same thing."

"It's fun to have fun," Maddy May said. "We'll always be here to remind you when you forget."

"As long as we get out of here alive," Remi said.

"Speaking of: Can we get back to that?" Nathaniel asked. Sweat made his face shine, highlighting the strain at the corners of his eyes. He was still losing blood. We had to get him to a hospital. (And while we were there, I might also need a transfusion, two dozen stitches, an IV, and a tetanus shot.)

Tentatively, I reached out and took his free hand, the one that wasn't holding his stomach closed. I wouldn't have blamed him for pushing me away or even refusing to touch a girl who hadn't liked him enough to live for him. Instead, a reassuring squeeze passed between us.

"We good?" I asked.

He nodded blearily. "It never would have worked with us anyway. You don't give a shit about space."

"I truly don't," I said with a chuckle. "NASA should allocate a portion of their budget to deep-sea exploration. We should see what else is on our planet before we go pillage other ones."

He winced, tucking his cheek into his shoulder. "You just couldn't be more wrong, Doc. They already get a fraction of what they did during the space race. And if we found an ounce of water on another planet, it would be more water than we've ever had in Earth's history–"

Propelled by his indignation, Nathaniel limped toward the staircase. Hannah leaped onto Remi's back. Maddy May ran ahead, blue skirt fluttering.

Behind us, the cloud of ghosts rose, stretching to fill the shape of the attic. I couldn't see Mrs. Deinhart. But I could smell her. And hear her ear-piercing cry: "No! Stay! There's nothing out there for you!"

Her voice followed us down the pitch-dark stairs, a looming threat. We ran as fast as we could, not daring to look back.

26

We had decided to live. Now we had to figure out how.

In the pinpoint of Hannah's phone light, we could see that Kenzie's body was gone from the hallway outside of the attic door. The axe lay on the ground where Nathaniel had discarded it. Remi snatched it up and immediately almost dropped it as she hissed in pain. With the pad of her thumb wedged between her lips, she sucked at an invisible wound.

"Ow, shit," she said. "I got a freaking splinter; can you believe it?"

Nathaniel, Hannah, and I stared back at her in bleeding, broken silence. Remi clenched her teeth in an abashed grimace.

Maddy May patted her shoulder. "It's okay, Rem. I have tweezers in my makeup case."

We went back the way we'd come, down the hallway toward the powder room. The sheet rope remained tied between two doorknobs. There was no sound coming from the locked bedroom of the possessed trying to escape or come after us.

"Is it just me or is the house gaslighting us?" Hannah asked.

"It's not just you," I said. "Remember: To keep the ghosts out of your brain, you need to hold on to something hopeful."

"I'm totally going to write in to *Specter Sightings* and tell them to add a fourth rule," Remi said.

"It's the Peter Pan rule," Maddy May said. "Think happy thoughts."

"Right. But instead of flying we get to not murder anyone," Nathaniel said.

"What if the loops downstairs are a way to make people feel hopeless?" Hannah asked. "If you have to pretend to die enough times, you give up and really die. Like what happened to the Drama Club."

"What do you mean? What happened to the Drama Club?" Maddy May asked.

Hannah stiffened, nervously looking around at the rest of us as she faltered to say, "Oh. Um. They collapsed in the kitchen after drinking really old wine...that might have been poisoned?"

"What?" Maddy May gasped, turning to me and Remi. "Why didn't you guys tell me? Was Keaton with them?"

"We were a little busy, Mads," Remi said. "Besides, we didn't think you even liked Keaton anymore—"

Maddy May took off sprinting downstairs. We struggled to keep up with her, trying to call after her and warn her about the rest of the party horrors she'd missed. But she refused to listen or slow down until she'd made it all the way to the kitchen.

The Drama Club was lying where we left them, on the kitchen floor, surrounded by broken glass and splashes of bloodred wine. Top Hat was missing, presumably still stuck in the primary bedroom with the other possessed.

"No, no, no. Wake up. You're just a little borracho, come on." Maddy May knelt on the floor beside Keaton, the pale chiffon of her skirt drinking up the wine on the floor and turning bruise purple. She scooped up Keaton's limp shoulders, cradling him in her arms. Tears shone in her eyes as she smoothed her Romeo's blond hair.

"'I will kiss thy lips. Haply some poison yet doth hang on them,'" she quoted.

Nathaniel staggered through the doorway, doubled over in pain and disgust. "Ugh! Don't kiss a corpse!"

Maddy May did not heed his warning. She leaned down and pressed her lips to Keaton's.

"'Thy lips are warm,'" Keaton quoted back, his voice faint. His sleepy eyes flickered open. "Sorry. That's your line."

"Oh, Keats!" Maddy May cheered, weeping and laughing as she rained kisses down on his cheeks and forehead. "I was so afraid you'd act five, scene three–d yourself!"

"Poison myself?" He chuckled, reaching up to cup the curve of her cheek. "Then I'd never get to kiss my angel Maddy May again."

He lifted his head and caught her mouth in another, deeper kiss. They held each other so tight, the tips of their fingers bleached white. Soon, the two of them were rolling across the wet floor, vigorously making out.

"Huh. So she really does like him," Remi muttered to me.

"She likes something about him," I said.

"'Give me my sin again,'" Maddy May moaned into Keaton's mouth.

Theater kids. So horny. So cringe.

In an attempt to give them some privacy (and tune out the wet smacks of their kissing), I turned to Remi, Nate, and Hannah, who were crowded in the doorway.

"Okay, so the loops apparently can be interrupted," I said. "Now, we need to find a way to wake everyone else up. Preferably without having to kiss all of them. And we have to make sure that no one else comes into this house. Ever again. You guys saw how many ghosts are here. Hundreds of people have died here. And people will keep coming back. Unless we stop them."

I thought about my parents, who would want to stop by to take measurements for new windows or bring in contractors to patch the holes in the basement walls and the kitchen leaks. They would eventually be taken by the house. Mrs. Deinhart only needed enough time to take away their hope. Then they'd die. And if not them, then the next group of people looking for the perfect place for a party. Or shelter from a blizzard. Or a warm place to sleep.

We couldn't let the manor take anyone else.

"Let's fucking wreck this place," Remi said. "No one can live here if we ruin it beyond what Arden's parents could fix with new paint and some flowers."

"Yes!" I said. "We need to make sure the only option left is to have the place condemned."

I knew by agreeing to this, I was officially giving up on my dream. Not just my dream, but my parents' dreams as well. No one would ever renovate the Deinhart manor. No one would ever sell it. And I'd never see Windsor College or spend ten years training to become Dr. Arden Lozano Flack.

But if no one else died here, it would be worth the sacrifice. No one ever got out of here without giving something up.

"Do we think the manor can even be destroyed?" Hannah asked.

"We know it can't be burned," Nathaniel said. "Blood rain."

"Fire isn't the only way to ruin a house," I said. "There are plenty of things that make a house unlivable. Structural damage, termites, black mold. Meth labs leave behind toxic fumes."

"Are you suggesting we come back to make meth?" Nathaniel asked sardonically. Sweat shone on his forehead as he struggled to hold his stomach closed and perform his "well, actually" act at the same time. "Is that your new career plan?"

"I bet we could buy a bunch of termites online," Remi said. "Just set them loose on the porch."

I shook my head. "Termites will take too long. An inspector will have to come to confirm the damage is severe enough. It has to be undeniably ruined. We need to be sure that we'll be the last people who ever set foot in here."

"The house can make dead bodies disappear," Hannah said. "What's to say it can't fix whatever we break?"

"Because it isn't infallible," I said. "It's not like the place is perfect. There are things wrong with it. The ghosts can keep the windows from breaking and put out fire with blood, but we've seen rooms that are in bad shape. Look around. This kitchen is disgusting!"

I gestured around us at the rusted-out stove and the deteriorating counters. The mold on the walls and the sun-bleached floors. It was the only room in the house that looked truly abandoned, like even the ghosts avoided it. And why would the ghosts leave behind the pyre full of half-burned art and weapons in the basement? Why not disappear it the same way they had cleared out the powder room?

"The ghosts can do everything except fix some leaky pipes?" she said. "Maybe they don't own a wrench."

"Water damage," Nathaniel said. He pumped his fist then pressed it to his mouth, badly containing his excitement. "Haven't any of you heard of haint blue?"

"No," Hannah said.

"Nope," said Remi.

"Yes," I said. "Of course. It's a pale blue people paint the roofs of covered porches. It looks like the sky. My parents swear by it for curb appeal. That and planting flowers that are going to die the second the house sells."

"Haint blue doesn't look like the sky. It looks like *water*," Nathaniel explained. "It's a Gullah tradition. It's to keep ghosts out of your house." He waited for a reaction that didn't come. Rolling his eyes in annoyance, he added, "Because ghosts can't cross running water."

"They can't?" I asked.

From what I'd seen that night, I wasn't sure I was ready to underestimate what the ghosts could do. They could possess entire rooms of people, turn regular high school kids into murderers, take souls while leaving the bodies in motion, control the doors, lights, and shape of the manor. Why would water slow them down?

"Think about it," Nathaniel said. "The manor doesn't even use water to put out fires. It's not like it doesn't have access. We saw the pipes in the basement. The toilets can flush. There's water here, but the ghosts won't use it."

"You've known this the whole time?" Remi asked accusingly.

"I know a lot of things!" Nathaniel sputtered. He tried to hold his hands up in surrender but bent over again to hold his stomach.

"Water damage will ruin a house. If it's enough water," I said.

I'd seen my parents walk away from plenty of properties that had bad water damage. Even just in one room, a leaky window could cause cracks in the wall and the floor and lead to mold infestations. Untreated water damage could sink into the house's frame and rot away the very skeleton of the place. If the ghosts couldn't cross running water, they wouldn't be able to stop the house from collapsing in an internal flood.

It was our best hope for stopping the manor.

"How many bathrooms are in this place?" Remi asked.

"Nine," I said.

On the kitchen floor, the rest of the Drama Club was slowly coming back to consciousness, stretching and humming and already searching for another bottle of wine.

Before they could start playing an improv game (or join Maddy May and Keaton's public display of dry humping), I asked, "Hey, do any of you want to help break some shit?"

"What shit?" asked Goggles.

"Everything. Start with the sink."

27

One of the bathrooms was already overflowing. Someone had tried to flush a slice of cake (with a fork in it) and the ancient toilet hadn't been able to take the heat. I turned on the taps on the sink and in the shower, then tore off the knobs. Just to be sure.

I rinsed my wounds as best as I could before tying them up with some of the leftover makeshift curtain bandages. Blood and velvet fused together, Velcro tight, so whether or not it was the most sanitary option, it was definitely effective.

I followed the water out of the bathroom as it crept down the hallway into the dining room, where Kenzie had mime-stabbed a bunch of people (who were luckier than me and Nathaniel). As the water slithered between their bodies, each person on the floor stirred to waking. Holding their heads and looking down at the chocolate frosting smeared across their clothes, they looked as confused and disoriented as the Drama Club had been.

Remi, Maddy May, Hannah, and Nathaniel had spread out to get as much water moving as possible. In the distance, I could hear the muttering of other people waking up as the ballroom and billiards room started to flood. Beyond that, in the basement, metal clanged against metal and water hissed out of pipes.

It was working.

Frigid wind screeched through the manor as the ghosts searched for somewhere to go. The power surged, making the lights flicker on and off. If a house could have a tantrum, the Deinhart Manor was doing its best.

"What's that?" someone asked, pointing at the wall where the ghost hands were trying to push through.

I chucked a bottle of bright blue curaçao at the hands. The bottle shattered, sending shards of glass and blue-raspberry-colored droplets in every direction.

"Fuck this party!" I shouted. "Let's rip this place apart!"

Thankfully, no one in the dining room questioned this. Or remembered that this was, in fact, *my* party. It was so easy, that it made me wonder whether everyone was just eager to shake off the unsettling feeling of possession or if they'd been waiting to destroy the house the whole time.

Maybe all anyone needs to riot is for someone to suggest it.

Bottles were smashed. The table was upended. The remains of Shaun's happy graduation cake splattered against a window, frosting dripping down in streaks.

I shoved the china cabinet with my uninjured shoulder

until it tipped over. Watercolor plates broke apart like stale rice cakes. I smiled.

In the hallway, phantom blood poured down the walls, searching for internal wounds to heal. None of it touched the water starting to rise at my feet. Not a drop. Ghosts pushed out of every dry surface. Grasping hands came through the walls. Featureless faces silently screamed in the ceiling.

No one noticed. Or, rather, no one *wanted* to notice. Living in denial of the ghosts meant they could stay busy running from room to room, laughing and shrieking with delight as they tore the house apart. The house was cacophonous with destruction.

I walked upstream to the second floor. The red carpet squelched underfoot. Some parts of the floor were already so saturated that the carpet threads floated like kelp.

Nathaniel stood outside of the primary bedroom with the axe slung over his shoulder. He stared at the sheet rope pulled tight between the two doors. Inside the bedroom, hands banged on the door, begging to be let out. Water lapped at the doorsill, struggling to find a way into the room.

I gulped, thinking about the possessed. Kenzie wielding the cake knife. Octavio's maniacal laughter. They had only been acting out loops, the same as everyone else. Except their roles had been worse than playing dead.

We couldn't leave them trapped here if there was a chance they could be saved.

"The water woke everyone else up," Nathaniel said. He looked over at me, face unreadable.

"You want to help them?" I asked, surprised by this uncharacteristic selflessness. "What if you get hurt again? Or worse?"

"It's probably better than knowing that we left them to die," he said.

I drew in a long breath, then nodded. "Do it."

He brought the axe down on the sheet rope. It unraveled easily, falling apart into shirts and scarves that floated away from us. Nate stepped back.

"Go ahead," he said, motioning to the doorknob. For added effect, he held his fist in his stomach wound.

There was the Nathaniel Graham I knew and barely tolerated.

I opened the door and leaped back, waiting for the flash of a knife or piano wire. Instead, there was silence, except for the shushing of water spilling into the room. Then, a hand gripped the doorframe. Octavio stuck his head out into the hallway.

"Is the party over?" he asked. His voice was soft and quavery.

"It's winding down," I said.

One of the sheet ghosts appeared in the doorway, shivering as drops of water dripped off the hem of her bloody drop cloth.

"I think I passed out," she said.

I remembered the new rule number four. *Hope.* The formerly possessed needed hope more than anyone else at the party. It didn't seem like they remembered what the ghosts had forced them to do, but if they did, it would probably be hard to hold on to a happy thought long enough to have a chance in hell of getting out of here. They needed something to hold on to.

So I lied.

"More like blacked out, girl," I corrected with a too loud, too sassy laugh that in no way belonged to me. "Were you guys playing Kiss or Shots with Everclear? That was so messy!"

Nathaniel looked at me in horror as he struggled to keep up with the kind lie. "Uh, yeah. It's like everyone forgot how to be. Did you guys get caught up in that dance party, too?"

"Oh yeah," said the other sheet ghost. The bloodied drop cloth slipped off her, leaving her with standing static hair. "I do remember dancing a lot."

"And drinking a lot," said Top Hat.

"It's a party," I said brightly. "You partied."

The tattoos drawn on Maze's arm were half-washed away, leaking purple-black down the tips of their fingers. Their eyebrows furrowed as they racked their brain for something they couldn't find. "Yara. Did something happen to Yara?"

"She's gone," I said, faltering. I couldn't just blurt out that she'd been murdered by ghosts, but I also didn't want Maze to go looking for her. "She left the party with Tanner Grant."

"Oh." Maze nodded, even as they looked at me with confusion and disbelief. "She always talked about how he was her first boyfriend. She carried a chunk of amethyst he gave her."

All the formerly possessed went back downstairs without

looking back. Except Kenzie Sullivan. She hung back, alone in the room. She was soaking wet from head to toe. Her clothes clung to her like wrinkled flesh.

"Kenzie," I said. "It's time to go. The party's over."

"I'm not leaving," she said. She stared into the slice of abyss between the torn sheets of wallpaper like she could hear something inside. *The call of the void*, as Mrs. Deinhart had called it. What did it sound like for Kenzie? "There's nothing out there for me."

"There's your whole life," I said. I took a tentative step over the threshold, following the flow of water into the room. "Everything that happens after high school. There has to be something you're looking forward to. Something to live for."

Behind the wet ropes of her hair, Kenzie's eyes flickered over to me. Her gaze was no longer vacant. Whatever had possessed her to stab me and Nathaniel and however many other people was gone. But she still wasn't herself. The girl who gave student council speeches at fundraisers and regaled the party with marching band stories was also gone. This Kenzie was, well, haunted.

"I tried to kill people," she said. "I tried to kill you."

My mind flashed back to the knife in her hand. The way the metal caught the limited light. The searing pain that continued to throb in time with my adrenaline-spiked heart. I shook the thoughts away.

"It wasn't you. You were possessed."

"It *was* me," she insisted. "Did you try to kill anyone tonight?"

"Hell no," said Nathaniel, out in the hall.

I glared at him over my shoulder. "What happened to helping?"

"I can't live among people I tried to kill," Kenzie said, speaking slowly like she was working her way through a formula. "And I can't live with myself knowing I tried to kill people."

I turned just in time to see her step backward. Into the abyss. I ran toward the split in the wall, shouting, "Kenzie! Don't!"

But it was too late. The water hadn't risen high enough yet. The house could still heal the walls. The wallpaper knitted itself together like epidermal cells healing a minor cut.

Sealing Kenzie Sullivan into the walls of the Deinhart Manor.

28

No amount of clawing at the walls would free Kenzie. Eventually, the ghost hands started to push back at my hands, threatening to pull me in as well. The ceiling started to lower toward me. Nathaniel finally dragged me out of the room, even as I screamed Kenzie's name.

"Let her go," he told me. "She made her choice."

We had to check the rest of the upstairs bathrooms. Each one was spewing out water at maximum capacity. Even without us having to say so, people had caught on that we were intent on flooding the place. Toilets and sinks were broken to bits. Bathtub drains were blocked off with curtains and toilet paper. The water flowed.

We checked the powder room last. It was empty. Everything we had brought with us (Maddy May's makeup, the extra dresses, my backpack) was gone. So was the money vase. Fifteen thousand dollars, eaten by the house. I had sacrificed my future to survive. The manor made sure I couldn't change my mind.

I was as trapped in Bucktown as Kenzie was trapped in the house.

White water rushed down the twin staircases, pushing us toward the rising tide of the first floor. The sound of water pouring into (and out of) every room was thunderous, nearly overtaking the noise of the partygoers breaking whatever they could find. The roar filled my ears like white noise.

Hannah and Remi splashed down the hallway with their arms around each other's waists, walking in step like a three-legged race. They were soaked and cleaner than they'd been in hours. The blood had washed out of Hannah's hair, leaving her once again pastel lavender from head to armpit.

Remi's uneven bangs were plastered to her forehead. She swiped at them anyway. "We broke pipes in the basement," she said. "Even if someone tried to come in and stop the water, they'd have to scuba down and find a new handle for the shut-off valve."

"Perfect," I said.

"There you all are!" Maddy May said, skipping toward us. Her face was flushed and her dress soaked with water and wine. She and Keaton were entwined by the pinkies, which was somehow more disturbing than watching them suck each other's tongues in the kitchen.

"Everyone has gone totally feral," she said. "I saw someone kick a window until the glass cracked."

"Wait, someone cracked a window?" I asked.

Maddy May frowned at me. "You can't tell people to

destroy the house and then get upset when they actually do it, Ardy."

"No, that's *great* news!" I said. The hope in my chest burned hot. *What if this works? What if it's* already *working?* There was a chance that no one else would have to die here. "If the windows break, we might actually be able to get everyone out."

"Was that in question before?" Keaton asked.

"Hush, sweets," Maddy May said, and kissed his nose.

"But how do you end a party?" I asked the group. I had only ever been to parties where everyone's parents pulled up at the end and made them leave. A party with no supervision could go on indefinitely (especially if Mrs. Deinhart had anything to say about it). "We have to get everyone out. No stragglers."

"No problem. I'll do it," Remi said. She held her hand out to Nathaniel. "Moose Tracks."

"That's not how a safe word works—"

Remi flapped her hand at him.

Grudgingly, he relinquished the axe.

Remi cleared her throat and spat a loogie into the water.

"Ugh, Rem." I recoiled. "That's so not hygienic."

"Some of us have open wounds here," Nathaniel said.

"Why are you two bleeding so much?" Keaton asked, staring at me and Nathaniel in our blood-soaked shirts.

"COPS!" Remi roared as loud as she could. Banging the flat of the axe against the walls, she stormed up and down the hallway, screaming, "Everyone run! The cops are coming!"

It must have been everyone's unified hope of escape that finally shattered the windows. One of the huge windows in the ballroom erupted and, with it, people ran as fast as they could out of the manor.

"You should go, too, Keats," Maddy May said.

"Why?" he asked. "Are the cops really here?"

Maddy May held his face and kissed him hard. "'Parting is such sweet sorrow. That I shall say good night till it be morrow.' Text me later."

"I will," he said, too in awe to question her. With a wave to the rest of us, he ran down the hall and disappeared into the ballroom.

Alone again, Maddy May, Remi, Hannah, Nathaniel, and I stood under the second floor. Water poured from overhead in sheets and crashed down beside us, sending up a fine mist.

"So...," Hannah said. "What now? We can't pretend like this never happened."

"We have to," I said. "The rumors are part of what got everyone killed. The more people wonder about the house, the more they want to come see for themselves what happened."

"People are going to go looking for Tanner and Yara and Kenzie," Nathaniel said. "They can't just disappear. It raises more questions."

"More questions mean more rumors," Remi said.

They were right. But any investigation into the manor wouldn't bring answers. No one would find the dead. They would only die themselves. There was no proof anyone had ever been here but us. And the only proof we'd been here was the destruction.

"We'll change the story," I said. "The three of them left early. To go to another graduation party that none of us were cool enough to know about."

"Plausible," Nathaniel conceded. "To an outside observer, I mean. If there had been another grad party, I would have scored an invite."

Remi heaved a sigh. "If I have to pretend to be uncool to save the lives of anyone who would come looking here, then so be it. But it's a stretch. Everyone knows I'm the beer pong champion."

"Then maybe they didn't invite you because they were jealous," Maddy May said.

"Definitely that," Remi said with a grin.

"Okay," Hannah said. "Let's go out the window."

Everyone started to move down the hallway. Except me. I hung back, letting the water lap against my shins.

"Arden?" Remi looked back at me.

"I can't go until I know everyone is out," I said. "I can't leave anyone behind."

Anyone else. I thought about Kenzie walking into the abyss and Tanner and Yara being absorbed by ghosts. I couldn't let anyone else die here. I *wouldn't* let anyone else die here.

"Look at your arm! Look at your shoulder!" Maddy May said. "You need to go to the hospital!"

"I will," I said. "After I know everyone else is safe. But *I* started this. I stole the key. I let everyone in."

"It was my idea to throw a party," Maddy May protested.

291

"We'll all stay," Remi said.

"No," I said firmly. I pointed at Hannah and Nathaniel. "You two need to go to the hospital. Now. Out through the ballroom window like everyone else. Go down the other side of the hill. Toward the gas station. Call an ambulance on the way. Say you got jumped and Hannah hurt her ankle trying to run for help."

Nathaniel scoffed. "We can't leave you here."

"If the water gets much higher, you could get necrotizing fasciitis or vibriosis or sepsis," I said.

"So could you!" Nathaniel argued.

I didn't budge. "I'll see you both at the hospital. *After* I make sure we aren't leaving anyone behind."

"You'd better," Hannah said. "You got stabbed more than Nathaniel."

"But we can all agree that I got stabbed *worse*, right?" Nate asked. "The worst?"

"You're definitely the worst, Nate," I said.

He cracked half a smile, letting one of his dimples out. "See you at the hospital, Doc. And, hey, don't throw any more parties. They're not your thing."

"Noted," I said.

Hannah kissed Remi goodbye. Then she and Nate made their way to the ballroom.

Maddy May, Remi, and I did one last check of the house. In some rooms, the water was so high that I wouldn't have been able to get in without swimming. Not knowing what was lurking under the water, we opted to do purely visual checks.

The house started to creak and groan around us. I imagined the running water soaking into every nook and cranny, filling up the wooden frame and bursting through the exterior bricks. More likely, the upstairs would get so heavy that it crashed down onto the first floor. We needed to be gone before that happened.

"Okay," I said. "I think that's everyone."

"Almost," Remi said.

"Almost?" I echoed.

She gestured toward the foyer. "She's still here."

In the entryway, a body was sitting on the floor, curled up against the umbrella stand. Claire hadn't seemed to notice that she was sitting in an increasing amount of water. It gave her the look of someone who had gotten into the tub too soon. In one hand, she gripped a single house key on a squishy frog key chain. She was idly carving into the wall. **STAY STAY STAY.**

"The house ate him, didn't it?" she asked without looking up. "Tanner."

"Yeah," I said. "It did."

Heaving a sigh, she swiped away a tear with the back of her wrist. "My friends told me not to date him. They said he wasn't good for me. I thought they were jealous because he was a senior."

I blinked. "Are you not a senior? What are you doing at a graduation party?"

"Tanner invited me," she said. "I'm a sophomore. Well. Almost a sophomore."

Tanner Grant was dating a freshman, what a fucking creep, I thought. I didn't say it out loud. He was already dead. I didn't have to spit on his grave.

"Sorry I scratched you earlier," Claire said. "I just wanted to go home."

"It's okay," I said. "It wasn't the worst thing that happened tonight. Do you have something you're looking forward to?"

She stopped scratching into the wall. Her fingers wrapped around the frog key chain and squeezed.

"My family might go to the river tomorrow," she said. "My mom was going to make one big sandwich for us all to share."

"That sounds nice," I said.

"Yeah," she agreed. "It does."

I held out my hand and helped her up. Remi and Maddy May joined us in the entryway. The four of us looked at the door.

I started to reach for the knob.

"Hold on," Remi said. She heaved the axe into the wall, next to the small mirror.

"No souvenirs," she said. "The story dies with us."

We all looked at one another, a moment of shared anticipation.

I opened the door.

Water spilled out onto the porch, leading the way for us. The door slammed closed like it was happy to be rid of us. I fished around in my pockets and found the key. The dead bolt clicked. I let the key fall down one of the many holes in the porch. It fell out of sight, hopefully soaking into the fresh mud the churning water made.

The outside air was fresh and warm, scented with wildflowers and dry grass. Mom and Dad's realty sign swayed in the breeze. COMING SOON. I pulled it down and tossed it aside. It disappeared into the overgrown grass.

We started down the hill, limping toward the lights of town.

The manor could do nothing but watch.

This book (lucky number seven) would not have been possible without the following people:

Kate Farrell, my editor at Holt, who challenged and inspired me to write something equally fun and scary. Together we found the line of how many people could die in a book and still have it be a comedy. Thanks for saving Maddy May's life.

Laura Zats, my agent. Happy tenth anniversary, Zatsy. So many of our dreams came true in the first ten. Can't wait to see what the next ten hold!

My partner, Erin, who has always been my biggest fan and changed my life in all the best ways, but most specifically by deciding to get deep into horror movies, which changed the course of my career. Who knew we would grow up brave?

Tehlor Kay Mejia and Casey Gilly, two authors I adore and admire who encourage me to write the most unhinged shit I can think of.

My copy editor, Erica Ferguson, and managing editor, Alexei Esikoff, who saved me from a variety of embarrassments.

Meg Sayre, for the most kick-ass cover design and illustration.

The Henry Holt/Macmillan team: Ann Marie Wong, Molly Ellis, Alexandra Quill, Elysse Villalobos, and Grace Tyler.

The 2023 Michael L. Printz committee: Valerie Davis, Ariel Birdoff, L. Butler, Amanda Kordeliski, Kaitlin Malixi, Emily Mills, Kali Olson, and Kim Dare. It is a mindfuck to write a book having just won the award of a lifetime. Good problems. Thank you, thank you forever.

My families: Anderson, San Juan, and Harbor, for their love and support.

And finally, for all the kids who got stuck in the suburbs because it felt like someone had to stay behind and try to make things better. Sometimes it feels like you're the only one who isn't in the city, but the suburbs need your voice, your perspective, and your art. Don't let them drive you out. Don't let them silence you. Don't lose hope of a better, safer, more inclusive world.